HELL'S HAPPY HOUR

He stood awkwardly in the flushed light by the window as Sindra went to the built-in bar. There were paintings on the walls, but standing here he couldn't quite make them out.

Sindra knelt beside a small refrigerator—the movement tightened the skirt around her ass. She took out a mason jar of dark liquid and poured some into two cups with a little cola. "I make a mind-blowing cocktail," she said. "I keep it pre-mixed."

She brought the glasses back to him, and they each drank. The stuff was both sweet and acrid. He couldn't quite . . .

"What is it?"

"Tarantula venom, partly," she said, as he began to twitch . . .

—from "How Deep the Taste of Love" by John Shirley

The Hot Blood Series

HOT BLOOD

HOTTER BLOOD

HOTTEST BLOOD

HOT BLOOD XI: FATAL ATTRACTIONS

STRANGE BEDFELLOWS

Published by Kensington Publishing Corporation

HOTTEST BLOOD

NANCY HOLDER
MATTHEW COSTELLO
BENTLEY LITTLE
REX MILLER
AND OTHERS

EDITED BY JEFF GELB AND MICHAEL GARRETT

PINNACLE BOOKS
Kensington Publishing Corp.
http://www.kensingtonbooks.com

PINNACLE BOOKS are published by

Kensington Publishing Corp.
850 Third Avenue
New York, NY 10022

Copyright © 1993 by Jeff Gelb

All Kensington Titles, Imprints and Distributed Lines are available at special quantity discounts for bulk purchases for sales promotions, premiums, fund-raising, and educational or institutional use. Special book excerpts or customized printings can also be created to fit specific needs. For details, write or phone the office of the Kensington special sales manager: Kensington Publishing Corp., 850 Third Avenue, New York, NY 10022, attn. Special Sales Department. Phone: 1-800-221-2647.

Pinnacle and the P logo Reg. U.S. Pat. & TM Off.

First Pocket Books Printing: January 1993
First Pinnacle Books Printing: September 2004

10 9 8 7 6 5 4 3 2 1

Printed in the United States of America

Copyright Notices

We respectfully dedicate *Hottest Blood*
to the memory of Dave Pedneau,
a friend, mentor, and author
who reminds us that
life is fleeting
but talent lives on.

CONTENTS

CONTENTS

INTRODUCTION

HOT . . . HOTTER . . . *HOTTEST*.

When the popularity of *Hotter Blood* proved that horror fans couldn't get enough of stories mixing sex and terror, we couldn't resist the challenge of topping our previous efforts.

Some of the stories in *Hotter Blood* suggested the direction *Hottest Blood* follows. As we began sifting through a mountain of submissions, we noticed that the best of them continued the tradition of innovation established in the first two volumes, pushing the envelope even farther to expand the boundaries of contemporary horror fiction. For every story included in *Hottest Blood* we read approximately twenty manuscripts, and those we selected map new territories in horror.

Our authors have stretched the limits of their imaginations to give you stories the likes of which you have never before experienced. We expect that, when you finish this volume, you will have been introduced to concepts, ideas, and images so wild, so creative, so *unusual,* that they'll haunt your thoughts and memories for a long, long time. That, of course, is certainly our goal!

There's been a lot of talk about the changing face of horror fiction, and our selection of authors represents superstars of the future, the ones who will chart the course that horror fiction must follow to continue its growth. Of course, it's always exciting to read a great story by an acknowledged master, but it's especially rewarding to discover a fresh new voice, whose earliest efforts will remain etched in your memory for years to come as having first been enjoyed within these pages. In *Hottest Blood* we offer both: the established professionals and the voices of tomorrow.

It's obvious from the stories in the *Hot Blood* series that sex and horror strike a responsive chord. The ongoing success of the *Hot Blood* books demonstrates that, while the combination may prove deadly, it's also intriguing and delicious . . . the ultimate forbidden fruit.

Indulge!

Jeff Gelb
Michael Garrett
January 1993

Hottest Blood

I HEAR THE MERMAIDS SINGING

Nancy Holder

Don't panic, you stupid bitch. Just write it all down and get it out.

They won't find this; they won't ever know you still hear the songs. You've conned them this long. What's to make them grow some brains now?

But so what if they do figure it out? What have you got to look forward to out here, you stupid, crazy loser? What the fuck is the big allure, these wide-open spaces they call the world?

Wide open spaces, ha! Tell me, girlfriend. Tell me about that wide-open space of yours, got you into all this shit in the first place. It was because you wanted that boy, and . . .

No. No, it went another way. Please, it happened the way you,

the way you,

you dreamed it all.

You dreamed it all. That's it, period, the end. I wish I could tell you different, hon, but just like on *Dallas,* it was all a dream. You know, the way you go off sometimes, like that girl in *I Never Promised You a Rose Garden;* you just zone out, and then

you hear the voices singing,

and you hear them sing you a story:

This, my life:

Once upon a time, I am the most precious of the Sea King's seven daughters, fondled and dandled, and loved by all. I rule gentle Pacificus for my father, and I am kind and generous.

I am the most treasured, the most beautiful. My tail sparkles and gleams, my hair undulates like sunbeam shafts through the water. My skin is pale and rosy as a pearl. And I live in the most splendid of the seven seas, wonder upon wonder: brilliant Garibaldis and purple sawfish laze and bob; anemone carpets of orange, pink, and yellow spread beneath me as I drift, combing my hair; castles of red coral dot my domain, and majestic jade-green kelp forests, towering in the currents, mark my borders. Elaborate curtains of sponges and starfish adorn my bower, and sea treasure and luxury surrounds me. Seahorses cuddle me; maidens attend me. Young lords come in great haste at my call.

Everything I can possibly want.

And when I am fifteen, I rise to the surface, as is my right, and come into the other world for the first time. The first gasp of air terrifies me, but quickly I get my bearings. New smells enfold me: oranges, pineapples, sandalwood.

And the first sight fascinates me. It is a ship, sailing upon the dark waves! Long and gray, laden with boxes. A freighter, carrying goods to other lands.

Oh, ship, oh, wondrous object! And then sharp flashes of lightning crack open the sky, and thunder's rumblings shoot across the waves. Water cascades from above—rain, it is rain!—and the bulging ocean tosses the ship like a bauble in its hand.

I am exhilarated. And I sing of its fierce magnificence, this world above, this angel-world. I strain to see men on the ship, for I know there must be some. Those who dwell here possess something called souls, something that allows them to live on, and on, though we of the water live for three hundred years before our bodies break upon the foam. What must it be like, immortality? To live for a hundred thousand storms, a million infinite songs?

The ship sails on, and I sing of its safety. It disappears, and so do I, back into my perfect kingdom.

But I think the whole night of the world I have caught but a glimpse of, and I am preoccupied all the next day. I do not hear the pleadings of my courtiers for my attentions; and the justice I dispense in my court is hasty and arbitrary. I hear sad songs in the spire and halls of my palace, lamenting my unfairness, and I determine to set all to rights on the morrow.

Yet the night was made for the upper world, and I rise again.

The sky is dark, and the round orb they call Moon glows like . . . like me. Beyond, a beach shimmers silver; and lush treetops wave in zephyr breezes. Enchanted, I swim closer. I hear laughter, and I sing of it. I sing of the joy of these angel-people, who walk and live forever.

I long to see one of them. Down below, I have seen only their dead shells—for I assume they must shed their forms and seek new ones, as the hermit crabs do; else how can they live forever? I want to see one move and walk. I want to touch one of them.

I am bewitched by the thought of meeting one of them.

And then, as if by magic, the moon shines on a glorious, sinewy man, riding a flat chariot over the waves. Each muscle of his brown body gleams in the magic light; his hair is long and blue-black and flies behind him like a tail. His legs are spread wide, and I am mesmerized by them. I swim toward him, singing a greeting.

He shouts in reply, "Cowabunga!" and I sing to him. I sing of cowabunga, hello; and as I gaze at him, my body hungers. I have only known this hunger for my father and my sisters, as we swim and stroke each other. My father has coupled with all my sisters, producing offspring; when I turn sixteen, he will couple with me.

But now I think of coupling with the legged man, though I can't imagine how. And I sing to him of my sexual desire, of my lust for his strange, exciting body. I sing and sing, and he shouts "Cowabunga!" in reply.

3

Then, like the night before, a storm churns the sea into a bombastic symphony. The young god falters on his chariot and tumbles into the sea. I have seen him do this several times before, and he has always recovered and swum to the beach. But now the chariot smacks his head as he surfaces, and his head sinks below the waves.

For a moment I do nothing, because I assume he will simply shed his shell if he is in danger. But something inside me tugs hard and tells me to go to him and carry him to the beach myself, though my father has expressly forbidden us to go near it. I ignore the feeling and sing to him of waking and swimming, but still he remains beneath the waves.

My eyes hurt. As you know, we of the sea cannot make the teardrops the angel-people do. For a moment I ponder that, wondering if that is the secret of their immortality, but my eyes hurt worse, pounding, and I find myself darting through the wild waves toward the spot I saw him last.

I find a shadow in the black water—we can see, even in the dark—and I put my arms around his chest and start for the surface.

And I cannot stop touching him, everywhere, as he lies limp in my arms. I kiss the back of his head, I nip it gently. I want to open for him, but I don't understand where his parts are. I don't know, but I'm shaking for him. The sea foams and boils around us and I nearly lose hold of him in my rapture, the rapture that is the deep. I sing of it, I sing of my need for him, my unfathomable yearning. I want the man. I want to couple with him.

The moon shines on his face as I reach the breakers and push him onto the sand. Mixed with my desire is a thrill of terror: If I beach myself I am doomed.

I stare at him, willing him to open his eyes. He lies inert. I run my hands over his body, and I find a hard, stiff shaft between his legs, and I smile: They are not so different, after all.

As I have done for my father, I do for him. I take him into my mouth and suck, for it gives intense pleasure. I suck harder, harder, though the flesh around his shaft is loose. Then I remember the stories of their clothes and realize he is

4

wearing some, and in my haste I rip them off his body, tearing them into pieces that are caught by the waves and carried out to sea like so many little jellyfish.

He is marvelous and thick. He is red and pink and he bobs in my mouth.

And he begins to gasp and sigh and move. He holds onto my head and pushes. He says, "Wha . . . wha . . ." and then he releases his hot stream into me.

Cowabunga, little mermaid. Cowabunga, angel-god of the flat chariot. Ah, a surfboard. Yes, of course.

He begins to awaken, and I lose my nerve. My father has told me all my life I must have nothing to do with this world, and I am his favorite, most treasured daughter. So I leave.

But I am ruined now, for the sea. I pine for him, for my legged man. I cannot endure without him.

I must couple with him.

I caress my tail; I find my opening and slide my fingers into it. It would not work, he and I. It would not be possible.

But it must be possible. I must make it possible. Without him, my body will dissolve on the foam and I shall become nothing.

Though I say nothing of my dilemma, my sisters strive to comfort me. They touch me and kiss me. My father takes me in his arms and squeezes my breasts as I love him to do. They gather round me, all my family, and I am the most loved, the most adored.

And yet, I am wretched.

I rise night after night to the surface. Sometimes he is there, and sometimes he is not. And he sings that he misses me, too: Cowabunga, cowabunga.

Cowabunga, little mermaid.

I begin to fade away, and my father grows worried. My sisters sing for my recovery from whatever strange illness has befallen me. Dolphins serenade me. The whales chant healing melodies. Even the smallest of snails hum and whistle to soothe me.

And I know I must do something, and do it soon.

Though my father would die if he knew, I go to the sea witch.

Vile is she, with fangs longer than any viperfish; and her bleeding eyes bob on stalks; she is covered with barnacles and pieces of black swallowers; she is an abomination.

She is my last hope.

Pieces of black swallowers, and the bones of dead angelmen, poisonous plants, and puffer fish. Horrible toxins she has found in leaking drums, dropped by the upper world. She mixes these up and tells me to drink when I reach the surface. She tells me to drink and that she will take my voice in payment.

My voice!

"Your life as a walker will be a living nightmare," she promises me as she hands me the bottle. "Death and madness are your answers there."

And I think of nothing but the dark-haired man, thrusting his shaft into me.

The bottle burns my hand as I carry it to the surface; the water bubbles, and blisters rise on my palm. I bite my lip and swim quickly, but I am wondering: What will it be like to swallow such a thing?

And I rise to the world of the air and the night, and I see the glorious beauty of the man, and I swim as close to him as I dare. I uncap the bottle and sing to him one last time, oh, cowabunga, and then I drink:

Lava slides down my throat. Burning it away, burning all away, my voice, my beautiful voice; all my songs, a bonfire in my throat. A conflagration, a holocaust.

In the morning, I awaken. And he is kneeling over me, and I cannot understand a word he is saying.

My life:

I still don't remember who I am, just some weird chick who tried to kill herself, got drunk, and nearly drowned.

He found me, gave me CPR. When I woke up, his mouth was pressed over mine and his breath thrust through my lungs, hot and humid. I had a strange thought: *Now his soul is in me; now I'm immortal*—which now I understand is tied up with all that stuff that got me in trouble in the first place.

My hand was wrapped so tightly around the Scotch bottle he almost had to break my fingers to get me to let go of it. We kept the Scotch bottle as a souvenir, and it was the first thing besides his fists that he hit me with.

Keep writing, girl. Keep going. You know you gotta get it out. But god, now you have to remember what a stupid bitch you are. You have to remember all that . . . that other stuff is a bunch of whacked-out bullshit

that you still believe,

that you still relive.

And you hear songs.

And you hear . . .

shit. You hear jack shit.

I'm glad for what happened. Don't get me wrong; we had some good times. Jesus, our sex was incredible. I never could get enough, and for a while, that was all we needed. I guess he got turned on by how weird it all was: Here was this young chick, couldn't talk, wanted it all the time. He felt like some big hero, taking me in. Found me some clothes of his sister's, took me to live with him in the little apartment he rented on the beach.

Yeah, it was great at first, and sex was enough. But I couldn't do anything. It was like I'd never seen a kitchen before. I wasn't steady on my feet, even. He was worried about that, thought I was a heroin addict or something. The way I shook and moaned. I told him with gestures that it was my legs, and he tried to laugh it off by showing me his surfer's knees. Knobby beyond belief. But I never went into severe withdrawal or anything, and I had that freckled, turned-up nose and those perky tits, and the tightest little snatch he'd ever had—he told me that a million times. It was good, living with Bobby. Yes, his name. Bobby.

Then I got knocked up. He totally freaked. Wanted me to have an abortion. No way. No way on earth; and I finally realized he didn't love me, not the way I loved him, or he'd

7

be jazzed. I was so mad. I was so hurt. I had given up . . . I knew I had given up something for him. And I was just a piece of tail to him.

I think he was hoping I'd move out, but I kept hoping he'd fall in love with me. He started drinking, and going out, and then he didn't come home until morning, still drunk.

"Don't stare at me with those eyes!" he would scream at me, and then he began to knock me around.

You'd think I'd tell him to fuck off and leave, but where could I go? I didn't even know where I was. Or who I was. And I had this despair inside me. This overwhelming sorrow, that grew stronger and stronger the angrier Bobby got with me. The more he regretted being with me.

Fish out of water, I told myself. That was what I was. A misfit. A freak. I deserved his fists, cuz I was such a drag. I was a burden. I was useless. It made sense that he lost his patience with me.

I was going down, really drowning. I started wandering down on the beach, staggering around for hours on end. My legs hurt worse and worse; I didn't know why, but I thought it had something to do with the baby. Just wandering up and down, all day, falling into the sand over and over, crying. People thought I'd gone out of my mind.

And then one day I found a knife on the beach. It was stuck in the sand and the sun caught it just so, danced off it. I pulled it out and stared at it, with tears running down my cheeks. My eyes burned in the bright light; they always hurt when I cry.

I thought, I'll just kill the fucker. I'll fucking kill him.

We went to a surfing tournament, and he did things like imitate the way I walked and squeeze my tits in front of the other couples, and all I could do was stare at him with tears running down my cheeks. Some of the other surfer chicks came over to me while he was in the waves and said, "Christ, Annie (everyone calls me Annie), why the hell do you put up with that crap?"

I couldn't talk, which was just as well. I had nothing to say.

Bobby won the tournament. There was a lot of partying to celebrate. He won some money, too. He drank more and more, and then he fucked me, hard, and I was scared about the baby. That it might get hurt. I thought of it, swimming around in its peaceful ocean, not knowing how ugly the world is. The sea, the sea, the beautiful, cowabunga sea, and it was going to have to come out and walk on the land with the two of us.

What if Bobby hit the baby?

I had packed the knife in my suitcase. I had pretended not to notice when I slipped it under the beach towels, as if it were some kind of accident; it was like someone was talking to me in my head: *Do it, do it, do it.* I thought about how I must have had a mother, and a father, and maybe brothers or sisters; how something really awful must have happened, since I didn't remember them. I dreamed sometimes that my father raped me, or my brother, or my mother abused me. But none of that felt right.

But then again, nothing in my life felt particularly right.

Anyway, Bobby got drunk. He sat facing me in our motel room with a bottle of Jack Daniels in his lap, and a strange smile on his face, and for some reason I was more afraid than I'd ever been before. Something was in the air, something sharp and dangerous and slashing. The air was too cold, and inside the sound of the surf, I thought I heard
singing: Whales gray and kind; or dark-nosed dolphins; or people; or
one person, one very special man.

Bobby said, "Whatcha looking at, you retard?" I shrank from him. I thought about the knife. My heart pounded. My body was dry as dust, and my skin prickled. My legs ached.

Jesus, they ached.

"I'm going out." He lurched to his feet. "And when I get back, Annie, you better be gone."

I stared at him. His face changed. He swore at me, came at me, hit me. Sliced my cheek open. "Goddamnit, I don't want that kid!" he shouted, and slugged me in the stomach. "I want you gone!"

I doubled over, my hands over my head. I wanted to ask, Did you never love me? Isn't there something about me worth caring about and sacrificing for?

Did I mention before that Bobby was only seventeen?

My legs couldn't hold me up, and I collapsed. He turned his back and walked out. My heart dissolved inside my body and I breathed out, in, long and slow, like it was new to me. I felt as if I were floating, looking down through water at what was happening. For a second, I thought I was going to rise up out of the motel room and fly over the ocean. I thought I was fucking dying.

I was so scared, I ran after him. I know, it's hard to believe: Here he had just beat me up and I was chasing him for more.

But I took the knife.

The waves were racing up the cliff near the motel, just soaring like a typhoon or a tidal wave or something. I had never seen surf like that, and it was violent and terrifying, but somehow it was wonderful, too. The moon was out and I let out a sob, almost a noise, as I looked up at it. The knife was too long to put in my purse, or a pocket; I had to carry it at my side. There was no hiding it.

I had the strongest compulsion to cut my legs; or maybe it was to cut one of them off. Like they were growths, and something wrong. Like they didn't belong to me, the way I didn't belong to anybody.

The baby. I could never let him hurt the baby.

But I added that in later; I remembered thinking that later. I was running after him, not from him.

The waves crashed on top of the cliff and they roared like sea monsters. Even at a distance, spray slapped my face. It was the end of the world, I thought, mine and everybody's. It was all over.

I ran toward it. I ran as fast as I could, even though white-hot pains shot up my legs and into my heart. Throbbed in my throat. Scalding, blinding pain coursed right through me and grew as I got nearer and nearer.

And then I saw Bobby, standing on the edge of the cliff with his arms outstretched, laughing. His head thrown back, wild and free, his hair streaming behind him like a tail; he was brown and handsome, and even then, I wanted him.

He shouted something, like a dare. He laughed again and began to sing, but I couldn't make out the tune. The waves crashed over him and he staggered backward.

I came closer. The water pelted me like stones. Angry ocean, I thought. Angry at him, angry at me.

Another wave dropped over him. I couldn't see him. I kept running. And I thought, Oh, God, when I reach him, I'm going to stick this knife into him.

I ran. I ran hard. I was going to do it. I would do it.

Another wave. He turned around and saw me. The laughter died. He screamed at me, "Freak! You fucking freak!"

And I was going to do it. I was going to really do it.

And then I heard the singing:

> *Beloved, beloved,*
> *most treasured.*
> *The littlest princess,*
> *the littlest mermaid,*
> *the joy of the seas,*
> *the father's lost darling.*

I heard it. I know I heard it. I heard it.

And the wave took him, just reached out with a watery embrace and yanked him off that cliff and pulled him into the water and

your voice moved the world and you screamed.

No, that's what you think when you're crazy. That's what you dreamed.

You pushed him. You know you did, and they knew it, but your lawyers were cagey and got you off as a nutcase. With your scratchy, pathetic voice, and those sad, kick-me eyes, the jury pitied you and let you off, into a barred, safe place full of therapy sessions and medication. The baby was a miscarriage. You were knocked out when they took it, but they promised you it was for the best and looked away when they said it.

Years of medication. And talking, talking, with a new voice. But there was a man in that wave, a powerful man with streaming gray hair and a long gray beard and a crown. There was a man, and he grabbed Bobby.

You stupid lying bitch. There was no man. There was not.

I'm better now. I don't need this shit. I'm better now, and I don't, won't, hear that singing anymore.

This, my life, once upon a time

no, goddamnit, no.

And now I'll wad these pages up and stick them in that goddamned Scotch bottle, and no one will ever find them cuz they'll sink like a stone.

Like a dead man.

Like Bobby—never found his body. Shed it. Found a new woman to live inside, hermit crab.

And I don't know why I'm writing this, except I feel so sick inside; I feel like I can't breathe and I'm drying up. Shriveling into nothingness, and I really wish someone would really help me. Because I am a crazy bitch, and no one on this earth wants me.

And now I'm standing on the cliff where I pushed Bobby, and throwing this bottle out to sea, cuz I can't get that damned singing out of my head. I hear it all the time, and it makes me dream. I hate dreaming. I know what the world is: hard, and mean, and ugly. You're a hungry puppy and it's the boot connecting with your stomach.

And the hunger's for something you can't name, anyway.

And the name of the tune is:

For a day and an hour, the bottle bobs upon the waters. Then it sinks down slowly, slowly, like a pearl in liquid gold, drifting into the outstretched grasp of the Sea King. He cracks it open like an oyster, extracting the morsel within. Reads quickly, as the ink begins to run.

Then he flashes to the surface and screams for his daughter. But she is already walking away.

Tears course down his cheeks, and while it is true that merfolk cannot cry, the laws of fatherhood transcend the laws of nature.

In the ocean blue, home of the little mermaid, sea fantasy and sea dream; aqua, purple, pacific, and serene.

"This, for a boy?" he wails to the cliffs, the waves. "This, for lust?"

And he dives back into the depths, back to his throne and his six beautiful, naked daughters and their sunken Grecian temples, and pulverizes with his fists the bones of the boy who ruined his daughter and drove her mad; pounds the bones, and no heart! No soul!

Pounds the bones, and the ashes
of the beauty of the sea.

> *I hear the mermaids singing, each to each,*
> *I do not think that they will sing to me.*

—T. S. Eliot

LLAMA

Bentley Little

Measuring:

The leg of the dead llama was three feet two inches long.

And everything fell into place.

Three feet two inches was the precise length of space between the sole of my lynched father's right foot and the ground.

By the time my wife's contractions were three minutes and two seconds apart, she had only dilated 3.2 centimeters and the decision was made to perform a Caesarean.

My wife was declared dead at three-twenty.

The date was March 20.

I found the llama in the alley behind the bookstore. It was already dead, its cataract eyes rimmed with flies, and the retarded boy was kneeling on the rough asphalt beside it, massaging its distended stomach. The presence of the retarded boy told me that secrets lay within the measurements of the dead animal, perhaps the answers to my questions, and I quickly rushed back inside the store to find a tape measure.

* * *

In 1932, Franklin Roosevelt bought a new Ford coupe. The license plate of the coupe, which Roosevelt never drove, was 3FT2.

My father voted for Franklin Roosevelt.

I thought I saw my wife's likeness in a stain in the toilet in the men's room of an Exxon station. The stain was greenish black and on the right side of the bowl.

I breathed upon the mirror above the blackened sink, and, sure enough, someone had written her name on the glass. The letters appeared—clear spots in the fog cloud of condensation—then faded.

In the trash can, partially wrapped in toilet paper, I saw what looked like a bloody fetus.

I left the llama in the alley undisturbed, did not tell the police or any city authority, and I warned the other shopowners on the block not to breathe a word about the animal to anyone.

I spent that night in the store, sleeping in the back office behind the bookshelves. Several times during the night I awakened and looked out the dusty window to where the unmoving body lay on the asphalt. It looked different in the shadows created by moonlight and streetlamp, and in the lumped silhouette I saw contours that were almost familiar to me, echoes of shapes that I knew had meant something to me in the past but that now remained stubbornly buried in my subconscious.

I knew the dead animal had truths to tell.

Weighing:
The hind end of the llama, its head and upper body still supported by the ground, weighed one hundred and ninety-six pounds.

My dead wife's niece told me that she was sixteen, but I believe she was younger.

I have a photograph of her, taken in a booth at an amusement park, that I keep on the top of my dresser, exactly 3.2 inches away from a similar photo of my wife.

The photo cost me a dollar ninety-six. I put eight quarters into the machine, and when I happened to check the coin return I found four pennies.

My father weighed a hundred and ninety-six pounds at his death. He died exactly one hundred and ninety-six years after his great-great-grandfather first set foot in America. My father's great-great-grandfather hung himself.

A hundred and ninety-six is the sum total of my age multiplied by four—the number of legs of the llama.

The Exxon station where I saw my wife's likeness in a stain in the men's room toilet is located at 196 East 32nd Street.

I do not remember whose idea it was to try the pins. I believe it was hers, since she told me that she'd recently seen a news report on acupuncture that interested her.

I showed her some of the books in my store: the photographic essay on African boys disfigured by rites of passage, the illustrated study of Inquisition torture devices, the book on deformed strippers in an Appalachian sideshow.

She told me that if acupuncture needles placed on the proper nerves could deaden pain, wasn't it logical to assume that needles placed on other nerves could stimulate pleasure?

She allowed me to tie her up, spreadeagled on the bed, and I began by inserting pins in her breasts. She screamed, at first yelling at me to stop, then simply crying out in dumb animal agony. I pushed the pins all the way into her flesh until only the shiny round heads were visible, pressing them slowly through the skin and the fatty tissue of her breasts in a crisscross pattern, then concentrating them around the firmer nipples.

By the time I had moved between her legs, she had passed out and her body was covered all over with a thin shiny sheen of blood.

When the retarded boy finished massaging the llama's distended stomach, he stepped back from the animal and stood there soundlessly. He looked at me and pointed to the ground in front of him. I measured the space between the retarded boy and the llama. Five feet six inches.

At the time my father hung himself he was fifty-six years old.

My stillborn son weighed five pounds, six ounces.

Five times six is thirty.

My wife was thirty years old when she died.

According to the book *Nutritional Values of Exotic Dishes,* a single 56-ounce serving of cooked llama meat contains 196 calories.

This information is found on page 32.

The young man did not object when I took him in the men's room of the gas station.

He was standing at the urinal when I entered, and I stepped behind him and held the knife to his throat. I used my free hand to yank down his dress slacks, and then I pressed against him. "You want it, don't you?" I asked.

"Yes," he said.

I made him bend over the side of the lone toilet, and although his buttocks were hairy and repulsed me, I made him accept me the way my wife had. All of me. He tensed, stiffened, and gasped with pain, and I felt around the front of his body to make sure he was not aroused. If he had been aroused, I would have had to kill him.

I slid fully in and nearly all the way out fifty-six times before my hot seed shot into him, and with my knife pressed against his throat I made him cry out "Oh, God! Oh, God!" the way my wife had.

I left him with only a slight cut across the upper throat, above the Adam's apple, and I took his clothes and put them in the trunk of my car and later stuffed them with newspaper and made them into a scarecrow for my dead wife's dying garden.

I hoped the young man was a doctor.

I realized the importance of measurements even as a child. When my sister fell out of the tree in our yard, I measured the length of her legs and the total length of her body. Her legs were twenty inches long. Her body was four-foot-five.

My mother was twenty years old when she gave birth to my sister.

My sister died when my father was forty-five.

Requirements:
I was required to pay for the knowledge gained from my sister's measurements.

My sister had two arms and two legs.

I killed two cats and two dogs.

My wife was Jewish. Before coming to the United States, her parents lived 196 miles from the nearest concentration camp and 32 miles from the city where Adolf Hitler spent his youth.

My wife was born in 1956.

I showed Nadine a book on self-mutilation, letting her look at photographs of men who were so jaded, who so craved unique experience, that they mutilated their genitalia. She was fascinated by the subject, and she seemed particularly interested in the photo of a man's penis that had been surgically bifurcated and through which had been inserted a metal ring.

She told me that the concept of self-mutilation appealed to her. She said that she had grown tired of sex, that all three of her orifices had been penetrated so frequently, so many times in so many ways, that there were no sensations that were new to her. Everything to which she submitted was either a repeat or a variation.

I told her I would make her a new opening, a new hole, and I took her to the forest and I tied her to the cross-stakes and I used a knife to cut and carve a slit in her stomach big enough to take me.

She was still alive when I entered her, and her screams were not entirely of pain.

She kept crying, "God!"

My white semen mixed with her red blood and made pink.

I wanted to kill the doctor who killed my wife, but I saw him only once after her death, and it was with a large crowd and the opportunity did not arise again.

So I rented a small apartment and stocked the shelves with medical books and arranged the furniture in a manner consistent with the way I believed a doctor would arrange it.

The apartment number was 56.

I made friends with a young man who, save for the beard, resembled my wife's doctor fairly closely. I invited the young man into my apartment, smiling, then I showed him the gun and told him to strip. He did so, and I made him put on the white physician's clothes I had bought. I forced him into the bathroom, made him shave, then made him put on the surgical mask.

I had purchased a puppy from the pet store the night before, and I had killed the animal by slitting its throat, draining the blood into a glass pitcher. I splashed the blood on the young man, and now the illusion was complete. He looked almost exactly like the doctor who had killed my wife.

I had written out the lines I wanted the surrogate doctor to say while I killed him, and I'd typed them out and had them bound in plastic.

I cocked the pistol, handed the pages to the young man, told him to speak.

End Exchange:
DOCTOR: I killed your wife.
ME: You wanted her to die!
DOCTOR: She deserved to die! She was a bitch and a whore!
ME: You killed my son!
DOCTOR: I'm glad I did it! He was a son of a bitch and a son of a whore and I knew I couldn't let him be born!

ME: That means that you deserve to die.
DOCTOR: Yes. You have the right to kill me. I killed
         your wife and son. It is only fair.

I shot him in the groin, shot him in the mouth, shot him in the arms, shot him in the legs, left him there to die.

In the newspaper article, it said he had bled to death four hours after the bullets had entered his body.

He had been a stockbroker.

I have clipped my toenails and fingernails once each week since my wife died. I save the clippings and keep them in a plastic trash bag that I store underneath my bed.

On the tenth anniversary of her death, on what would have been our son's tenth birthday, I will weigh the bag of nail clippings and then set the bag on fire.

I will swallow ten teaspoonfuls of the ashes.

The remainder I will bury with the body of my wife.

I will use the information gained from the weighing to determine the date and manner of my death.

John F. Kennedy was assassinated on the date of my birth.

My initials are J.F.K.

Cataloging:

My store has sixteen nonfiction books containing information about llamas. There are five fiction books in which a llama plays an important role. All of these are children's books, and three of them are Hugh Lofting's Dr. Doolittle stories.

I have killed sixteen adults since my wife's death. And five children.

Three of the children were siblings.

The llama has changed my plans.

The llama and the retarded boy.

I stare out the window of my store at the dead animal, at the retarded boy next to it, at the occasional gawkers who pass by and stop and whisper. One of them, I know, one of them over whom I have no control, will eventually notify the authorities and they will take the carcass away.

I cannot let that happen.

Or maybe I can.

For the presence of the llama in my alley indicates that I have done wrong and that a sacrifice is demanded.

But who is to be the sacrifice, the retarded boy or myself?

Neither of us know, and we stare at each other. He outside, next to the animal, me inside, with my books. Through the dirty window he looks vague, faded, although the llama still seems clearly defined. Is this a sign?

I don't know. But I know I must make the decision quickly. I must act today. Or tonight.

I have measured the body of the llama and it is four feet ten inches long.

Tomorrow is April 10.

WHERE THE HEART WAS

David J. Schow

Victor Jacks ambled through the back door to ruin their lives on Thursday. Which was a pain, since Victor had been pronounced dead the previous Saturday.

"Stubborn sumbitch." Renny reached under the bed for the ballbat. He was on his hands and knees, forced to paw around until it finally came out with dustballs and hair kitties chasing it. Renny, who was allergic to animal dander, sneezed ear-poppingly. This trebled his rage.

Renny's life was one that Victor's back-from-the-dead encore was designed to ruin. Barb's was the other. Just now she was backed into a corner, shrieking like an ingenue in a fifty-year-old horror film. Unlike those World War II heroines, she was naked. Renny still had his socks on. Apart from his Timex, he was garbless, but for the baseball bat. This he refused to wield in the name of mere modesty.

Victor looked a bit shaggy, having been deceased for the better part of the work week. His shoulderblades, butt, and legs down to the heels were blue-black with dependent lividity. His eyes were so crusty that one was welded shut. His hair was lank and wild, the most alive thing about him; his skin tone hung somewhere between catgut and bottled pig's knuckle.

He crackled as he moved. That would be rigor.

He had obviously been walking for some time. At each of

his joints the dry flesh had split into gummy wounds with chafed and elevated flaps. The distance from the morgue to Barb's bedroom was about twelve pedestrian miles.

Provided, that is, Victor had come here directly, after sitting up on his slab and deciding to ruin their lives, Renny thought. And that pissed him off even more.

Renny's next explosive sneeze spoiled his aim. He wiped his nose with his forearm. Barb kept screaming, totally out of character for her, and Renny wished in a mean flash that she would either faint or die.

Enough.

At the crack point it was the batting that mattered, not the invective. The bulb end of the bat smashed Victor's dead left ear deep into the dead left hemisphere of his dead brain. Victor wobbled and missed his zombie grab for Renny. He didn't have a chance.

Renny was foaming and lunatic, swinging and connecting, swinging and connecting, making pulp. It was what he had ached to do to Victor all along. What he had fantasized about doing to Victor just last week, when Victor was still alive. His yelling finally drowned out Barb's, who was shrunken fetally into her corner, her eyes seeking the deep retreat of trauma.

Renny's eyes were pink with rage. Flecks of froth dotted the corners of his mouth. He kept bashing away with the bat, pausing only to sneeze and wipe. Victor put up as good a fight as a dead person could, which is to say, not much.

While the Renny on the outside was cussing and bludgeoning, the Renny on the inside was smirking about several things. Number one: zombie movies. In the movies, reanimated corpses boogied back from the dead with all kinds of *strength* and *powers*. What a bagload. Cadavers had all the tensile strength of twice-cooked pasta. Even in the movies you could put them down with a headshot. What threat, where?

Deeper down, Renny was *enjoying* himself. He thought Barb watched too much cable. When he had first proposed murdering Victor—just as a hoot, mind you, nothing serious—she burdened him with *probable cause* and *airtight alibis* and *where-were-you-on-the-night-of.* Ridiculous, in a world where people simply dropped off the planet on a daily basis, never again a peep. You break his neck, you dump him in the first available manhole, the sewer is a disposal system, end of story.

Barb had wanted to play faithful and loving right up to the climax of the drama. Loving, hah. Faithful, not since she'd met Renny.

In the end it hadn't come down to murder, but right now Barb sure was reaping some drama.

Things were so lively right now that Renny had busted a workout sweat and Barb's vocal cords were rawing. He finally turned around and told her to shut up while what was left of Victor Jacks twitched in a pile on the floor. The business end of the bat was a real mess.

"Is he dead?" said Barb, cowering.

"I don't think he's gonna move no more right now." Renny would have wiped his begored hands on his pants; his pants had been off since just after dinnertime. He let his hands hang in the air as he looked around, uselessly. He said *sheeeit,* slow and weary. It didn't help.

"How? How did he? He . . . we . . . I don't . . . it just." Barb was still having a bit of trouble being coherent.

"Victor was always a stubborn sumbitch, you *know* that one, babe."

Barb stood up and risked moving a little closer to what was left of Victor. "Maybe he, you know, didn't really die. Went into a coma or something."

"Barb, Victor was dead. He was dead last week and he was *still* dead when he walked in on us. He is the deadest thing I ever saw."

"You knocked his head off," she said dully.

"Stopped him, didn't it?"

"What're we gonna *do,* Renny? He's all . . . ehh."

"Shush. What we're gonna do is call the morgue and tell them some pervert snatched the body and mutilated it, and dumped it here as a joke. Some old boyfriend of yours. You can make up a description. Nobody'll bug us."

"What makes you so smart?"

Renny had to stop a moment to ponder a good answer to that one.

"I mean, you think they'll buy it?" There she went again. Barb was one of those people who strolled through life obliviously, thinking a call to the police would sling her free of any sort of trouble. Now she was just as convinced that the Authorities—capital *A*—would swoop down at any moment to point *j'accuse*.

"Babe, just dream up a good description. Say he was a Mexican in a green windbreaker."

"But Renny, I'd never go out with no Mexican, and how come I have to say he's my old boyfriend? I mean—"

Renny sighed, held her by the shoulders, met her eyes. "We'll *deal*. Trust me. Please." He forced a smile for her. It was like jamming a finger down his throat to chuck up an emotion. He needed to divert her, to say something that would get her mind off police procedure, so he said, "Uh, got any towels?"

Renny mopped up. Barb brought a big Hefty bag. Renny stuck the bat back under the bed. Touching it again made him reexperience the sheer satisfaction of pounding ole Victor right back into death, and this gifted him with a healthy and urgent erection.

Barb glimpsed what was coming up and managed to finish him off before the police came knocking. Once again she told Renny that she'd never done *that* with Victor, and Renny smiled and stroked her head, keeping to himself the private notion that Barb could probably suck the stitches off a hardball through a flexistraw. Victor Jacks would never have hung with a china doll. Renny would never have been tempted by one, either.

Then the Authorities arrived, and Renny and Barb set about making up stories.

Funerals never were much of a hoot. Neither Barb nor Renny had RSVPed many in their combined forty-odd years, but this time they dutifully duded up in basic black, and held hands, and dabbed at crocodile tears as the rearranged remains of Victor Jacks were boxed up and delivered six feet closer to Hell.

Half an hour after the services, both of them were naked and neither of them was very depressed.

Most annoying of Barb's bedplay habits was her wont of lighting off to the toilet as soon as . . . well, right after. Renny had once joked about it: "I make all that effort to give you something, babe, and you just go piss it away." Barb had made a face. Crude, her face told him. Not funny. Then, hi-de-ho, off to the can again.

Fine. Renny grunted manfully and rolled to his right side, his favored side for dozing. Swell.

In the bathroom, Barb watched herself in the mirror for a long time, not quite sure what her surveillance was in quest of. Victor had hit her in this bathroom. He'd also done it to her, same day, in the tub, which was too small for love. Victor's tendency to boil over all at once was frightening, a pit bull on a very iffy leash, thought Barb. Whether it got hostile, life-threatening, might depend on a dozen factors. When it last ate. Whether it was pissed off. Whether it liked you. Whether it liked your smell. Victor Jacks had been like that.

But when Victor got to the part where he put his big hands all over her, large, powerful, warm hands, unbuttoning and unzipping her, making her naked and telling her she was wanted, touching her in places only *she* touched—curve of ass, inside of thigh, underside of breast, smooth-shaven armpit—oh, my. He made her moist, filled her up; she would practically *hallucinate,* and she had always slept gorgeously afterward. The sex was never violent between them; only the occasional backhand was.

Barb knew she would never get around to enjoying the way men apologized, every time, *after* they smacked her.

When she met Victor Jacks, she was a waitress-newly-turned-exotic dancer. Petite-chested, with good hips and sturdy, if not long, legs, she figured it was virtually the same aggravation for better tips and weirder hours; she fancied she needed more weird in her life. She got Victor. All he lacked was a puff of smoke to appear in.

When Victor met Barb, he was comfortably into pharmaceutical dexedrine pops and on the cusp of crystal meth. He made do with the odd frame-weld for RUBs—Rich Urban Bikers—and bashed big-blocks for muscle-car meatheads with too much leisure cash. He paid Barb to table-dance and made her sit, just sit, while he looked at her. Management did not approve. Victor did not make a scene. He merely smiled and showed Barb's bosses more money. To Barb, whose concept of foreplay was someone bigger than her saying *shut up and lay down,* this was romance with a big *R* indeed. After a week of this bizarre courtship, she went out with him . . . and he stayed in with her.

When Renny Boone met Barb, he was so chemical-free you could almost see his halo. To Barb, by this time shellshocked by two years of biker-speed tantrums and eight-ball insomnia, Renny's well-cut bod and addictionless turn smelled like that myth come true, the Better Life.

"You look like you could use a rest," Renny had told her, and, so telling her, he took her straight away to bed.

Five days later the two of them were still trying to dope out some rationalization that might convince, say, a jury, that she, Barb, and he, Renny, were Meant To Be. But Barb lacked the heart to dump someone as spontaneous and romantic as Victor Jacks.

Truth was, Renny preferred Barb as a rental. And that Victor wasn't such a bad dude. He'd even nailed the chronic carburetor wheeze suffered by Butch, Renny's black '66 Impala.

Truth was, Barb preferred Victor's flashfire spats to shaking her ass for the beery swine who bellied up to the runway at Nasty Tramps.

So Truth held sway, and Victor stayed ignorant, dangerous, and sexy. Barb had Renny for the topics she could never broach to Victor. And Renny had Barb, the way cowboys have spittoons. And they all lived happily ever after for about two more weeks, until Victor came back to the house, unannounced, to fetch his set of Allen wrenches, and . . .

. . . Well, you can imagine.

The tool excuse had been Victor's cover story. That afternoon, unbeknownst to Renny and Barb, Victor had fallen in love again—this time with a smokable amphetamine called ice. He was pretty saturated, on top of his morning handful of vitamins, when he walked through his front door and caught Renny and Barb doing the bone dance on the sofa bed. The speed made his anger instantaneous, his reaction time zero.

Victor snarled. Literally snarled, lips curling. He came for his betrayers, face bright crimson, the sclera of his eyes pinking. Two steps closer he stopped, stiffened, pawed at his left arm, and fell stone dead of the most concussive goddamn heart attack his mesomorphic build could contain. Victor's fulsome, romantic-if-crazy heart shut down like a phone sex line with no callers, and all that was left was for the coroner to scribble *death by chemical misadventure* in the appropriate box.

Which brings us back to Barb, in the bathroom.

She flushed the toilet. Flushed, then blushed in a matchhead flare of anger as she remembered Renny's idiotic joke about her having to urinate after sex. She would never forget it. Crude, Renny could be so crude. Maybe dumb, too, dumb enough never to have heard of Honeymooner's Cystitis, an inflammation of the urinary tract that was easy to get when you had too much foreign juice rammed up your tubes. And perhaps uncaring as well: Maybe Renny didn't care what havoc forty-five minutes of the missionary position could wreak on even a healthy girl's poor need to pee.

In her mirror, by nightlight, she spotted a hickey on her neck. Crude.

But she loved the way Renny liked to chew on her, just nibble and bite and suck all the right places, as though he was desperately hungry for her, physically starving. She always orgasmed first, even when she tried to outlast him, and when she was coitally zoned, she wanted him to leave marks. Little ones she'd see in the morning, when she felt the delicious ache of their workout.

She liked to tease Renny about all the women he must have learned his bag of tricks from. If she had a headache or a rotten mood, Renny could bang it right out of her. Victor would never touch her at her time of the month; Renny didn't have that problem. He made her feel more desirable on her doggiest days, and feeling desirable made Barb feel womanly indeed. Renny even understood about her having to go back to work at Nasty Tramps, now that Victor was no longer winning the bread. In fact, Renny had suggested it. What a guy.

Crude, dumb, uncaring, and boy-howdy opportunistic. Yeah, Renny was a prize, for sure.

Except that today, somehow, Victor had found time in his schedule to come back from the dead. Maybe she'd seen too many of those damned monster movies, after all, and lacked the emotional capacity for astonishment . . . beyond the histrionics, that is. She looked her reflection eye-to-eye and reminded herself that Victor had done a lot of uppers in his thirty-two years on the planet. Hell, he was probably turning in his new grave right now—at 78 RPM.

The bathroom light was harsh and made her feel lonely. Fortunately, she knew it was a loneliness she could drive away. She wanted Renny on her, inside of her, the fastest way she knew not to feel lonely anymore.

She found him semiconscious and semierect. Renny functioned best with a five-minute nap between rounds. Barb woke him up with her mouth; she didn't say a word. They made a great deal of noise over the next forty-five minutes. Renny always lasted longer once he'd primed his pump; his words.

They were both on their backs, kicking away the sheet to let their own sweat cool them, when Barb said, "Did you hear that?"

"Hear what?"

"Little scritchy noise. Like a mouse."

"Probably that stupid cat of yours."

"No, he doesn't make noises like that."

"Then it probably *is* a mouse. This house is—"

"No, listen."

Renny listened. If the thing making the noise was a mouse, it was dragging off a dog for a bit of fun.

Barb pounded his shoulder. "It's under the bed!"

"Jesus Christ." Renny stayed calm and leaned overboard for a look-see.

From beneath the dust ruffle, the baseball bat shot out like a piston, hitting Renny foursquare in the chin and making him see night sky. It still had clots of Victor drying on it. Then something whipsnaked tight coils around Renny's throat and dragged him down to tussle.

Renny made a gargling noise in the dark as he was reeled in. Discombobulated, he thought he was being engulfed by a giant wiggle-worm with a whole lot of little worms attached. He dug his heels into the rug and fought to breathe. Barb was already making those screamy gasps that truly *bugged* him, deep down.

It was a hand on his throat. He peeled it off. As he did, another appendage trapped his hand.

Renny pulled back and dragged his rubber-limbed assailant out from under the bed—the preferred place of concealment for seasoned, traditional bogeymen.

It was Victor again.

Moreover, it was Victor as he had been buried that afternoon. Bones all smashed. No head.

Renny was instantly mummified in a barbwire-tangle of leathery muscles and nonliving rubber flesh; it was like trying to wrassle a waterbed. What *used* to be Victor's arms and legs—now freed from bones and framework—coiled and constricted into tentacles that were much quicker than Renny's fists. They slithered snug around his windpipe, his chest, his stomach, and Renny could feel it coming: the big squeeze that would make the life jump right out of him.

Now Renny was making those screamy noises.

He was clawing at his own face when Barb, no longer wailing, charged back from the kitchen, brandishing the biggest meat cleaver Renny had ever seen.

Victor had threatened her with the cleaver once; that was how she'd known where to find it.

And Barb had, in fact, seen too many monster movies. Especially the ones about psychos and kitchen implements; you could get every-damned-thing on cable nowadays. She hacked and chopped and slashed and hollered and only nailed Renny by accident once.

The grabby Victor-thing began falling to pieces faster than a clay pot run through on the wheel with a cutoff needle. Tearing a suffocating creeper of skin free from his mouth, Renny flailed to a sitting position and sucked air.

"Barb—you cut me *open,* goddamnit!"

"I *missed,* honey, I'm *sorry,* okay? That thing was all over the place!"

She helped him stand. He was wobbly, unused to needing help, to being nearly beaten. Their feet buried in the desiccated meat on the floor, she felt him shake. He hugged her tight and genuinely.

"I know. I know, babe . . . but that thing is ole you-know-who again."

"Can't be. No way." She pressed her face into his neck, not looking.

He lifted a scrap of now-inanimate flesh and turned it to the faint light, so Barb could see the tattoo. A cherubic, comic-book devil-child looked back at her from a corona of flame.

"Aww, *shit*—it's Hot Stuff, Renny!"

"Yep." Jesus, wasn't there *anyone* whose life hadn't been touched by Harvey Comics?

Victor Jacks had gotten his ink at a Sunset Boulevard parlor called Skin Illos, at the behest of Nikki, who had been his girlfriend of record prior to Barb. Barb had heard you could bleach tattoos by using a laser. She hadn't been able to work up the spit to suggest this to Victor prior to his very timely demise.

"Renny . . . hon . . . I don't want to make you *mad* or nothin, but—"

"But?"

"What if Victor . . . you know, keeps coming back every time we, you and I . . . you know."

31

"Victor ain't coming back again."

"What're we gonna do?"

"What I wanted to do originally. Dump him in the sewer. What's left of him. Let the rats chow down."

"Guess we're gonna need another Hefty bag, huh?"

Barb grimaced at the sliced-and-diced assemblage of tissue on the floor. It relaxed and settled, shifting softly. Renny stared at it, too, panting, with shiny eyes, the sweat leaving his chin in droplets.

"But first, babe, hand me that meat cleaver."

The manhole cover weighed ninety-five pounds, give or take. Renny had the advantages of a prybar and good upper torso strength. Thus were the headless, autopsied, dismembered, broken-boned earthly remnants of Victor Jacks consigned to L.A. County's waste-disposal network.

Hacking Victor into itty-bitty bite-sized morsels had given Renny a peculiar thrill—the same excitement that had granted him a full-on chubby while bludgeoning Vic-baby the *first* time.

Sucker just wouldn't give it up. Renny had to admire that, begrudgingly.

And if Vic-baby somehow managed to make a third curtain call, why, that'd be the tits, too. Because Renny was starting to enjoy the new, fun things he could do with his hands.

Like what he might do if Barb lost her marbles and started that gawdawful shrieking again . . .

Nahh. Just a vagrant thought. No problem there.

Renny yanked his fingers clean and the lid seated with an iron clank. An old pal of his had once broken three fingers by not letting go soon enough, after chasing a frisbee into the sewer. That made Renny think again of Barb. Maybe it was getting time to let *her* go. True, she'd come to his rescue and handled herself well enough tonight, but what if Victor was some kind of *curse* or something, specific to her?

You don't pull back your hand in time, you lose. And it

wasn't his fingers that Renny had been parking inside of Barb most of the recent past.

Just now, in fact, he was up for another bout. His body urged him to hurry home to her. She would be fresh out of her bath, tasty and scented, and Renny wanted to ride her until she screamed for real.

"Do you hear something? A noise, or—"

"Oh for *christ* sake, Barb!"

"I'm serious. Stop it."

Feeling like a wiener, Renny backed out and listened to the doubletime of his own heart, backdraft from his urgent need to climax, soon-sorta-like-immediately. Barb listened intently—she resembled a grade schooler trying too hard to concentrate—not for sounds from the heart, but telltales of nearing monsters. She was still head down, ass up after coyly asking Renny to do her *that way,* and she clung to the mattress as though it could render her some psychic truth.

"I don't hear anything, babe, except maybe your own paranoia bouncing back at us from the walls." Fed up, he grabbed his smokes off the nightstand. Pretty glib, he thought, for a guy who was strangling on a rope of living dead ligaments about an hour ago.

"I thought I heard the seat fall down in the bathroom."

"My fault. I left it up." When Renny strove to impress, he could be the most courteous, thoughtful man on earth. Then, as he procured what he wanted, he let the courtesies slide. Like tonight: He'd left the seat up on purpose, a territorial assertion he knew she'd notice, yet tolerate. The brilliant trick of Renny's life was that he made sure people always noticed him when he was being a swell guy, so there was less risk of him being singled out when he was being a turd of ethics. *Voilà:* He was known far and wide for being fair, wise, and trusty. No way he'd ever sleep with another man's partner, or murder someone, or even *think* of doing the deed.

Even to someone already dead.

Renny could take blame artfully, too—whamming it back

33

the way a tennis pro returns a smartass serve. Like the toilet seat thing.

"I admit I left the seat up, babe. Your house, your rules. But that fuzzy cover on the tank makes it fall down again, and—"

"Shh!"

He smoked in silence, having scored his point. Barb took the cigarette from between his lips, stole two quick puffs, and replaced it as though afraid of being caught tampering with the evidence at a murder scene.

Renny gave up and went to use the bathroom. He left the seat up.

"Barb, there's water all over the bathroom floor. I think maybe your pipes are backing up. Roots, maybe."

"Oh, no! Is it all, you know, messy?"

"Just water. Like a big splash, all over."

"Renny!"

That brought him back quick enough. What a man.

As he skidded in barefoot, he caught Barb shrinking and pointing. Something had just moved near the juncture of wall and ceiling above her cosmetic table. Renny squinted. The something was low-slung, slid along lizard-fashion, and was now watching them both coldly from seven feet up.

"What the hell is it?" said Renny. "A rat?"

"You ever see a white rat with no hair, with eyes that big? Jeeezus, Renny!" Barb could see pretty well in the dark after all. "Where's the bat?"

Renny almost chuckled. "I'll get the damned thing. Whatever it is."

She stopped him, open palm to naked chest. "No you won't either, Renny. Now, I've been doin' some thinking, and you're a nice guy and a good man and a good male protector and all that, and I haven't been holding up my end on this deal, and like you said, this *is* my house . . . so let me do this. It's my turn."

When Barb let loose with stuff like that it stopped Renny deaf and dumb: How could he even consider dumping a woman this good?

She watched his cigarette glow near the bedroom door.

"You just stay right there and hit the overhead lights when I tell you, okay?"

"Yes'm."

"Go!"

The hundred-watter Barb kept in the ceiling fixture blinded them. The thing on the wall recoiled and dropped behind the mirror. Renny and Barb heard it hit the floor and scrabble into the shadows.

"See it?"

"I see it," Barb lied. She shielded her eyes and groped around until she found the bat.

"I don't see it."

Renny could see the tail of Barb's cat, poking from beneath the dresser. It was a miserable calico Renny felt was responsible for every one of his sneezes since he and Barb had linked up. When it wasn't skulking around the kitchen trying to eat everything in sight, it was shedding pounds of hair and clawing the furniture to ribbons. It had some kind of inane cat name Renny could not retain. It didn't listen when Barb told it no. It never had.

It had probably knocked the toilet seat over, numb little fart.

The tail twitched in that spastic way that announced the cat was revving up for the old chase-and-disembowel routine. Barb told the cat *no,* loudly. It didn't listen.

She tried to block it with her foot, but the cat executed a tight dodge and zipped under the dresser, way ahead of her. There followed an unseen, brief, and violent encounter that *sounded* pretty awful, though neither Barb nor Renny could see any of it.

The cat's tail whapped Barb in the chest. The cat was no longer connected to it. Tufts of calico fur followed, held together mostly by blood.

Barb began making cave-person noises and wedged herself into the combat zone, dealing short, blind strokes with the bat. The bureau began to scoot with each hit, bunching the area rug.

The intruder darted out from the far side. It looked like a hand.

"Barb, it's a *hand!*"

"What!" Barb backed off, frantic and hollow-eyed. "What! What! A hand? I don't *care!* It hurt my cat!"

"Barb, it ran under the bed." Renny stepped back from the edge, just in case Barb started swinging again.

Hot for combat, Barb spun. "It hurt Rumplecatskin!" The kill light was in her eyes.

She swept aside the dust ruffle. Two eyes returned her gaze from about a foot in. Then it charged, before she could bring the bat into play, and got a tight grip on her throat.

It was Victor's hand, all right. He'd grabbed her throat enough times for her to make a lightning ID. Whatever else had befallen Victor's mortal parts, his right hand was still strong and mean as ever. Barb's wind was cut and in seconds she'd see the purple spots. Victor knew *exactly* how to throttle her.

She collapsed into a heavy, spread-legged sit-down as Renny dived across the bed, not as fast as he could have been. He didn't really want to touch it. The severed wrist terminated in a reddish-white bag of muscle, like the fat, nontapered tail of a gila monster. Renny grabbed that end and tried to yank it off.

Goddamnit, but this was getting to be much more trouble than *anything* was worth.

Barb's face had shaded to mauve. Renny crawled in tighter, bent back the clutching index finger, and heard it *pop* as he broke it at the base joint.

Shouldn't he just let it polish Barb off? Would this all be over then?

Nope, he thought as he levered the middle finger out of the flesh of her neck. No way he was going to be beaten and humiliated by disorganized body parts. He cocked the finger away savagely and smiled when he heard it snap.

There were eyeballs on the back of the hand, and they swiveled a full one-eighty to glare at Renny. The pupils dilated. Barb was sucking wind in big horsey gasps, her face flushing crimson.

Renny remembered the first time he had ever shaken this hand. Howyadoo. Victor Jacks was the sort of guy whose very existence dared you to be better than him and promised to humilate you if you tried.

The thumb and ring finger could not hang on alone; apparently Barb had smashed the pinky, a lucky hit with the bat; it jutted crookedly, alienated from the choking operation. Renny pried the hand free and chucked it across the room as Barb fell down. The hand bounced from the wall to the floor, leaving red impact smears. Clumsily, it tried to locomote.

Barb stumbled over and started stomping on it. She got gook all over her heel, slipped, and nearly fell again. This enraged her enough to bash the hand with the bat until it didn't move anymore.

Both of them squatted down at a safe distance and got their first really clear look at it.

Apart from the killer hand and about four inches of forearm, there were Victor's eyes. Eyes that had always been the color of pastel-blue enamel, opaque eyes that did not deal in emotional shades, with the hairtrigger flecks of silver buried deep like vague rumors of madness. The eyes were seated across the first three knuckles on the back of the hand and looked roped down by strings of muscle and threads of optic nerve. One eyeball had just been imploded by Barb's death-dance. At last Renny could recognize the bulbous bag that hung off the far end of the wrist.

"That's his heart."

The whole assemblage reminded Renny of something that Victor might jerry-rig on his auto workbench. He was known to be miraculous when it came to solving your vehicular woes with a bent coathanger, spit, and a soldering iron.

"His *heart*." This was not the sort of news Barb was eager to hear. "His *heart*, oh godddd . . . how could it be his *heart*, they took it *out*, you beat him to *pieces*, didn't you break his hand? *Last* time?"

Renny honestly could not recall.

"I mean . . . he didn't have no *head*, Renny! What'd the eyeballs do, *roll* here by themselves?"

As they watched, the heart-end caved in, voiding blood in a final death spurt. It made a large, wet, wide stain on the finished wood of the now-exposed floor.

It appeared to Renny as though it had farted. It was kind of funny. "Wow. You *really* broke his heart."

She began slapping him. The blows were openhanded and basically harmless. "Renny, goddamnit, that's not funny! That's his fucking *hand!* It's been around my throat plenty of times, and for a minute there I could actually *see* him, like he'd come back whole to beat me up again, and *it's not funny!*"

Barb was a pace and a half from an asylum. Her tirade petered out and left her sobbing. Renny did the right thing and tried to hold her. She let him. If he had given her a Kleenex, she would have dislocated his jaw.

"Okay, okay. Sorry I'm such a jerk."

Pangs of selfishness could occasionally make Renny feel guilt, or something like guilt. More important right this minute was the abrupt deduction he'd made while keeping an untrusting eye on the no-longer-moving hand thing.

Victor had been slabbed and gutted . . . and had come walking back. He'd had all his bones busted and he'd come *blobbing* back. And Renny had dumped Victor in the sewer and Victor had come back again, from the sewer. Up through the toilet, just like those urban legends about scuba-diving rats, and snakes, and crocodiles, all of which the eyeball-hand resembled.

"Look, babe, I know what this thing needs. I'll make sure there ain't nothin' left this time."

"And how do you plan on doing that?" Barb had regained enough of her equilibrium to peek at herself in the bureau mirror to ensure she didn't look *too* messed up.

Renny lifted the interloper by its broken pinky. He could feel himself piling up jungle smarts by the minute.

"You got any charcoal starter out back?"

It stank. Truly. It sizzled when it burned, a roundly unappetizing spectacle that Barb forced herself to witness.

They both watched it cook down and Renny periodically batted the chunks apart with barbecue tongs until it was reduced to black goo and bone ash.

Barb plodded back inside to take her third shower in twenty-four hours. There was just no washing Victor off her life.

Renny watched the goo smolder and bubble on the coals. Kind of like pork, the smell.

He rubbed the smoke from his reddened eyes and finished up, not really wanting to enter the house again. He no longer wanted to play bed games with Barb. He just wanted to get some sleep.

By the time Barb had toweled off, she discovered Renny deep in slumberland. Igg, she'd have to change the sheets, despite her shower. A job for tomorrow. She sat on what was, de facto, "her" side of her own bed, successfully not waking her partner in crime.

Renny was different, she knew. Their relationship had turned. Flowers decay. Banquets spoil. Water evaporates. And their sneaky victory had soured. At first it had been a delicious, shared secret; now it had become a horrid quickmire that bonded them like a pair of panicked dogs struggling to uncouple.

She felt, well, *dead* inside, to hammer a phrase. Blown out, wasted, spent, scorching at the edges. She did not want to feel anything so much as she wanted to feel nothing.

Renny was sleeping with his mouth unhinged, as usual, just beginning to snore. That snore would tell her that she was far, far away from his thoughts. She gently grabbed his nose and tilted his head so he no longer faced her. The incipient snore died with a gurgle.

She felt unusually sensitized, to the point where the dust on the sheets and comforter bothered her. Grit was in her eyes, and she fancied more dust layered upon her soul, like wet snow. The thought that it might be the powder of dead bones made her start crying, and she never stopped.

Caught up in her own grief, she missed seeing the tenacious little gob of charred protoplasm as it wormed past Renny's slack lips, to slide easily down his esophagal tract. Soon it would renew its work deep inside of him, where the heart was.

THE LAST CROSSING

Thomas Tessier

*E*ven when you know it's likely, when you have lived with the fear and uncertainty for weeks, it still comes as a terrible blow to be told that you no longer have a job. Dale Davies had been a trader on Wall Street for more than twenty years. He was a quiet but efficient man. He had risen to a certain level and then held his position. He was never a threat to the ambitions of his more aggressive colleagues. He was not brilliant, but the only people who seriously lost money with Dale were those who would have lost it anyway.

There is a kind of poetry of money, a rhythm to finance that generally follows the heartbeat of society at large. Everyone in business knows that there will be highs and lows, steady periods, slumps, occasional jolts, and shocks. Through it all, the market goes on like life itself.

But this new slide into stagnancy was particularly worrying. It was longer and steeper, and for the first time in memory there was no bottom in sight. Dale sensed early on that it might prove to be a transforming moment, such as happens only once in every two or three generations, when things change fundamentally. If that were the case, he had no doubt that sooner or later he would find himself among those culled from the herd.

He was smack on fifty, a dangerous age: too far from

young, too close to old. He believed that his best work was still ahead of him, but Dale knew he was probably wrong. All he wanted to do was carry on where he was for another twelve or fifteen years, to last the course.

He didn't. It was not his fault. Nothing to do with him or his performance. The firm was downsizing, and Dale was downsized out. The same thing was happening everywhere, a slaughter on the middle ground. The young wouldn't go, because they are young and in touch and cheaper to keep on. The old men on top wouldn't go, because they were, after all, on top. So it was Dale, and others like him, who were thrown onto the street.

He was given his notice on a Friday. He tottered out of the building and hesitated. He should go straight home to New Jersey and break the news to Cynthia, his wife. But he wasn't ready for that yet. Cynthia was a woman with lingering social pretensions. The hard fact of Dale's unemployment would not go down well with her, and sympathy would not be her first response. Joanne, their youngest child, had celebrated her nineteenth birthday last month by moving in with a heavy-metal drummer in Hoboken. Things were tense all around. Dale went into Gallagher's. He needed time to think and calm down. He needed a drink.

Call him old-fashioned, but he believed that the dry martini was a divine creation. It seemed to go from the mouth right into the bloodstream, with welcome effect. But there was still a grim reality to be faced. Good Lord, Dale thought, what is happening? All that wariness and anticipation had failed to weaken the blow. It hurt, worse than he ever expected.

He had grown up reading novels about the exciting, ruthless, high-stakes world of business, and he had longed to be a part of it. He studied through the silly sixties, pursued his dream, and finally achieved it. Twenty years—but where did they go? The world had changed so much, and yet here he was, sitting in a fine old gin mill around the corner from the market, feeling just like a character out of Sloan Wilson or John O'Hara. His life nothing but an empty cellophane wrapper.

There was no future, no job waiting for him elsewhere. Dale was at his peak, but in the marketplace he was finished, or would be by the time this slide ended. A desk in a small brokerage out in the suburbs was the best he could hope for, and in itself that would be a kind of death. His clients wouldn't leave the firm to go with him—not for Dale Davies. He was finished. It was all over but the paperwork.

He hit a few other bars, heading vaguely west, away from the financial district. Too many young Turks gargling happily. They were on the escalator going up, alive with their futures. It was not their fault, Dale told himself. They, too, would eventually take it on the neck. Still, he hated them.

It was dusk when Dale realized that he had wandered all the way to the Hudson. The lights of Jersey City were fuzzed by fog. Over there, in the clean suburbs beyond, was his home: across the river, to hell. Not yet. The night had barely started, and Dale was in the mood to cut loose. Let me get robbed, or beaten. Let me be thrown in the gutter. Let me flirt with some pretty young lady in a dangerous joint. Let there be an operatic moment in my life, and let it be tonight.

The immediate prospects were not encouraging. Dale was in a shabby dockside area full of rotten old offices, warehouses, meat-packing plants, and dubious shops cluttered with second-hand junk. But then he found a place, and almost at once he knew that it was the place he had been looking for all his life. There wasn't any name on the small sign overhead, but the flashing lights promised a BAR and GIRLS, and that was good enough for starters.

He went through a narrow doorway, down a flight of creaking stairs, and paid five dollars to a guy with no neck. Then he was allowed into the main room. He banged his right shoulder against a post thicker than a telephone pole—there were a few of them scattered about the big cellar, he saw, when his eyes adjusted to the gloom. There were faint lights strung along the stone walls, a long bar off to one side, some rickety tables and chairs placed in dark corners. The music was loud but not unbearable.

Dale made his way carefully to the bar. He bought a gin and tonic, asking for extra tonic, as it was a good time to slow down and pace himself for a while if he was going to make a real night of it. There were quite a few customers: men on their own, as he was. And there were a lot of fairly undressed young girls out on the floor: some dancing, some lounging around with disinterest, others working the crowd.

Dale saw stockings with garters, thong bottoms, string tops, gym shorts, hot pants, tiny tennis skirts, halters, T-shirts that were cut off to leave the breasts partly exposed, as well as some skimpy or filmy pieces of lingerie. The girls, who included the odd black and Asian in their number, had good bodies, and some of them were strikingly pretty. The place was kind of a dump but it was definitely no dog pound, Dale thought.

"Mardi Gras?"

She was blonde, with layered curls. She was short and cute, with a thin tube top that barely covered her breasts. Below, she had V-shaped panties that were cut high on each side. Dale found himself thinking of a babysitter they had used for a while, years ago. It wasn't the same girl, of course, but the association was quite pleasant. Lisa, as he recalled.

"What?"

"You want to Mardi Gras?"

"I'm sorry," Dale said. "I don't know what that is."

"Mardi Gras. It's, like, lap-dancing."

"Lap-dancing? What's that?"

"Okay," the girl said, smiling sweetly. "We'll go sit down on one of the couches, where it's nice and private, and you give me five dollars when the next song comes on, and as long as that song is on I'll sit on your lap and wiggle around and rub you up and down and cuddle you. You know? Like that." She tugged down the top of her blouse a little, an artfully nonchalant gesture he appreciated. But still Dale hesitated. "I can tell you one more thing," she went on. "They play long songs here. Not like some places I know, where it's two and a half, three minutes. All the songs on this album are like four, five, six minutes long."

"Really?"

"Sure." The girl moved closer, pressing her soft upper body against his arm and at the same time placing her hand just below the small of his back. "Come on, give it a try anyway. Then if you don't like it, at least you'll know."

"I can touch you?"

"If you're nice about it."

"Okay."

Dale put his hand just below the small of her back, and they made their way across the large room to a dark alcove where there was a battered couch. He noticed that the girl was wearing thick white cotton socks on her feet. That's why she was so short: The other girls, most of them, were in high heels. He preferred the socks. They were suburban, New Jersey, wholesome, and yet somehow more wicked.

Why didn't Cynthia dress like this? Why didn't she act like this once in a while? Well, nowadays, she would neither look nor sound anywhere near as appealing as this fine young creature. It was a shame; even years ago, when she could have done this sort of thing with great success, Cynthia never had. It had to be his fault, for never telling her, teaching her. He never asked. The two of them had failed each other. Well, she had, anyway. Where was Cynthia's natural lust, her creative sexiness? But where was his, come to that? He had been timid all his life, in the office and at home. In bed. He had taken life as it came to him, which is what Cynthia had done. In some ways, it had never arrived for either of them.

Dale felt so sad that he had a moderate erection even before the girl settled on his lap and began using her body to play with him. He had his feet up and was sitting back against one arm of the couch. She spun around gently, put her face to his belly, and slowly slithered up his chest. Her tube top was pulled down, and her bare breasts—not large but firm, buoyant—brushed across his face, and he kissed them. She took his hair and pressed his face to one breast, then the other. Dale's hands moved down over her back, gliding to her bottom, her taut thighs.

She stood up on the couch, and suddenly she was in his face. He put his mouth against the thin cotton fabric. She turned and deftly bent away from him, her fanny still in his face. He moved his head forward, touching her there. And that was the moment he didn't want to end, not ever. The smell and feel of her sent his mind swirling off in a dozen dizzying spirals. She touched Dale, her hand stroking him lightly, but that wasn't what mattered. It was this closeness —she was a stranger, he didn't even know what her name was—this sudden profound intimacy, much more intimate precisely because it was not the act of sex itself, that made him tremble and ache. In the cellar of this dead factory, warehouse, whatever, to have this contact, this moment.

"I love you," he said faintly.

"The song's over, honey."

But she didn't move. Dale extracted a twenty, put it in her hand. She touched him again. He ran his tongue along the inside edge of her panties. He tasted her. Pushed his tongue into her. Anyone watching? He didn't care. Everything was on the line.

"Oooh . . . honey . . . hey."

He gave her some more bills.

"Oh, God."

"What?" she asked quietly, not moving.

"You have to be home."

"It's okay, I told them I'd be late," she replied after only a brief hesitation. "My folks are asleep by now. Don't worry, I won't wake them when I get in."

"I'll be late getting back."

"You stopped for cigarettes, or milk. Gas."

"I . . . love . . . you."

"Mmmmmh . . ."

Suddenly he splashed her face.

"God . . . help me."

A murmur, but she caught it.

"You don't need any help now, honey."

"Lisa?"

She laughed softly as she moved off him. "Samantha," she corrected. "Sammie. I'm here from four till midnight, every day. You're sweet. You must eat right. I hope you come again."

"Yeah . . ."

"Look for me?"

"Yes, I will."
"If you don't see me, ask."
"Lisa."
Laughter. "Sammie."
"Right. Sammie."

He stumbled around, found his way, lost it, wandered again. The fog was worse now. Rare to see it in Manhattan, and never as thick as this. The streets were choked with mist, the buildings gauzed. It had the effect of dimming all lights, giving them the weak glow of oil or gas lamps. The cars and trucks inching along cautiously seemed like vehicles from another century.

Dale somehow made it down to the pier and got the passenger ferry to Jersey City. As usual, just later and drunker. Though not too much later, and not nearly drunk enough. He had lost the desire to have a roaring great night in the city. The romance in it, spurious at best, had vanished somewhere. Besides, he had to navigate his car home. He could drink more at home. Rip through the night and then pass out. Why the hell not?

The air was damp and raw, but Dale stayed out on deck as the ferry slowly pulled away. Amazing, how little there was to see! The bright lights of the city were feeble specks beneath the fog. Too bad it wasn't daytime, the whole of Manhattan would look like some ghastly cocoon, he thought. It would look like a dead thing, but it would be teeming with tiny insect life.

Dale went inside. There were only a few other passengers on the ferry. Business types going home, sitting apart from anybody else, each in his own bell jar of solitude. A tipsy young couple standing in a corner, bodies tight, a pint in a brown bag passing discreetly back and forth.

Dale sat down opposite a girl who was on her own. He looked across at her just long enough to register that she was a little on the young side, a teenager. Somewhere in that area. She was staring right back at him, so he glanced away. Schoolbooks. It wasn't smart, a youngster out alone at this time of night.

His eyes drifted back to her legs. Pretty. She was wearing a denim jacket and a short skirt. Her legs parted. Bare thighs. Her legs parted a little more. White panties, just a tantalizing glimpse of them. Dale stared for some minutes.

He looked up at her face. Pretty, very pretty, and somehow familiar. She smiled at him, but it was shy, not the bold smile of a blatant come-on. He looked down. Her jacket was open, and her blouse was unbuttoned to the fourth button. Was that really the curve of her breast? She shifted slightly on her seat, as if to help him see that it was, but then she straightened up and the shirt flapped and that exquisite vision was gone. Her legs moved back and forth slightly. Peekaboo.

Dale gazed at her face again. She was still smiling at him, but there was puzzlement in it now, as if she expected him to say or do something and couldn't understand why he didn't. Where had he seen her before? The more it eluded him, the more certain he was that he knew this girl.

"Sammie?" he asked quietly.

She said nothing, but her head tilted a fraction of an inch and her eyes seemed to narrow with interest.

"Lisa?"

The ferry docked with a bump. People were up and moving to the exit. Dale waited until they were all gone, as did the girl. Then he rose from his seat and took one step toward her.

"Do I know you?"

"Do you?"

Dale didn't know what to say. Then she got to her feet and stood in front of him. Waiting, apparently, for him to make some kind of move. She adjusted the schoolbooks in her grip.

"Do you need a ride?" Dale asked. "My car is parked in the lot outside."

"Thanks."

The night was clear, the fog blown away by a sharp wind from the northwest. Dale felt the chill, but it didn't seem to bother the girl. Her long sleek legs flashed as they hurried toward his car, and her blouse hung open in the harsh air.

He turned on the heater, watching her intently as he waited for the engine to idle down. She put her books on the floor and sat back, smiling.

"Where do you want to go?"

"Where do you want to take me?"

"Home."

"Sounds good."

"My home," Dale said.

"I know."

It was so outrageous it made perfect sense. Dale could see exactly how it would play out. It was late. Cynthia would be up in bed, sound asleep. Probably snoring. And when she slept, she really slept. Dale would bring the girl in, take her downstairs to the now seldom-used family room, make her a drink, and then see what happened. Later, he would drop her off wherever she had to go. It was like a movie. It was delicious. He accelerated, and soon Jersey City fell behind them.

"I'll make you a drink."

"Thank you," she said enthusiastically.

"How old are you?"

"I'd better not say."

"Well, I bet you've never had a martini."

"No, but I'd love to try one."

"The martini is one of man's greatest achievements."

"Mmmm. Sounds good."

She took his right hand and placed it on her thigh. So warm and soft, yet firm, and gloriously bare. It was such a beautiful feeling that Dale nearly had tears in his eyes. He looked across at her: blouse open, now revealing a lot of breast, those dream legs that seemed so amazingly long, the girlish smile, the finger held to her lips—such a vision. When you find such beauty you can't just walk away from it. Before this night was finished, he would lay his face on her flat belly and cry. With sadness, yes, but also with joy—for being granted this moment at all.

Twenty miles flew by. The house was dark, a very good sign. He pulled right into the open garage, so that no snoopy neighbor would see the girl on the way into the house. She left her books on the floor of the car. They went inside through the breezeway, through the kitchen and downstairs to the family room. He turned on only one small table lamp.

"Ooh, it's nice and warm in here."

"Yes," he said.

The girl threw off her jacket and then flopped onto the sofa like a child. She wiggled and stretched her legs, and her skirt bunched higher. She sat up suddenly, turned, and leaned across to look at the books on the shelf nearby. They were Cynthia's. The collected works of Danielle Steel. But Dale was gazing with awe at the girl's backside, those legs and the way the flimsy panties clung to her heartbreaking fanny.

"Do you want that martini now?"

"Yes, please."

"First take off your blouse."

She smiled. She undid the remaining buttons and slipped out of the blouse. Some cheap gold chains hung between her so-lovely breasts. He went to her and touched one nipple with his cheek in an act of homage. She was still smiling, but with curiosity now, and he knew then that she had never behaved like this before, not with a boyfriend, never. It was new for her, too.

"Come on."

He led her to the bar at the back end of the room and showed her how a martini was made. There had been some noteworthy times in Dale's life, but nothing to compare with this, to have a sweet young thing standing there half-dressed while he fixed a martini. In his own family room!

"Take off your skirt."

She did so. He gave her the drink. While she tasted it, he came closer and ran his hands over her body, dizzy with wonder. She pretended not to notice, concentrating on the martini. Dale was awash with joy. Tomorrow might be the first day of a new era in his life, an Age of Lead, but still he had been given this one final moment of poignant, surpassing beauty.

"How do you like the martini?"

"Wow."

"Good. I'll be right back," he said.

"Okay."

She took her drink to the sofa and stretched out, waving her legs until they found a comfortable position. Dale knelt beside her and put his cheek on her belly. There had never, he thought, been a moment like this in my life.

"I'm going to lick you all over," he said softly.

"Cool."

"In a minute."

Dale went into the unfinished section of the basement, where he kept tools and stored things he didn't really want. He picked up a small hammer, the light little one he used for tapping nails in the walls when he wanted to hang a picture. Then he dashed up the stairs to the kitchen, then the half-flight to the top level, past the empty kids' bedrooms, down the hall to the master suite. The door was ajar. She was snoring. Well, it was more than just snoring. She sounded like a factory in western Massachusetts in some previous era.

One good swing. It made an awful sound. But then there was a tremendous silence. Dale lingered. He became aware of wetness on his cheek. He pulled his shirt off, wiped his face, and tossed the shirt aside. He left the hammer where it was.

Down the hall, down the half-flight, down the regular stairs again—suddenly there was so much motion in his life! Amazing. But when he got to the family room, the girl was gone. He looked around the empty room, catching his breath. Nothing, no one. He ran to the car, but the schoolbooks were gone as well.

Dale sat down on the sofa in the family room. He should be angry with himself, with fate and all of its indignities. But it was no use. A great lassitude came over him, and it was all Dale could do to finish the martini.

DAMAGED GOODS

Elizabeth Massie

You put your penis here," Darla said.

Paul, sitting in the tall grass next to her, rolled his eyes in embarrassment.

"You hear me?" Darla repeated. She had her yellow cotton skirt up over her knees, and although she retained her pink panties, she poked her index finger with firm direction at the space between her thighs. "I'm the lamb, and it goes here. God, you're dumb."

Paul pulled out the nub of wild mint he had been chewing and turned on his butt, moving so Darla was no longer in his sight. He stared, instead, at the pasture in which they sat and at the shallow river running nearby. He wasn't certain where the pasture was; he and Darla had been rightfully blindfolded in the van until they were placed in the grass. The sun was behind the two of them, setting in the warm, late spring sky just over the woods to their backs. The men with the sunglasses were in those woods, hiding and silent.

Waiting.

"You're so fucking dumb," Darla continued. "Don't care about nothing except yourself."

Paul closed his eyes and tucked his head. She was right. He was afraid of responsibility. He wasn't good at it and he was afraid of it. Several years ago when he had been living at home, his mother had asked him to watch his baby brother. A simple request. "I got to get this down to the bank. Just let Timmy stay in the crib. I know you can do it. Just twenty minutes, you hear?"

Paul had heard. And Mom had left. But what a mistake she had made, giving him a chore. Silly old Mom. Paul loved Tim, and he liked to play with the little boy. Paul had forgotten that his brother could not eat peanuts, that baby Tim had no teeth and couldn't chew. Paul thought a nut-eating contest would be fun. For each peanut Paul had eaten, he had put one in the baby's mouth. He sang as they played.

"Old MacDonald had a farm, ee-ii-ee-ii-oh. And on his farm he had a cow, ee-ii-ee-ii-oh."

Almost the whole can of Mr. Peanuts was gone after three verses. Paul got to giggling, and he thought that Tim was giggling, too—his face was all shiny and tight and he made funny noises in his throat. But, as Paul found out, the baby wasn't laughing. And Mom didn't laugh, either, when she came back from the bank to find the baby was dead.

But here was responsibility again. And Darla with her dress hiked up and her ass raised to the soft blue sky.

"I can't," Paul said without looking back.

"Hell you can't. All mens can do it. You got a dick, don't cha? It squirts, don't it?"

Paul cringed. Darla wasn't supposed to know about what men's things did. She wasn't yet eighteen. But she knew, all right. She had had a couple babies and a couple operations, too. She lived in the special church home where Paul lived. She did sex things with any man that could walk: residents, orderlies, old drunks from the street that she called to from her third-floor window.

Paul, on the other hand, two full years older than Darla, had never done what she had done. He thought about it, although he tried not to. He watched Darla during dinner or activity time, and he got a knot in his pants. Sometimes he even pretended his fingers were hers, late at night when the lights were low and the sheets were up over his head.

Sometimes he sweated like a horse, he wanted it so bad. But this was daylight, and this was out in the open, and there were men with sunglasses in the trees. This was not pretend.

"Some lion you is," said Darla. She passed air through her lips in a noisy declaration of contempt, and Paul could hear rustling as she pulled her skirt down. He looked back. Her eyebrows were a thick, angry tangle.

Darla wasn't ugly, but she was scarred. Her nose was crooked where some man broke it one time, and the puckered remnants of a long knife wound cut across her throat. Black hair cupped the curve of her cheek in a thin cap. She squinted, because her eyes were bad, but she wouldn't wear glasses. Paul wanted to do what had been asked of him, but he wasn't sure he knew how. He was nervous, even if it was for God.

In his nervousness, he began to sing. He couldn't help himself. He sang on key, soft and trembling. "With a baa-baa here and a baa-baa there, old McDonald had a lamb, ee-ii-ee-ii-oh."

Darla laughed at him, and he wasn't sure why.

"Old MacDonald had a farm, ee-ii-ee-ii-oh. And on his farm he had a lion, ee-ii-ee-ii-oh. With a—"

Then Darla grabbed Paul sharply by the shoulders. Her face squinted up like her eyes. "You might be stupid, but I ain't. I know what's going on here. And I ain't going to let you ruin it. It's for the world, goddamnit, do you hear what I'm saying? We'll be famous, you fucker, not to mention going to heaven for sure. It ain't long to go now, and you better be ready or I'll chew off your nose and send you to hell myself."

Paul watched her face. He felt tears pushing at his eyes, but he worked them back down. She was right, and he knew it.

A new preacher had come to the church home last week. He had walked around for a long time, and Paul had seen him go up and down the halls, all serious and stately in his black suit and white shirt, a big Bible with a tasseled bookmark streaming from the middle pages. He had short brown hair and his ears were sunburned. Paul watched when he thought the preacher didn't know he was watching. But then the preacher had come right up to Paul as he sat looking at cartoons in the rec room. Without even asking, the man turned off the television set, took Paul out to the backyard, and read to him from the Bible.

"The lion shall lie down with the lamb," the preacher had begun, and Paul nodded because a preacher was a man of God and knew what he was talking about, even if it made no sense to Paul. "Do you know, son, that that line is the prophecy of the end of war and the beginning of true peace?"

Paul nodded again, and out of the corner of his eye he watched as a squirrel with a torn, bloodied back pawed an acorn from the ground.

"I have had a sign, and I have shared it with others who understand. They sent me here, to find you."

Paul suddenly thought he was going to go to the electric chair for killing his baby brother, after all this time, and the preacher was to give him his last meal and pray with him. Paul started to cry.

"Weep not," said the preacher. "For blessed are the pure in heart. They shall see God."

Paul's lip twitched, and the tears continued.

"Blessed are the damaged ones, for they will bring perfection to our world."

The preacher told Paul of the Holy Plan and kissed him before he left.

Now they were here. This was the day. It was secret, of course, because the masses, so the preacher said, would not understand the seriousness of what was going to take place. There was only one audience, and they were in the trees now, waiting patiently. Only One was missing, and He would arrive very soon.

Paul and Darla, the chosen ones, the damaged ones, were here to be the lion and the lamb. At their union, all the evils of the world would be bound and thrown to the pit of fire and onto Satan's head.

Paul reached under his shirt and scratched his chest nervously, leaving long fingernail lines. He looked past Darla's shoulder. Soon He would come. Then it would be time to act. Paul would either get over his embarrassment and do to Darla what he'd always wanted to do in the late-night hours, or he would let the world continue to fight and kill and torture and tear itself into a million pieces.

Darla said, "Hey."

Paul blinked but said nothing.

Darla said, "Hey."

He looked at her. "What?"

"I'll rub you. It'll help."

Paul shuddered at the thought. But he became instantly hard.

"I'll rub you and it'll be easier. Big shit, you can think of somebody else if you want, I don't care. Damaged goods is what they wanted, but you can think of someone else, okay?"

Paul said, "Okay."

Darla smiled then, the first time since the blindfolds had been removed. With the sun behind her head, she almost looked like an angel.

And then there was a shadowy sparkling from the trees, and Paul knew that He had arrived. The long car with its secret windows pulled up behind the outer edge of trees and stopped. Men in sunglasses became briefly visible as they shifted and stamped in silent respect.

"He's here," whispered Darla.

Paul reached under his shirt and scratched frantically.

Out of the woods came the preacher, and behind the preacher He came. Darla and Paul sat motionless. Paul felt his muscles kick into spastic idle; he shook uncontrollably.

The preacher wore his black suit and white shirt. He smiled a beautiful smile. The Man with him was tall and white-haired and wore a gray suit and sunglasses. He said nothing but stood in command of them all.

The preacher said, "The lion will lie down with the lamb. In this will be the beginning of peace, and all nations will lose their love of war."

Darla's eyes were turned up in an expression of near-worship. Paul scratched his chest, making it burn.

"Thus it is said," continued the preacher. "When she who is the lamb and he who is the lion lie together, and become as one, the veil of hate will be rent."

The Man with the preacher crossed his arms. His hands were soft and strong, His fingernails trimmed and clean.

"Blessed be the lion and the lamb."

Darla whispered, "Amen."

"Please," said the preacher. "Make the prophecy come true." With that, the preacher fell silent.

Darla looked at Paul. "I'll rub you," she said.

Paul's fingers became still on his chest. He watched as Darla moved her hand to the snap on his pants and popped it open. The zipper was undone, exposing Paul's white briefs. Darla's touch and the cool spring air on the cotton stirred Paul's organ again. It tingled in anticipation and pushed at the cloth. Paul wanted to cover himself. He wanted Darla to suck him and make him explode.

"Come on, lion," said Darla. "Lie with me."

Ee-ii-ee-ii-oh, thought Paul.

Darla slipped her hands beneath Paul's hips, and he instinctively rose up so she could pull his jeans down to his knees. Then she loosened his shoes and tossed them aside. His socks followed, and then the jeans, one leg at a time. Paul sat back on the prickly grass. He wondered if little Tim would have been proud of his big brother now, the new savior of the world.

The yellow skirt with its elasticized waist came up over Darla's head. Her pink panties appeared to be damp. Darla touched her thighs, her belly button, the damp pink panties.

Paul realized that she was not going to remove her own blouse, nor his shirt. Not that it mattered: The business ends were already exposed. He wanted to touch his penis but was afraid. He would let Darla take charge. She knew what to do. Blessed be the lamb who sucks the dick of the lion.

Darla caught Paul's hand in her own. She moved it to the panties and worked his fingers down inside. Paul gasped at the feel of coarse hair. "Oh," he moaned.

He thought he heard the Man echo, "Oh."

"Come on," Darla said, her breath hot on Paul's face. "I'll rub you and you rub me."

Paul's fingers began stroking the thick hair below the elastic. No longer could he feel the burning scratches on his chest; his own breath came in horrified, ecstatic jolts. Darla found his erection with the palm of her hand. Paul arched his back, pressing into her touch.

The Man with the preacher opened his own pants, and from the corner of his eye, Paul saw him reach in to stroke himself.

But Darla took his attention back with a firm squeeze. "Lie with me." Her voice was barely audible. "Stop wars. Bring peace." She slipped her hand inside his briefs and brought his organ out into the sun. Passion, embarrassment, anticipation, and fear cut his heart. Paul groaned.

The Man and the preacher groaned, too.

Somewhere beyond the holy union, sunglasses, moving to the edge of the woods, winked in unison.

Darla tore the seams of her panties and tossed them out with Paul's socks. She ripped away Paul's briefs with sharp nails. She folded, and her mouth took Paul's penis in a wet caress.

"Ee-ii-ee-ii!" Paul shrieked. He felt the swelling pressure, the urgent demand as her tongue studied him. He wanted to stop for a moment, he was rushing ahead too fast, he could not think of what was happening and he wanted to, he wanted to have memories of this and think of it again and again, but it was too fast. Too fast.

"Wait!" he screamed.

Darla dove backward, dragging Paul with her. She threw her legs apart and shoved Paul into the wet place beneath the dark hair. Paul bucked instinctively, furiously. He was so swollen he knew he would rip her open, but that was fine. That was good. The lion tearing the lamb for the peace of the world.

And then the divine, glorious explosion.

"Oh, my God!" shouted Paul.

"Oh, God!" shouted Darla.

"Oh, God," grunted the Man near them.

Paul fell, face into the sharp grass, arm crumpled up under him, folded against Darla's breast. His groin and stomach continued to shudder with aftershocks. He could hear Darla's pants. He could feel the sweat of her body. It was warm, like a beautiful, peaceful bath.

"Yes," said Darla in his ear. "We laid down together. Lion and the lamb. We done it." It sounded as if she were weeping with joy.

Paul began to laugh for the same reason. "We saved the world," he sang. "Ee-ii-ee-ii-oh, we saved the world from war!"

He heard the preacher laughing, too.

Then the preacher said, "Well, sir, that do the trick?"

Paul used his untrapped hand to wipe a gnat out of his eye. He squinted up at the men near them in the pasture.

The Man had his penis out of his pants, and it was erect. His mouth was a straight, tight line across his face. His eyes were still invisible behind the glasses. There were sweat droplets on his cheeks and hands.

For the first time, the Man spoke: "Not quite. Almost."

"Shit," said the preacher, and Paul flinched. Preachers didn't talk like that, not at the church home, anyway. "We got another go-round," the preacher went on. "If you'd like."

Paul worked himself up off of Darla. He sat and brushed dead grass from his legs. Darla lay still, basking in the glory of her success.

The Man wiped his mouth, gazed out past the river, then back to the preacher. He said, "Why couldn't I go for golfing?"

"Different strokes," said the preacher, and he laughed again, once.

Darla opened her eyes and looked at them all.

Then the preacher swung his foot and caught Paul in the ribs. "Get up, morons," he said. He kicked Paul again.

Darla sat up immediately. Her mouth hung open, bad teeth showing. "What the hell are you doing?" she said. "What is the matter with you?"

Paul began to shake. He stood and looked over at his torn underwear in the weeds. He glanced down at his exposed penis. With a surge of supreme humiliation, he covered himself with his hands.

"Thanks for saving the world," said the preacher.

Darla jumped to her feet. "What the fuck's going on?" she screamed. She raised her hand to strike the preacher, but he caught it and twisted it. Darla dropped to her knees.

"I've got State of the Union tomorrow," the Man said to the preacher. "Teddy got off on hunting, Ronald on his horses. Sports just don't cut it for me. I have to have my stress release or who knows what wrong decisions I might make?"

The preacher said, "You don't have to convince me. I'm just happy to be part of the smooth running of the government. 'Remembereth me as thou dwelleth in thy kingdom.'" He smiled a chilling smile.

"Another go-round," said the Man. "Please. That would be good."

The preacher pulled a small pistol from his black jacket. His smile was gone, but in its place was not anger, just emotionless duty. "To the river," he said.

Darla was crying. She stayed on her knees until the preacher put the pistol to her head. "To the river," he said. "We don't have time for this shit."

Darla stood up beside Paul. The preacher led them to the river's edge. He took white strips of cloth from his pocket. He tightly gagged Darla's mouth. Then he gagged Paul.

"Silence of the lamb," said the preacher. "And the lion." He laughed.

Paul began to choke against the dry cloth. He could not swallow. He felt his nose could not take in enough air. Had the wars stopped? Had the peace come?

"Hands back," said the preacher.

Darla shook her head violently. The preacher put the mouth of the gun against her teeth and she stopped. She put her hands behind her back, and the preacher tied them with cloth. Then he looked at Paul.

Paul put his hands back.

"Good little lion," said the preacher, and he secured Paul's wrists. "You won't be shot, though. Morons drown so much more naturally."

There was a rumbling from the woods, and Paul looked behind to see a van moving out into the pasture. The Man stepped back to give it room. It stopped, and the engine was cut.

Darla's eyes widened in hope. Paul tried to stumble forward. Rescue, oh, God, yes, thank God, thank God! He uttered a choked whine of agonized appeal.

The driver of the van swung out and around, then opened the sliding door on the side. Two blindfolded people climbed slowly into the daylight.

A young blindfolded man. A young blindfolded woman.

"They're going to save the world, too," said the preacher.

Ee-ii-ee-ii-oh, thought Paul.

The preacher baptized Darla and Paul in the brisk, running water of the river.

HILLBETTYS

Graham Watkins

*T*here was no warning, none at all. One moment Ron was driving up a run-down mountain road, listening to his stereo; the next he'd rounded a sharp curve and seen the rockpile covering the pavement ahead. There was no way he could stop in time, and the front of his Mercedes slammed into the limestone chunks with a sickening crunch.

After sitting stunned for a few moments, he finally unhooked his seatbelt and opened the car door. On shaky legs, he climbed out and stood staring at the damage; it took only a few seconds for his relief at being uninjured to change to rage.

Clearly, the car wasn't going anywhere. The engine might run, but the front end was crushed in against the wheels. He cursed the rocks, kicked one of them; then he aimed his fury at the tipster he'd met at an antique show in North Carolina, the man whose stories had sent him on this trip in the first place. The old trader had told tales about an out-of-the-way shop up in the hills where the proprietor had no notion of the true value of her merchandise, and even given Ron a map to find the place.

Turning away from the car, he began surveying his surroundings. To his right was a rocky slope dotted with clinging trees, rising on up toward some unseen peak or ridge; to his left, an abrupt dropoff. Ahead and behind, nothing but woods and the tortuously winding road. There wasn't a sign of human habitation anywhere; the road itself and a rutted dirt trail leading up the hillside a few hundred yards back were the only signs that anyone had been up here since the days of Daniel Boone. He'd already traversed at least five deserted miles since leaving the main road. Going on might well lead to help sooner, but he had no way of knowing that; besides, it was steeply uphill. A resident of the urban hills of Knoxville, Ron allowed his choice to be determined by the slope of the road, by the known—even if the known did constitute one hell of a long hike.

Still cursing under his breath, he started walking. It was not yet noon; with any luck at all, he told himself, he'd be able to find a phone before nightfall. But even that wasn't a certainty. He couldn't remember seeing much of anything down on the main road either, not for quite a few miles. What he'd do if he found himself out wandering these hills after dark, he didn't know.

"Hey, sonny," a voice called before he'd covered a hundred yards. "Kindly looks lak ye done had y'seff some trouble thar!"

Stopping, he looked for the source. Up the rutted mountain trail a short distance stood a woman waving at him. She appeared to be perhaps forty, and she was dressed in the uniform of the mountain woman: long dress, heavy shoes, semipermanent apron.

"Yeah," he called back. "Yeah, there's been a rockslide, and I've wrecked my car. Do you live around here?"

She smiled; as he came closer he could see that she was really pretty good-looking, that she'd probably been stunning in her youth. Her black hair was heavily streaked with gray, but her eyes still seemed bright. "Why, shore," she answered, her hill accent extreme. "Our place is raht on up the hill here a ways."

"Do you have a phone?"

"Shore. C'mon. Lahk I said, its a ways!"

Smiling back at her, he turned onto the steep path. "Hey, I really appreciate it," he told her. "Mrs. . . . uh . . ."

63

"The name's Reardon," she supplied, cocking her head and looking him over. "Ye look lahk a city boy fer sure!"

He nodded. "Yeah, Knoxville. I'm Ron Maxwell—Dr. Ron Maxwell."

Turning, she took a few steps up the hill, motioning for him to follow. "Doctor, huh? Whatcha doin' up here? Makin' a house call?"

"No," he grunted sourly. "No, I was up here to—"

He stopped, fell silent. There was another woman waiting up there, and for a moment all Ron could do was stare. Daisy Mae, he'd always assumed, was strictly an Al Capp fantasy; yet, allowing for a few minor differences, there she stood on that rutted road, not fifty feet away. Barefoot, clad in tiny shorts and a tied plaid shirt that left her midriff and much of her upper chest exposed, she was dressed so much like L'il Abner's wife that Ron wondered if it could be coincidence. Like Daisy Mae, her hair was blond; unlike the comic-strip heroine, it was silky and straight, and it reached far down her almost unnaturally long legs.

"'At's my oldest," Mrs. Reardon said, not failing to notice what he was staring at. "Martha Jean. Martha Jean, this here's Doc Maxwell. He done had some trouble down 'ar on 'at ol' road."

"Hey, Doc Maxwell," the blonde said. Her voice fitted her appearance: low-pitched, sultry. Evidently, deliberately so.

"Ron," he said, his own voice just a little weak.

"C'mon now, you two," the older woman said. "Y'all can talk later. My youngest is up thar a-fixin' some vittles. I 'spect ye c'ud use a bite, cun'cha?"

"No—well—I don't know—I really need to use that phone—"

"Wal, it's up yonder too!"

Ron tried to keep up as the two women almost scampered up the hillside. He wasn't really able to, and they were forced to slow down and wait for him. The trail seemed to go on forever; at the point where he was beginning to wonder if there actually was a house up there at all, it suddenly came into sight. Large, rustically but sturdily built, it looked quite old. Across the front stretched a full porch supported by barked but otherwise unaltered tree trunks, the steps leading to it rough-hewn. Inside, the impression of age persisted; few of the well-worn furnishings appeared to belong to the twentieth century. Giving him little time to look around, the two women guided him to the kitchen, where he'd been told the telephone was located. At the doorway, he was again stopped cold.

If Martha Jean was a Daisy Mae clone, then the girl working at the wood-fired stove was Moonbeam McSwine without the dirt. Shorter than her sister, she was dark-skinned, dark-eyed, dark-haired—and outrageously appealing in her tied shirt and shorts. Mrs. Reardon, obviously amused at his reaction, introduced her as Cindy Ann.

"Uh—could I see the phone, now?" he asked after a long pause. He was still staring at the dark-haired girl.

"Sho 'nuff," Mrs. Reardon answered amiably. "It's over on yonder wall thar."

With mumbled thanks, he went to it; the instrument looked like it might have been one of the first dial phones ever produced, one generation after the crank. "You have a phone book?" he asked.

"Uh-uh. An' it wu'nt do ye no good if'n we did. Ye cain't call nobody 'ceptin' th' op'rator. Jis dial th' *O* thar."

There was a faint buzzing hum in the phone when he picked it up; as instructed, he dialed the zero. Immediately the sound ceased, the phone went dead. Clicking the hook restored the hum; dialing zero—or any other number—eliminated it.

"What am I doing wrong?" he asked after several tries.

Mrs. Reardon took the receiver from him and tried it herself. "Well, drat!" she exclaimed. "Ol' Bertha Sue must be a-goofin' off again! That, or she was called away fer sumpin'." She hung up the phone. "Ain't nuthin' ye kin do but wait, Doc," she said. "Jis sitcher seff down thar at th' table. Cindy Ann, you 'n' Martha Jean get some vittles on here, an' git the Doc a glass o' cider."

"I don't know," Ron said doubtfully. "I don't want to impose. Maybe I should go back to my car, see if someone else comes along . . ."

Mrs. Reardon waved her hands impatiently. "T'ain't gonna do no good t'go back down thar t' th' road, Doc. Ain't a lot o' folks use that thar road; one, mebbe two cars a day. There's times there ain't none." She laughed. "An' we done had one today, raht?"

He couldn't really argue; he himself had seen no other traffic there. Besides, he told himself as he watched the two women put food on the table, the scenery down there might be good but it was much better up here. "Okay," he agreed. "Maybe you're right. And I think a glass of that cider might be nice!"

The cider was very good indeed, flavorful and mildly alcoholic. The food was better; Cindy Ann could open a country-style restaurant in Knoxville and get rich overnight. By his standards, it was a huge lunch, but he ate heartily nonetheless; he couldn't remember having eaten potatoes, corn, ham, and gravy prepared as well as this.

Afterward he received a bit of a shock: On asking where the bathroom was, he was directed to an outhouse, and upon returning he learned that the Reardons did not even have running water; that water was hand-pumped from a well. He hadn't imagined that anyone still lived so primitively, even in these remote Kentucky hills.

Over the course of the next couple of hours he tried the phone repeatedly—but without results. Each time Mrs. Reardon counseled patience—"Ol' Bertha Sue's bound to come back sooner er later!"—and each time he allowed himself to be persuaded. Between tries he spent most of his time in the Reardon living room, sipping the wonderful cider and talking with Martha Jean and Cindy Ann—and, in the process, learning a bit about the Reardon family. Martha Jean was twenty, Cindy Ann eighteen; their father had been dead for many years. They had no other siblings, no living relatives; the women were on their own. To his surprise, he learned that neither of them had ever attended public school. Mrs. Reardon had taught them the rudiments of reading and math, what the girls referred to as the "three *Rs.*"

Nor had they ever been employed. "Well, I don't understand!" he exclaimed. "How do you live?"

"Don't take much," Cindy Ann replied in her slow, sleepy drawl. "We got our gardens, we got our hawgs. We get 'nuff t'eat."

"Yes, but you can't pay—oh, let's say the phone bill!—with that!"

Here the younger girl looked hesitant—nervous, it seemed to him—and glanced at her sister. "Sho' 'nuff," Martha Jean answered quickly. "But we do awraht. We need some money, we c'n allus sell a hawg. We raises us some real fine hawgs up here, Rahn!"

He shrugged, let the subject drop. The afternoon slipped by gently, its passing cushioned by the cider and the two girls, who were utterly charming in spite of their sometimes almost grotesque accents. The Reardons seemed to enjoy his presence; at dinnertime a place was set for him, apparently as a matter of course. While they were eating, Mrs. Reardon informed him that it was useless to even try the phone again until the next morning. Bertha Sue, it seemed, left work around six and did not reappear until nine the following morning. If you had a fire or a medical emergency in the night, well, that was, presumably, just too bad.

It was also taken as a given that he'd spend the night. They had a spare bedroom, Mrs. Reardon told him, and first thing in the morning they'd see what could be done about his predicament. Feeling he had no choice, he accepted her invitation with thanks.

As night began to fall, Ron got another surprise: The Reardons had no electricity. Oil lamps and candles that he'd assumed were merely decorative were lit, and before long Mrs. Reardon began dropping hints that it might be about time for bed. It wasn't much past nine; for Ron, it felt like going to bed in the middle of the day. He had a sinking feeling that someone was going to be knocking at his door and offering breakfast at—or even before—sunrise.

Again, though, he felt he had little choice. Taking his leave of the two girls, he allowed Mrs. Reardon to show him to his upstairs room. As he stepped onto the stairway and put his hand on the banister it leaned far to one side, almost causing him to lose his balance. Mrs. Reardon made a clucking sound.

"Got to get attair thang fixed," she observed. She pointed to a cracked support near the bottom. "Dang thang, hit got wet and split open. You whatcher seff thar, don't let it throw ye." He nodded, then followed her up the stairs to the guest room. Mrs. Reardon gave him a small oil lamp and a quick course in how to use it, then left.

Alone in the room, he kicked off his shoes, lay down on the overly soft bed, and allowed his gaze to roam. The furnishings, like virtually everything else here, were antique; except for a so-far nonfunctioning telephone, the Reardons lived without any sort of modern convenience. He was glad that the telephone was here, even if it wasn't working: It eliminated any "Twilight Zone" fantasies, any notions that he might've fallen through some sort of a time warp.

He was still thinking about that when the door of his room squeaked slightly and started moving open.

Instantly alert, he sat straight up in the bed, but when he saw that the intruder was Cindy Ann, he grinned and relaxed. Knocking, apparently, wasn't a convention that was observed here. He watched her as she closed the door and turned a small wooden bar that he'd not noticed previously; it dropped into a slot in the thick wooden doorframe, locking the door.

Giving him a slightly tremulous smile, she came to the bed and sat down. "Y'doin' okay, Rahn?" she asked. "Y'need anythin'?"

He smiled back, perhaps a little suspiciously. "I'm fine," he replied. "I don't need a thing. Maybe you'd better go."

She scooted a little closer. "Now, Rahn," she said with a smile that was by now almost overtly seductive, "I ain't a-goin' nowhere, not jis yet! 'Cause if'n I do, y'know what's a-gonna happen!"

He looked a bit confused. "What's that?"

Her eyes opened wide. "Why, you're a-gonna go over t'

Martha Jean's room, or else she's a-gonna come in here! We ain't ignorant, Rahn! We know how menfolks are!"

He had to struggle not to laugh. "No," he told her. "I had no intention of going to your sister's room, and I doubt that she—"

She pushed closer, pressing her bare thigh against his leg and running a hand down his chest. "I think," she sighed, "that ye lahk to talk too much! You just let ol' Cindy Ann look after you, Rahn, and ye won't hafta worry none 'bout Martha Jean!" By the time she'd finished speaking, her hand had dropped below his belt and she'd crossed her other leg over his knee.

Visions of back-country shotgun weddings started running through his head. "No, now wait a minute," he protested, pushing her hand away. "I don't think we should be—"

Ignoring his words, she kissed his cheek; she reached for her shirt, and before he could protest she'd pulled the knot. It fell open, revealing two of the most attractive breasts he'd ever seen. She shrugged it off, kissed his lips, began unbuttoning his shirt.

With much less conviction he continued to try to argue, to try to push her away. She was having none of it; her lips moved around his face, his neck, his ear. He started sweating; in spite of himself he started to respond. One of his hands was already on her silken thigh, the other headed for those magnificent breasts. This doesn't happen, he told himself as she smiled up at him engagingly and deftly undid his belt. It doesn't. Women don't act this way, back country or no. Maybe I already fell asleep?

But he really couldn't buy that. "No," he managed to croak. "No, Cindy Ann, you don't want to do this, you—"

"Yes," she murmured. "Yes, I do!" She unzipped his pants and quickly reached inside; when she wrapped her fingers around his erection, it became almost painful.

The thoughts of setups and shotgun weddings did not actually go out of his head, but they certainly got pushed down, far down. Slowly at first, then with increasing vigor, he began cooperating with her. Within minutes his clothes were gone; she took her shorts off, but she was still wearing a tiny undergarment, almost like a G-string but more rudely made.

For the moment, he paid little attention; he was too busy caressing, licking, and nibbling at her breasts. She moaned softly; her small nipples became quite hard. Lifting his head, he kissed her, and she kissed him back with an almost violent passion.

Finally he reached for the wispy undergarment, but she stopped him with her hand. "No," she said, gently but firmly. "Cain't. But don't you worry, Rahn. I know how to make a man happy!" With this she pushed him back on the bed and lowered her head to his lap. Her head tipped up, her eyes fixed on his, she began licking his penis.

It was his turn to moan then, as she took it between her lips. She was startlingly expert, alternating quick movements with slow sensual ones, using both her tongue and her lips to perfection. He watched her, saw her glance up at him repeatedly, saw her smiling as she continued to push him higher and higher.

His only regret was that it didn't last longer, but there was no way he could hold out. He warned her that he was imminent, but her response was to take him deeply into her mouth; when he filled it with his semen she unhesitatingly swallowed it all.

Afterward she snuggled against his side, and he forgot all about the oversoft bed. He still didn't sleep in it, however; her hands kept moving on his body, and after a while he was ready to go again. This time he did take longer, and after another intermission and a third performance, he fell asleep.

He awoke to a banging on the door. "Cindy Ann!" he heard Mrs. Reardon calling. "Cindy Ann, y'up? Answer me, girl!"

Groggily, he moved to shush the girl, but he was too slow. "I'm rahtchere, Ma," she called back. "We'll be raht on out, y'hear?"

From outside the door, he heard a long, drawn-out sigh,

followed by the sound of feet clumping away. He groaned, covered his face with his hands. "Christ!" he muttered. "Now your mother knows you were here all night! Jesus!"

"Well, a-course she knows," Cindy Ann said. Still naked except for the G-stringlike panty, she was distractingly beautiful in the pallid morning light. "She sent me in here, after all!"

Yet again he stared, his suspicions welling back up. "What?"

She smiled, kissed him. "Don't matter none, Rahn," she told him, her voice conspiratorially low. "You jis lissen to me, do what I tell ye. Now, when we go down to breakfast, ol' Martha Jean, she's a-gonna be after you. You jis say no, an' y'say it lahk y'mean it! Then, after you eat, you skedaddle! Don't you lissen to Ma tellin' you 'bout no phone. That ol' thing don't work and never has. She done rigged it up to buzz so's the fellers 'ud think it did!"

He scowled. "What in hell are you talking about?" he demanded. "Why would she do that? She——"

"Rahn," she said in a near whisper, "Ma put the rocks on the road down thar so's you'd whang yer car into 'em. Ye ain't the first feller to come lookin' for a antee-kwee shop what ain't here!" Her face became very serious. "But you're a-gonna be the first one t' leave, if'n ye do what I tell you! And if'n ye do, mebbe ye might wanta have a little talk with th' sheriff! I cain't take this stuff no more, Rahn. I ain't like Martha Jean, I jis don't lahk it!"

A little chill ran up his back in spite of the warmth of her still-close body. "What's going on here?" he growled.

"Rahn," she said patiently, "Ma don't get her money by sellin' no hawgs! She gets it from a-robbin' fellers like you!" She drew a little closer. "And the fellers, well sir, they ain't in no shape to go tellin' th' county sheriff 'bout it! No sir!"

He began visualizing Mrs. Reardon waiting outside the door with dagger or pistol, and he questioned Cindy Ann on the Reardons' methods. She might, he told himself, be a part of the plot; she'd certainly kept him distracted all night. But if she was, why say anything about it now?

She looked down, seemingly embarrassed. "Don't you

worry 'bout it," she said. "Jis 'member what I tole ye. Ye gotta say no to Martha Jean!"

He heaved himself out of bed and began dragging on his clothes. "I assure you," he said, "there's no problem with that!"

In spite of his assurances, she groaned. "That's what the last feller said!" she cried. "Jis exactly! You ain't a-gonna lissen, you ain't a-gonna believe!" She jumped up and stood with clenched fists. "I'm a-gonna hafta show you! You looka here, Rahn; you look here and you'll see, you'll see what's a-gonna happen if'n ye don't lissen!" With that, she jerked down the little G-stringlike affair and tossed it aside. The menstrual pad Ron had believed it concealed was not there. She threw herself down on the bed and spread her legs wide. Her pubes were high and heavily haired; the lips were very obvious, as if swollen. "Look!" she demanded, pulling at them with her fingers.

"This is hardly the time," he said dryly. "And I must say, I'm not really in the—"

"Look!" she hissed, opening herself more widely.

He did. At first, what he was seeing didn't make sense; he thought perhaps she had some sort of disease. When it did, his eyes almost started out of his head.

She'd pulled both sets of her vaginal lips open; both were larger than might be expected, but Ron hardly noticed that. What captured his attention were the teeth.

Bright white, each one half an inch long or more, recurved like a snake's teeth and serrated like steak knives, there were four rows of them, one row lining each inner and outer vaginal lip.

"Now you kin see what we are!" Cindy Ann spat. "Martha Jean's built the same way, and so's Ma! You believe me now, Rahn?" Tears filled her eyes and ran down her cheeks. "The las' feller didn't, and Martha Jean, she cut him all up! I don't wanna—"

Ron had taken a few steps backward. "Christ. Christ," he muttered. "Jesus, I can't—my God! Vagina dentata, I've heard of it, I thought it was just tales, I—"

"I only killed one feller," she went on, her eyes pleading.

"Jis one. I tol' him no, I tol' him I'd make him happy, but he tore off my panty and he forced me—I didn't mean to, I didn't!"

Ron was standing near the door by then. "Not possible," he said, addressing himself. "A trick, a fake. Can't be. How could the mother get pregnant? How could the girls be born? Can't be, it just can't."

"If'n the man squirts quick, we can get pregnant," she said tearfully. "Martha Jean had a li'l boy a couple years back. Ma killed 'im. When he come out, her lips was turned all inside out!"

He started back toward her, reaching out as if to touch them, to prove to himself he was being tricked. "No!" Cindy Ann cried, closing her legs. "No, they're pizen! Y'cut y'seff on 'em, even jis a little, and it'll make ye so's you cain't move at-all!"

He couldn't believe this either, but even so he pulled his hand back. His head was swimming; a sense of nightmare overtook him. He rushed to the door and began fumbling with the wooden latch.

"No, wait!" Cindy Ann cried. "Wait! Don't let 'em know you know! Rahn, I don't know what they'll do!"

He couldn't hear the warning. The door opened; headlong, he rushed out and down the stairs.

And almost ran right into Martha Jean, who was evidently waiting for him.

"Well, g'mornin', Rahn," she purred. She was wearing a thin shortie nightgown, and it was evident that that was all she was wearing: Her nipples and pubic hair were quite visible through the sheer material. She reached for him. "We oughta find us a place where we c'n sit and talk for a while," she murmured. "Without Ma or my li'l sister!"

"No," he muttered. He started to pass her, but she stepped in front of him. "No, I gotta go, I gotta—"

But she pushed closer to him. "Now, Rahn," she said, her tone teasing, "I know mah l'il sister! She might've showed you a good time, but she don't wanta do it raht. Now me, I'm not lahk that! You jis come 'long with Martha Jean now, let me—"

He began backing off. "No," he told her. "No!" He held out his hands, palms first. Tousling her hair, an exaggerated expression of lust on her face, she continued to push her body closer to his.

Ron continued to back off, trying to ward her off with his hands. He couldn't have imagined being in a situation like this: A stunningly beautiful and very obviously unarmed woman advancing on him amorously, and he was terrified.

Eventually, he could back up no more; his back touched the stair banister, his heel hitting the first step. Martha Jean came on, cupping his face in her hands, kissing him, pushing her tongue into his mouth, straddling one of his legs with hers. Looking down, he saw that her nightgown was pushed up to her hips, and he could see that her vaginal lips were spread in an unnatural fashion, like the jaws of a mantis or a spider, sideways, and that they were resting against his thigh . . .

Panicked, he pushed her violently away; she staggered but quickly regained her balance. Her hands on her hips, she glared at him. "What's wrong with you?" she demanded. "You act lahk you're skeered o' me!" She cocked an eyebrow at him, and a suspicious look crossed her face. "Cindy Ann ain't been a-tellin' you no silly tales, has she? She does that sometimes, she—"

"Look," he told her, desperation obvious in his voice. "I have to go, I really do, I—"

She smiled again, as if she'd decided that it was impossible that Cindy Ann had exposed their secret. "Aw, yer jis shy!" she declared. She came forward once more, trapping him on the stairs.

As he frantically looked around for a way out, he remembered the cracked banister support. With some vague idea of using a piece of it as a club, of threatening her with it, he reached down and grabbed it, jerked at it.

But, cracked or no, the hard oak did not give way. Paying no attention to what he was doing, Martha Jean pressed close to him; still yanking at the support, he lost his balance and sat down hard on the steps. Seizing the opportunity she slid onto his extended leg, again pushing her nightgown up, again exposing her genitals. He heard his pants tear, then felt a sharp biting pain in his thigh.

He let out a screech; Martha Jean grabbed his neck with both arms, and he immediately felt his leg going numb, felt the numbness spreading rapidly upward. With all his strength, he jerked once more on the support. This time it came loose in his hand.

He didn't even look at it; he knew he had only a fraction of a second to get her off him. Without thinking, he jabbed it at her, as hard as he could. He heard a thud and a ripping sound.

She grunted loudly and stopped moving. Ron looked at his own hand, by now growing numb, and saw that the banister support had split, leaving one end tapered and sharp. His wild thrust had buried it in her lower abdomen, and blood was gushing out around it.

"Oh . . ." she muttered, looking down at it. "Oh . . . ye kilt me, you . . ." She looked up at him with the expression of an injured child. Then her eyes rolled back in her head and she slid off his leg, sprawling on the floor in front of him.

Ron could see that she wasn't dead, that she was breathing still. He struggled to get up. He could not; his legs felt like they were coated with lead. His arms were equally rigid, as was his neck. He could move only his eyes.

Hearing the sound of running, he turned them to the side. From the other room, Mrs. Reardon appeared; she stopped short, and her hands flew to her mouth.

"Oh, my Gawd!" she screamed. "Oh, my Gawd, Martha Jean, Martha Jean!" Babbling, she rushed to her daughter's side. "Oh, Gawd! Gawd! He done kilt you, he done kilt you!" Her eyes wild, she turned to glare at Ron. "You son of a bitch!" she hissed. "I'm a-gonna cut you up in little pieces, one little piece at a time!" She grabbed the wood, ripping it out of the girl's belly; in her rage, she didn't notice how her daughter's body spasmed.

But then she was stalking toward Ron, the stake in her hand, a manic look on her face. He could not doubt her intentions, and he was absolutely helpless to do anything about it. Almost idly, he wondered how much of it he was going to feel.

As she came within a yard of him, he heard Cindy Ann's voice. "No, Ma!" she was yelling. "No, you let 'im be!"

Mrs. Reardon glanced up. "You go t' yore room," she snarled. "I'll have a word with you later, girl! And you c'n put that there thing up; we won't be a-needin' it none!" She came on, raising the stake, ready to make the first stroke.

A deafening explosion roared in Ron's ears; he saw Mrs. Reardon's body careening backward, saw the piece of wood go flying across the room. Behind her, more blood stained the carpet; she regained her balance long enough to stare beyond him—apparently at Cindy Ann—in disbelief. A huge red stain was spreading across the front of her dress. She crumpled to the floor, just a few feet from the now-still body of her other daughter.

Ron couldn't move his head, but he saw Cindy Ann come walking past him, tears covering her cheeks and an ancient-looking bolt-action rifle in her hands. "I'm sorry, Mommie," she whimpered. "I'm sorry, I just couldn't letcha. Not no more. Not no more . . ." She dropped the gun and fell to her knees, her body racked with sobs.

Quite a while later, she regained enough of her composure to turn her head and look at Ron. "It's a-gonna wear off," she said. "I dunno how long it's a-gonna take, 'cuz I dunno how much pizen Martha Jean got inta your laig thar. But it won't kill ye, Rahn."

She was right, but it took several hours; several hours during which he had little choice but to lie there on the stairs and think about the unbelievable things that had happened in this house. Cindy Ann stayed with him almost the entire time, watching him and avoiding the sight of her dead relatives.

His head and neck muscles were the last to feel the effects of the paralysis, and they were the first to come out. As soon as he could move his mouth, he tried to speak.

"Sorra," he mumbled, his tongue still thick. "Sorra it hadda be dis way."

"T'warn't your fault," she told him.

He lifted his arm experimentally, laboriously. "Know dat," he answered. "Wha cha wanna do wit' the—uhh . . ."

"Don't care. Bury 'em, burn 'em. Don't matter none. They's daid."

"Mayee we oughta burn . . . whole . . . fucking house down!"

She shook her head. "Cain't. I gotta live here." Putting her face in her hands, she started to cry again.

"Fuck that," he said, beginning to get a little movement in his legs now and talking more clearly. "You're coming with me, back to Knoxville. Get yourself a real life, by God!"

"Cain't," she repeated. "Rahn, ye done seen how I am! T'ain't natcheral! I c'n make a man happy, but I cain't do it raht, cain't have no babies ner nuthin'!"

He grinned at her. "Cindy Ann, in all the time we were talking you never asked me what kind of a doctor I was. I'm a goddamn dentist. If there's one thing I know, it's how to pull teeth!"

ABUSE

Matthew Costello

There was just a scattering of guys in the theater. Always just a scattering, each one picking his own little island of seats, all those empty seats with just one man slumped down in the middle.

And what a theater. What had this been before? An auto-parts store? A Lightning Lube place? A Kentucky Fried Chicken?

Billy Pratt looked for his own bank of seats. He heard someone snoring, he saw the outlines of heads, heard a cough, someone clearing his throat. Billy sat down, expecting the guy to hawk a louie into the air.

It was that kind of place.

The action had already begun on the screen.

There was a blonde, so good-looking she could have been some goyisher jock's prom date, a sweet virginal thing keeping her thighs locked together, the creamy white flesh crazy-glued all nice and tight.

It will be better if we wait, Tom, she'd coo.

While Tom's balls began to glow with a burnished blue.

Yeah, this blonde looked like that, her sweet blond hair and cherry-red lips. Now she was opening those lips, sticking out her tongue, a human viper, tasting the air before chowing down on some short hairy guy's meat puppet.

Billy Pratt settled down in his chair. He unzipped his

jacket. He watched the blonde work, in the dark, watching the giant screen. No little video, this was a head with a mouth the size of a Volkswagen bug.

Billy was alone, away from everyone, everything.

He reached down and felt the outline of his stiffening cock through his pants.

He didn't think, then, of the strange dichotomy, the weirdness of "The Uncle Billy Show," Billy and his Amazing Time Shack, the weird and wacky world of Uncle Billy's TV pals: Cave Boy, Two-Headed Girl, and Marco, the evil if ineffective magician from the future who liked to make bad puns.

He didn't think of his show, the kids who watched it, the ratings (slipping, God, slipping so fast and who the hell knew why?).

The blonde locked her blue eyes right on the unworthy object of her amazing ministrations . . . a premier blowjob being wasted on one ugly son of a bitch.

Billy heard a cough, the hum of the heating unit, pumping out smelly hot air.

He was alone.

The cop coughed. It sounded like a nervous tic. But it was a signal. The cough alerted his partner, the kid, that they had *one*.

Sergeant Walter Bruno had bitched when they told him what the hell he had pulled for duty.

"Shit," Bruno said in the Day Room. "This is fucking lower than fag baiting."

Though he had done that, too. Sure, he had logged hours milling around the men's rooms down by the train terminal and the airport, making cow eyes at guys who seemed to take just a bit too long to shake their pee-pee. The only plus of queer hunting was that he got to play baseball with their heads.

But this—this was shit. And to make things worse, they gave him a young punk, Collins, for a partner. Kid couldn't take his eyes off the screen.

Bruno looked over at Collins. He could see his eyes

reflecting back the glow of the screen. What the hell's the matter, kid? Never see a blowjob before? Shit . . .

Bruno coughed again. Collins turned to him.

Bruno nodded.

Think we got a live one, the nod meant. Collins sat up in his chair a bit. Bruno tilted his head in the direction of a guy sitting off to the side.

Collins's dark head nodded back.

Now Bruno would have to watch the guy instead of the show, looking for the telltale signs of someone choking the chicken, greasing the pole, playing flapjack with the old one-eyed snake.

Catch the fucker, and maybe kick his ass for being such a jerk-off . . .

The blonde didn't finish the guy off. No, she stopped, leaving his cock hard, glistening with wetness and maybe a trace of her red lipstick. Then she stood up.

"I want you to fuck me," she said. "Fuck me hard!"

Just like real life, Billy thought. That's what all the babes I date say. Fuck me, Billy. Fuck me hard. Wasn't a one who ever said, Fuck me soft.

The blonde hiked up her skirt, showing a picture-perfect ass. She turned around and bent over. The cameraman pulled off an interesting shot right through her legs, looking back at the hairy dwarf-man.

"Fuck me!" she hissed.

He didn't need any more encouragement.

Nor did Billy. He pulled down his fly. He heard the sound the zipper made, so loud. Billy looked around, at the other patrons. Most of them doing the same thing, he thought. Right? Why the hell else would you come here? This isn't Fellini we're talking about. Billy heard the cougher.

His zipper was down. His cock was half hard.

The hairy dwarf-man was slamming it into the blonde. There were a lot of close-ups now of her mouth, her lips curled in ecstasy, enjoying the ride, licking her lips.

While Uncle Billy had his favorite two characters out,

sitting on his lap: Mr. Hands and the One-Eyed Wonder Worm.

And for a few minutes, all the other shit went away.

Even Bruno had to check out the action on the screen. Jeezus, he thought. I'll probably have a boner on when I get up to make the collar. But hell, it's so fucking dark in here. Who'll see?

Bruno felt on the seat next to him, feeling for the flashlight. He had a flashlight.

Yeah, that blonde was sexy, so damn sweet. The wife was sure getting a workout. My week at the Adam and Eve Theater, and her little slice of shriveled poontang had been getting a nightly workout like no tomorrow.

Might need something else tonight though, Bruno thought. Maybe a quick run past the strip, check out some of the ladies, give them the once-over, grab some free action. Do some community relations.

Bruno looked over at his young partner, his eyes glued back on the screen.

Collins had asked, driving in the patrol car, "What's the big deal? Why do we have to hassle these guys?"

"Because," Bruno said, "it's against the law, Collins. Duh! Against the fucking law, and we're lawmen."

"Capiche?"

Bruno watched the guy to the side, saw his shoulder move, and Bruno knew—with an expert's unerring sixth sense— that the guy was playing with himself.

Course, he thought, I could be wrong. Could be fucking wrong. Screwed up twice last week, two guys sitting there with nothing but smiles on their faces. But that was no big deal. Just shut off the flashlight and slide back to my seat for the second feature.

No big fucking deal.

Got to move now, though. The guy could be a quick-draw artist. Might shoot his load too damn fast, zip up, and get out of here, without a bust.

It was time to move.

And Collins had to be there, to see the light go on, to witness the *exposure*. Had to have two cops, or the collar was no damn good.

You needed a witness to prove public indecency.

Bruno sat up straight in his seat.

There was a close-up of the dwarf-man. His face contorted. He was going to come. Gotta hurry, Bruno thought.

He coughed twice.

And now he moved with the speed of a TV cop making a billion-dollar cocaine bust.

Mr. Hand was moving into high gear now.

Billy Pratt didn't want to spend any more time in the theater than he had to. Just grab a bit of something, safe moments in the dark, alone, watching this.

The blonde had the guy ready to pop, slamming her buttocks back into him, grinding away on his dong. God, it was a thing of beauty. He flashed on images of babes from his past, cute brunettes and stacked redheads who got off on making it with a kiddie-show host.

Mr. Hand's pistons were burning up the road.

Billy opened his mouth. He tasted the hot air, hermetically sealed against the outside, against reality.

He nearly moaned.

When a small pool of light fell on his lap. His first instinct was to look down. He saw the light illuminating his cock. His hand frozen on it, locked to the stick shift at the moment of impact.

Then Billy looked left, just as someone said:

"You're under arrest for public indecency. Please cover, er, yourself and stand up. You have the . . ."

There were words, words Billy had heard from cop shows. This felt like a script. I didn't do anything. I didn't kill anybody, I didn't just eat a zillion dollars worth of crack.

"Cover yourself, you freak," the cop barked. "And get the hell up."

Billy nodded, forcing his prick back into his pants.

He flashed on Cave Boy, Marco, the toys, the little Uncle

Billy Time Travel play tents, the Time Traveler ride-on toys, the millions of kids who tuned in.

Shit, he thought. I fucked up, I really fucked up.

He begged a god that he didn't believe in to please be kind, to just let him get a ticket, or whatever the hell happens.

Just don't let them find out . . .

They stood him outside and pushed him against a car, a shabby Plymouth, now looking like what it was, an unmarked cop car.

The young cop frisked him, while the older cop looked through his wallet.

Please, he thought, don't let him figure it out. Make him a real stupid cop. Please . . .

But the cop looked at the California driver's license.

"Los Angeles," he said.

Billy looked over at him. The fat cop rubbed his chin. He nodded. Then—oh, Christ—there was a sick glimmer in his eye.

The cop looked up, a smile on his face.

"Bill Pratt . . ." he said. He took a breath. "Billy Pratt . . ." Now the cop laughed, out in the cold, great gusts of human steam erupting from his mouth while the name exploded out of his mouth. "Uncle Billy." The cop came close to him. Billy knew that it was as bad as it could be.

"Uncle Fucking Billy." He turned to Collins. "We just nailed ourselves a celebrity!"

He popped open the back door to his cop car.

Inside, the movie was nearly over.

That was good.

Because now the cops were gone. Yes, the man thought. The cops would be gone all day.

It helps when you can spot them.

They wouldn't be here for the second show, for the movie that he really came for.

It was the fourth time he'd seen it. The girls got tied up and guys pretended to hurt them. It was pretend.

That wasn't so good. It wasn't real. But it helped the man remember. Sitting in his seat, he could remember.

The theater was nearly empty. Everyone got scared away by the police. There were just a few other people.

But now it was so safe. The cops were gone.

The movie began.

It opened with scenes of this girl whipping another girl. She wasn't really hurting her. She was hitting her much too lightly. But she yelped nicely. She made nice yelping noises.

There were close-up shots of her buttocks. The man saw red marks.

Real, or makeup? The man didn't know.

The man slowly tilted his head back. Just stretching, that's all. If anyone were to see me, to give a damn. I'm just stretching. Then the man turned and looked at the nearly empty theater.

It was a ghost town in here.

It was perfect.

The man fumbled with his pants and opened his fly.

He was hard already. The whipping did that. That and the anticipation.

He slumped down in his seat.

He took a breath.

It was so exciting. Exciting, and safe . . .

Safe sex . . .

He dug into the pocket of his overcoat. He felt it, hard, forced to the proper shape. That had to be done quickly, before it turned rigid, frozen into some useless curl. He had moved fast, molding it quickly.

He took another big breath. The bright colors of the film, the echoing sounds of the movie, made bright lights flash in his brain as if he'd faint.

He felt it in the pocket. And then—quickly, as if he were pulling out a piece of gum—he pulled out the hand.

It was dry . . . and cold. He had cauterized the end.

The fingers were thin. She had taken nice care of her nails. They had been painted a blushing pink, nice and long.

The man had repainted them once.

Soon, though, he'd have to get rid of the hand. They were good for only so long.

He'd have to get a new one.

And that was fun, too.

The woman had screamed when she saw his serrated saw. The man remembered that, listening to the movie now.

The girl being whipped had her head buried between the legs of the other girl, and still the pretend whipping went on.

The man fit the rock-solid hand over his prick.

It fit perfectly. Of course, I measured it, he thought.

He made the hand dance up and down, while he watched the movie . . . with ever-growing interest . . .

FOREVER IN MY THOUGHTS

Don D'Ammassa

*T*oni felt the touch of eyes tracking her progress across the office. It wasn't the first time she had attracted unwelcome admiring stares from a man, despite a body that was just a trifle too slender to be sexy, but they'd never previously affected her so strongly. There was a definite sensation of physical contact, a feeling of feather-light pressure up one thigh, over her hip, moving higher.

She stopped and turned quickly, caught the new clerk, Evan Something-or-other, abruptly dropping his head, pretending to be studying something on the desk. Toni's mouth twisted into a quick, unpleasant smile. Dream on, she told him silently. Evan was slightly overweight—not grossly so, but with his pale skin, thin and undisciplined hair, narrow-set eyes, and puffy cheeks, he appeared unwholesomely swollen if not actually obese. And his lips were too full and wide for his face. He reminded her of another man, another face, one that had haunted her nightmares since high school.

"Hey! Earth to Toni. Anybody home in there?"

She turned, blinking, and found herself facing Marian Darby, her nominal supervisor and closest friend. "Oh! Sorry, Marian. Guess I was daydreaming."

"Not about *him,* I trust." Marian inclined her head in the new man's direction. "I still don't understand why Maggie hired him. His work experience is limited, and he gives me the creeps."

"Probably works cheap. Didn't you tell me Maggie's running over budget?"

"So who isn't? Look, I could use you for a couple hours of overtime tonight. You don't have a hot date or anything, do you?"

It was a rhetorical question. Marian knew Toni well enough to understand that she never had dates, hot or otherwise; they'd been friends back in high school, when Toni had been abducted, raped, and beaten by an unidentified assailant. The conversation turned to the backlog of unfinished projects sitting on Marian's desk and, for the time being, Toni forgot about her new admirer. But twice more before the day ended, she jumped at a sudden, phantom touch, and on both occasions there was hasty movement from the other side of the office, as though he had turned his head away at that precise moment.

Toni spent the rest of the week researching old product-cost standards in the records-storage area of Eblis Manufacturing, the company where she had worked since graduating five years earlier. It was the following Monday before she returned to her own desk, and during the interim, she had completely forgotten about Evan.

Her overflowing "In" box had just been sorted into three piles of successively lower priority when a vague uneasiness caused her to raise her head and look around.

The office wasn't quite right. It was still recognizably the same room, but it was somehow simpler. The paintings on the wall were mere blobs of color, lacking detail. The row of filing cabinets was recognizable, but the labels on each drawer were simply white rectangles. All the desks except her own were clean and orderly, empty chairs tucked neatly in place, and when she glanced down, she realized that most of the paperwork she had sorted was mysteriously absent. A pale moon shone pearly white through a window on the far wall; it was dark outside, even though it had been early morning only minutes ago.

"Sure gets lonely working here late at night."

Startled, she turned and found Evan standing beside her desk. Except that it wasn't quite the Evan she knew; he was still overweight and his clothes were wrinkled and threadbare, but he held himself with an air of assurance and his voice was deep and forceful.

"I don't mind it so much now that you're working here with me," she replied warmly, even as alarms were ringing wildly in her mind. What was she saying? What was happening here?

"Do you suppose anyone suspects? About us, I mean." Evan suddenly reached out and touched her shoulder, cupping it with the palm of his hand. A thrill of sexual tension heightened her senses even as her mind jerked with revulsion. Against her will, Toni turned in her seat, inclining her head back as his face descended and those too-wide lips closed over her own.

"Toni, wake up!"

She blinked as the office suddenly became brightly lit and crowded once more. Marian Darby was standing at her side, frowning. "What is it with you lately?"

"God, Marian, I'm sorry. I think I fell asleep." She shook her head emphatically. There was a sour taste on her lips.

"Must've been one helluva weekend." Marian dropped a new set of reports on the desk, already losing interest.

As soon as she was out of sight, Toni rose and went to the ladies' room, where she washed her face so vigorously that she had to reapply her lipstick.

When she returned to the office, Evan was staring in her direction. She met his gaze levelly and he turned away almost immediately, but not before she saw him smile knowingly.

It happened again during the afternoon, shortly before the day ended. Two of the three piles of work had been disposed of and Toni was feeling rather pleased with herself. Her back hurt from leaning over the desk, so she pushed her chair away and stretched her arms, head back and eyes closed.

When she opened them again, she was no longer in the office. Or anywhere else that she recognized.

Toni rose from the couch as though bitten. Where was she? It was obviously an apartment, sparsely furnished: only a couch, floor lamp, and a television in the entire room.

"Here we go."

She spun on one heel, eyes widening as Evan emerged from behind a half wall that led to what looked like a kitchenette. He held two wineglasses, one of which she accepted.

"Cheers!" He raised the glass to his lips and drained it, and she found herself doing the same. It tasted like grape juice.

"Why don't you sit down? You know how wine makes you light-headed."

Toni knew no such thing: She had a remarkably high tolerance for alcohol, as a matter of fact, and it was the only vice she allowed herself. Nor was she convinced that this was really "wine" in any case. Nevertheless, she immediately felt dizzy and collapsed onto the overstuffed couch.

Evan took his place beside her, much closer than was necessary.

"Are you okay?" He leaned forward, staring into her eyes.

Within herself, Toni wanted to jump up and run from the room, preferably after using her nails to claw out Evan's eyes, wipe out that confident expression. It reminded her too much of that other, the unshaven face that had smiled and smiled as he slapped her again and again, until she could no longer prevent him from removing her clothing.

"I'm just a little bit tipsy," her traitorous lips formed words that horrified her. Tipsy, indeed. A ridiculous word. She might have gotten "pissed," "bombed out of her mind," or "blown away," but never "tipsy." "I feel like I'm going to fall right off the edge of the world."

"I'd better hold onto you then." And his arms were suddenly around her and she was pressing her face into his chest while his hands moved from shoulders to waist and then to her buttocks. Toni wanted to struggle, scream at the top of her lungs, but instead she leaned back, pulling Evan down on top of her as she raised one leg and wrapped it around the back of his thighs. He shifted his own weight and brought his left hand around to cup her right breast, bringing a surge of ecstasy so intense that she arched her back convulsively, closing her eyes as the sensation burned through her nerve endings.

There was a sudden sense of weightlessness as she fell to the floor.

Toni opened her eyes, blinking rapidly, convinced that they had slipped off the edge of the couch. Except that the apartment was gone. She had, in fact, fallen off her chair and lay beside it, one leg folded painfully back, the other stretched out under the desk.

"Here, let me help." Several people were standing around and one, Bill Eversole, had extended his hand down from what appeared to be a nearly infinite distance. "Are you all right, Toni? You took quite a fall."

Obediently, she grasped his hand and let him pull her up. Sharp pains lanced through her left knee and she rubbed the point of her right hip with one hand, still struggling to understand what had happened.

Across the office, Evan stared silently, his face betraying an awareness of power that mirrored Toni's most nightmarish memories. She mumbled an apology and raced to the ladies' room, where she crouched over a toilet until she could stop retching.

Toni agreed to work late again that evening, even though Marian had to attend a PTA meeting and would be unable to keep her company. Determined not to think about the unpleasant experiences earlier in the day, she concentrated on the matters at hand and cleared up most of her backlog by eight o'clock. She was about to page the guard and leave when a thought occurred to her.

She rose and crossed to Maggie Lawrence's work area.

The desks were all locked, but it was a simple mechanism she had learned to circumvent years before when she lost the key to her own. It took only a few minutes to find Maggie's copy of Evan's employment application. She discovered that his last name was Wade and that he lived in Managansett, was twenty-three years old, unmarried, a high-school graduate, whose previous work experience was with several temporary-placement services.

She replaced the paperwork and then unlocked Evan's desk, but the only personal item she found was a paperback novel titled *Lust in the Ashes,* apparently part of a series about life after an atomic war. Several pages had their corners turned down, and when she read these, she discovered they invariably involved rape or other violence.

Her sense that something was seriously wrong grew worse, not better, and she left the building as quickly as she could manage.

That night, Toni experienced the most realistic dream of her life. If it was in fact a dream.

Her first impression was that she'd been in an accident. She lay half buried in a pile of unrecognizable rubble, apparently unhurt, although her clothing was so badly torn that she might as well have been naked. When she tried to stand up, she discovered that her left ankle was pinned tightly to the ground by a fallen beam of some sort.

"Can someone help me?" Her voice echoed off the half-collapsed roof above; through several gaps, she could see bolts of lightning playing through a sky filled with roiling thunderheads.

"Toni? Is that you?" It was a male voice, accompanied by the sound of someone making his way through the wreckage. She turned to see Evan Wade stumbling in her direction. Despite the destruction through which he moved, his clothing was neat and clean.

"Over here!" Her emotions alternated between relief and revulsion. Her apartment building must have exploded, she realized; probably a gas leak of some sort. "My foot is caught."

He reached her side and crouched to evaluate the situation. "No problem," he said softly, then placed both arms around the rough wooden surface. She saw his back tense as he strained to lift it, and he whispered, "Pull your foot out now." When she had done so, he released the beam, which fell back with a crash and a small cloud of dust.

"What happened?" Toni sat up, rubbing her bruised ankle until she realized that what remained of her blouse concealed nothing of what lay underneath. And somehow she had forgotten to put on a bra that morning. Despite the hot, dry air, goose pimples formed on her exposed flesh.

"The damned idiots," Evan responded bitterly, turning to face her. "Just when it looked like the world was finally on the road to peace, someone decided to push the button."

"Oh, God, no!" Toni raised both hands to her mouth, coincidentally allowing him a panoramic view of her bare breasts. "What'll we do?" But within her mind, Toni was struggling to control her own body. This is all nonsense, she thought. It has to be a dream.

"Don't worry," Evan said reassuringly, reaching out to pat her bare knee. "I'll make sure nothing happens to you."

Without transition, they were walking together along a street. Buildings on either side had been reduced to crumbling ruins, funnels of smoke rising into the still angry sky, scattered fires flickering here and there. Toni noticed that although she was barefoot, there was no sense of pain as she walked over the ragged, broken ground.

"We can shelter here for the night." He indicated a small office building whose roof had fallen in, but it was in much better condition than anything else they'd seen. The front door was missing, so they entered without hindrance and soon found an intact office with an undamaged couch. Evan found some candles and they were soon huddled together as darkness fell with unnatural suddenness. Throughout this transition, Toni felt stunned, her body playing the part as it had been written, while her mind insisted this was a nightmare conjured up from her previous hallucinations and the discovery of the apocalyptic book in Evan's desk.

But when his hands started moving over her body, the sensation was too real to ignore. Toni turned her head toward him, intending to shout obscenities, seeing once more that subtle curve of the mouth, all too similar to one she had seen years earlier, and in her nightmares ever since. But the words she actually spoke were unexpected, and appalling.

"Oh, Evan, I need you now more than ever. Can't you make me forget this horrible world?" Toni wanted to vomit as her body began to move rhythmically under Evan's. The remains of her blouse and his untouched shirt had disappeared, and he was squeezing her breasts—breasts that she now realized had gotten a good deal larger during these past few hours.

"God, you're so good! Don't make me wait for it!" Toni was stunned by the words she felt compelled to speak, terrified by the touch of alien hands. Evan literally tore off what remained of her jeans—she had apparently forgotten to put on panties this morning as well as a bra—while his own pants seemed to have dissolved away. She had a brief glimpse of an impossibly long appendage before he slammed his body down onto, and into, hers.

Her last thought before unconsciousness overwhelmed her was that no matter how hard she scrubbed, she would never feel clean again.

She woke in her own bed, alone, unsurprised to discover that the world was intact, that no nuclear war had taken place, and that her breasts were back to their normal, unexceptional dimensions. "You're losing your goddamned mind, Toni," she muttered aloud, wondering if she had made a mistake in discontinuing her therapy sessions with Dr. Brodsky. The violent moodswings that had plagued her ever since the assault had ceased, though, and she had believed herself adjusted, if not entirely healed.

She started to rise, intending to get a glass of water, but when she moved her legs, there was a stinging sensation, as though something sticky had dried on her inner thighs. She took a hot bath instead and scrubbed her thighs until they were red and raw.

Toni almost literally ran into Evan Wade at work that morning, turning a corner just as he reached it from the opposite direction. Without thinking, she retreated, one arm half raised defensively. He smiled familiarly, his eyes meeting hers for a split second too long, then moved on.

That evening, the dream took up where the previous one had ended. They were chased through the ruins by hideously deformed mutants, then became separated due to her stupidity rather than his error. Captured by the mutants, she was stripped and tied naked to a cooking spit over a low fire, only to be rescued in the nick of time when Evan appeared, armed with an automatic rifle that never needed to be reloaded. After dispatching several score of the mutants, he freed her, for which she was so grateful that she made passionate love to him in the ashes of the fire, even though hot coals burnt her flesh.

The following morning, she discovered a dozen tiny blisters on her buttocks.

Her life fell into an uneasy pattern in the days that followed. Although there were no more incidents while she was awake, she dreamed of Evan every night. She was convinced that he was somehow invading her thoughts, manipulating her imagination while she slept. At times she found herself quietly weeping with frustration. There was no one she could talk to about the situation, not even Marian, who was beginning to make pointed comments about her productivity and the consequences if Mr. Nicholson noticed her absentmindedness. What she believed to be happening was clearly impossible, and if she claimed otherwise she'd end up in an institution.

Evan never approached her at work or elsewhere, confining his attentions to her dreams. At times she believed he was quite conscious of what he was doing; at others she wondered if he might be unaware that he was somehow dragging her into his own wish-fulfillment fantasies. It was not a difference that mattered; the results from her point of view were identical.

Eventually Evan tired of the nuclear scenario. During the days, or rather the nights, that followed, he rescued her from pirates, terrorists, and a psychopathic killer. They survived plane crashes in stormswept mountains, were shipwrecked on abandoned but bountiful islands, were trapped in a sunken submarine, and thwarted an invasion of alien creatures who, despite their entirely inhuman appearance, had crossed the galaxy for the express purpose of raping human women. In every instance, she rewarded Evan's efforts with her body, the single element in her dreams that did not vary from scenario to scenario.

Toni began to suffer from flashbacks even when Evan was not involved. The dreams and memories of the man who had assaulted her in the woods behind the Sheffield estate returned as fresh and hateful as in the days immediately following her abduction. As the days passed, his face and Evan's seemed to grow similar, as though in this aspect, at least, her own fears were beginning to reshape his projected fantasies. After several fruitless efforts to affect her own part in the surreal minidramas, she had retreated into a numb acceptance. Several people told her she appeared unwell, and indeed she moved with none of her previous easy grace. Psychosomatic or not, each morning she discovered a fresh collection of bruises and scratches. All of this could have resulted from uneasy thrashing in her sleep, but Toni was unable to avoid noticing that the injuries always coincided with those she had dreamed about and always replaced those of the previous day.

She might have continued this apathetic acceptance indefinitely if Evan had not read the vampire novel.

Toni had gotten into the habit of walking by Evan's desk several times during the course of a day, trying to see what book he might be reading. The pirate dreams had occurred while he was reading C. S. Forester, the shipwreck after Peter Benchley, and the psychopath coincided with his purchase of *The Silence of the Lambs*. So when she saw the dark cover decorated with two dripping fangs poised over a punctured planet Earth, she knew pretty much what to expect that evening.

She found herself in a large wooden cage with a dozen other women, all of them completely unclothed, and even though she had managed to remain relatively detached during her recent dream experiences, their utter terror communicated itself to her. Nor was she unaware of the fact that each and every one of them bore an uncanny resemblance to herself; they might have been her sisters, if she had ever had any sisters.

"There's no hope for us now," one of her fellow prisoners was insisting. "They've taken over the whole world. There's no one left to fight them."

"It's not over yet," protested another. "There's still time to strike back."

Several black caped figures appeared from the darkness, one of whom opened a door on the side of the cage. One by one, the prisoners were pulled out into the dim light, where one of the vampires would seize hold of his victim, bend to rip out a throat with gleaming fangs, drain the blood until the woman's struggles ceased and her limp body fell to the floor.

Toni was the last to be taken, and for once, her mind and body worked in consort, struggling against the powerful arms of the red-eyed monstrosity that held her. The fangs were within an inch of her throat when the vampire suddenly jerked, eyes widening with surprise. The restraining arms fell away from her shoulders and Toni stepped back far enough to see the wooden shaft that had suddenly emerged from the creature's chest.

The room was a sudden pandemonium as archers systematically finished off the rest of the undead creatures. When they had all fallen and turned to dust, one of the rescurers rushed to her side. It was, of course, Evan Wade.

In this dream Toni was so grateful that she rewarded him with something special: oral sex.

And that was the straw that broke the metaphorical camel's back. Even the man who had broken her forearm, shattered her nose, and bruised several of her ribs before making free use of her body had not subjected her to this indignity.

The following morning she rose calmly, called Marian, and told her she was too sick to come to work. After a long hot bath that made her feel no better, Toni dressed and drove to her uncle's house on Cape Cod. He was in Florida for the winter, but he always left a key so she could look in on the place from time to time. Behind the panel of a false closet, she found her uncle's collection of handguns and rifles, chose the revolver that he'd taught her to use after she'd been released from the hospital, located the right ammunition, and loaded it. Satisfied, she replaced the panel and drove back to Rhode Island.

Although she had eaten neither breakfast nor lunch, Toni felt no hunger as she sat in her car in the parking lot behind the apartment building where Evan Wade lived. The clock on her dashboard moved slowly but relentlessly forward, and she became more alert when it passed five o'clock. There was no clear plan in her mind, but she knew that the time had come to confront Evan, to show him she was not completely powerless and that he would either leave her alone or suffer the consequences.

At seventeen minutes past, she saw him climb out of a battered Datsun and start toward the rear entrance. With one fluid movement, she opened the car door and slipped outside, the revolver concealed in her purse. She moved quickly across the lot at an angle, to intercept him just short of the entrance. As she approached, he caught the movement out of the corner of his eye and half turned in her direction. At that moment, she withdrew the revolver from concealment, raised her arm, and opened her mouth to speak.

Evan turned in her direction, eyes widened in recognition, and then his lips curved in a sarcastic, knowing smile. Toni blinked, and Evan's face was replaced by that of the man who had raped her. The two identities flickered back and forth, then slowly merged into a single gestalt, an amalgam of the two.

The gun seemed to fire itself; Toni never consciously realized that she'd pulled the trigger. There was a startled look of dismay on Evan's face just before the bullet struck him in the forehead. His body flew back against the wall of the building, then slid to the ground.

Toni was momentarily paralyzed, uncomprehending. Someone else must have shot him, she thought; I only meant to frighten him. I never would have pulled the trigger. But there was an acrid smell from the handgun, and she let her arm drop to her side. "It was an accident. I didn't mean . . ." she said in a soft voice.

And then she saw a station wagon signaling to turn into the parking lot, and panic reanimated her limbs. She had accelerated into the late-afternoon traffic before anyone spotted Evan's body.

Marian told her the news early the next morning.

"Did you hear about poor Evan? Someone shot him last night."

Toni made what she hoped was a suitably shocked face. "That's horrible! Do they have any idea who did it?"

Marian shrugged. "If they do, they're not saying. Probably a mugging. There's no place safe anymore, I guess."

"Did he have any family?"

Marian shook her head. "Maggie said he was brought up in an orphanage."

"I suppose we ought to go to the funeral."

"Well, that would be a little premature. He's not dead yet."

Alarms began to ring inside Toni's head and she felt a strange sense of detachment. "I thought, I mean, how serious is it?"

"He was hit in the forehead and there's some brain damage. He's in a coma, according to the radio. They don't know if he'll pull through or not. I called the hospital, but they said they wouldn't know anything until after he'd had a chance to recover from surgery. I'll call again this afternoon."

The morning was an eternity. Toni was certain that Evan had recognized her; he could identify her if he recovered consciousness. She fantasized about sneaking into his hospital room, disguised as a nurse, suffocating him with a pillow, but her fantasies were far less convincing than those she had experienced at his instigation. And she knew she could never muster the nerve to act.

At shortly after four that afternoon, there was news, both good and bad. The bad, from her point of view, was that Evan Wade's condition had stabilized, and the hospital felt confident that he would not die in the foreseeable future, barring unforeseen complications. The good news was that, although he had intermittent periods of consciousness, he was totally paralyzed, could not speak or even blink his eyes, and the doctors believed it might be permanent.

She left work that evening in a calmer frame of mind, if not entirely at ease. After an unusually heavy meal, she took one sleeping pill and went to bed, determined to finally experience some untroubled rest.

Toni found herself lying on a bed of filthy straw in a dark room with a barred door. Even as her internal self collapsed into a pool of self-pity, realizing that she was still subject to Evan Wade's unconscious desires, the door creaked open and three men entered, one wearing an elaborate clerical costume, the others outfitted as medieval men-at-arms. They lifted her to her feet and half-pulled, half-dragged her from the room.

They passed along a narrow corridor to a wider, torchlit chamber, at the opposite end of which three heavily robed men sat at a long table. Her escort forced her past an array of devices she only vaguely recognized: a rack, a brazier of glowing coals, a strangling post, a rack of whips and flails. Toni had never been particularly interested in history, but she realized she had been thrust into the era of the Spanish Inquisition.

Don D'Ammassa

"You are accused of trafficking with demons!" the voice thundered across the room. "In order to save your soul, we shall use pain to drive the forces of evil from your body."

And just before the soldiers lifted her body onto the rack, Toni caught sight of the Grand Inquisitor's face, half concealed in the shadow of his cowl. It was the face of Evan Wade.

Toni suddenly realized there'd be no rescue this time.

BLIND DATE

Julie Wilson

Sally Jameson's temper boiled. She moistened her lips, glanced away from the man standing before her, and surveyed the crowd of divorcées and never-marrieds packed into the smoke-filled banquet room. Sally knew the odds of being propositioned at a singles function were relatively high, but she never expected anything like this. Perhaps she had misunderstood. Having finally regained her composure, she uttered a nervous laugh in response. "I beg your pardon?" she said.

The man's face remained expressionless. He stood approximately five-foot-nine and sported a slender build, so average in appearance that he could blend into any gathering. He brushed an eyebrow with a forefinger, his diamond-studded signet ring glittering beneath the glow of a chandelier. "I apologize for having been so blunt," he said, "but it's really not as harsh as it may sound. I admit that I'm eccentric, and few people understand my sexual needs, but some of us get off on different things, that's all." He cleared his throat, then repeated the offer: "I'd like to pay you to have sex with someone you've never met."

Now Sally was more angry than before. She had heard him correctly after all, and how dare he insinuate that she might demean herself in such a way! She had been reluctant to attend the singles mixer for fear of being approached by egotistical jerks like him, had even dressed in loosely fitting clothes to conceal her full figure, and now she deeply regretted having come. She didn't know anyone here, and she was ready to go home. Her heart really hadn't been into meeting anyone tonight anyway.

But before she could give him a piece of her mind, the man continued. "Please understand that I'm not soliciting you to have sex with *me*," he said. "You can feel free to choose your own partner. I only want to watch. But your partner has to be a stranger. Someone you've never met before."

Sally wanted to turn and walk away. The nerve of this man! But she had to hear more, to learn what kind of pervert stood before her. Maybe she could lure him into a trap and call the cops. But was his proposal actually illegal? She couldn't recall if any porn stars had ever been charged with prostitution, and wasn't this a similar arrangement, a man and woman being paid by a third party to have sex? Sally silently shook her head, recalling her own run-ins with the law as a teenager. The thought of cooperating with the police, even after years of law-abiding behavior, was still unsettling.

"I see that I've offended you," the man whispered, his expression still unchanged. "I'm sorry. Perhaps I should speak with someone else." He paused and gazed into her eyes, then added, "But five thousand dollars is a lot of money to be paid for something you would probably like to do anyway."

Five thousand dollars! And she wouldn't technically be a hooker, would she? At least maybe not in the legal sense of the word—she didn't know for sure. If times weren't so rough, she would turn up her nose and walk away. She would summon a security guard to throw this rich creep out on his perverted ass. But John Jr. needed a whole closetful of new clothes; in fact, the toe-holes of his tennis shoes had already been a source of embarrassment to Sally, who hadn't seen a child-support check in months. She was already late with the rent, and the landlord was beginning to get nasty. Five thousand dollars would go a long way toward getting her back on her feet financially, and she wouldn't even have to risk a larceny rap. She had kicked that particular vice years ago, but was it really wise to venture into something so vile and disgusting now that her life had virtually started over?

"I assume that since you haven't slapped me or walked away that you're considering my offer," he interrupted her thoughts.

Sally opened her mouth but found it difficult to speak. What would be the consequences if she said yes? But of course it would only be this once. No one else would ever know. And she could be cautious, and protect herself in case this depraved stranger had something else up his sleeve. After all, if the Burt Reynolds look-alike at the bar had approached her tonight, she might well have slept with him anyway. The only difference under this arrangement was that she would have an audience.

"Suppose I said yes," she finally said, the words coming slowly, and forced. "Where and when would this take place? And where would I find my partner?"

The man lit a cigarette without offering her one. Despite the fact that Sally didn't smoke, she was offended, but not surprised, that he could be so inconsiderate. "Go to any man in the room and ask him to step outside. I'll make the arrangements and we'll leave immediately. We'll check into any motel you wish." He exhaled a plume of smoke away from her, then continued. "It's really quite simple, though I'm embarrassed to admit such a timid fetish. Still, we have to do whatever we can to find pleasure in this cruel world."

Sally was disappointed in herself for contemplating the offer. But she had done a couple of one-night stands before and had survived with both her conscience and dignity intact. Hell, she'd even spent a night in jail, many years ago when her mother had refused to post bail. And hadn't she only moments earlier fantasized what it would be like to curl up in bed with the man at the bar who had given her the eye? It had been months since she'd last made love. Sally's lips trembled as she probed further. "Is that all there is? Just quick sex and it's over?"

He cleared his throat again. "Nothing more than the fact that you'll both be blindfolded." He dropped his cigarette butt and thoughtlessly ground it into the linoleum floor. "That's part of the reason I get off on this. The two of you will have sex without ever having actually seen each other's bodies. I'll know something about each of you that neither of you will know."

It was kinky but, despite the warnings of her conscience, worth further consideration. "What if the one I choose won't go along with it?" she asked.

The man almost laughed this time. "How many men in this room would turn down a chance to make love to such an attractive woman?" He reached out to touch a flipped-up curl of shiny brown hair at her shoulder. Sally cringed but tried not to show her displeasure. "Believe me, they rarely refuse such an opportunity, and I usually don't even offer them money," he continued. "But if your first choice won't go along with us, we'll simply go to someone else. It won't take long, I assure you."

Five thousand dollars would pay a lot of bills. "But he has to wear a condom," she said nervously. "I won't consider it without that." She couldn't believe what she was saying! Would she actually go through with this?

"By all means," the man said. "I wouldn't have it any other way."

Sally pushed the red plastic frames of her fashionable eyeglasses up the bridge of her nose. "I don't have much time," she said. "I've got to pick up my son in a couple of hours."

For the moment, she couldn't find a reason to say no.

Sally waited inside the ladies' room, pacing nervously as the man propositioned the Burt Reynolds clone in the empty hallway. She took a deep breath and eyed the rest-room door. Maybe it would be best to leave, to escape the temptation. Why venture to the wrong side of the law again? She had been so distracted by their unorthodox conversation that she hadn't even gotten the man's name. Of course, neither had he asked for hers, and he probably wouldn't give her his real name anyway. The anonymity of the setup seemed a major part of the turn-on for him, and as much as she hated to admit it, Sally knew that her libido had been hooked. She would make love to a man whose name she didn't know; in fact, she would perceive him only by touch and would never even see him without his clothes.

But, no—this was wrong. How could she have come this far?

Sally burst through the rest-room door, determined to pick up John Jr. at the child-care facility and cry her eyes out at home, when a familiar voice echoed from farther down the hall.

"Where are you going? We're all set!"

She turned to see her propositioner standing beside the man of her choice, and from the look on his face, her potential partner was just as nervous as she. Sally's face was pink with embarrassment; thank God there was no one else around to see what she had gotten herself into.

While her partner secured a room, Sally and her propositioner waited in her partner's car in the parking lot of the Relax Inn Motel, an establishment near the freeway, where Sally believed she would be less likely to be seen by someone she knew. Clutching her purse in her lap, she tried to remain calm. Garth Brooks was wailing a country tune on the radio, while the windshield was speckled by droplets of light rain.

The short drive to the motel had been tense. Sitting alone in the backseat, the man had instructed the two of them not to speak, explaining that their only communication with each other must be exclusively physical. Of course, there hadn't been much that Sally had wanted to say anyway. How does one make small talk under such strained circumstances? *How's the weather? Where are you from? What's your favorite position?*

Sally felt her chest tighten with nervousness. The man remained motionless, void of expression. She swallowed hard and glanced in his direction. "I don't like this arrangement," she said. "I want half of the money now."

The man shrugged, his face dimly visible in the dark backseat. "How do I know I can trust you?" he huffed. "How do I know you won't bolt out the door and run away with my money?"

She moistened her lips and took a deep breath. "At least prove to me that you've got the cash."

With a groan of aggravation, the man retrieved his wallet from a hip pocket and fanned a thick wad of hundred-dollar bills in her face. "Does this make you feel any better?" he snarled.

Sally raised her brow and looked out the windshield. Her partner was exiting the registration office now, the key to a motel room dangling from his fingertips.

"Don't tell him about the money," the man warned her. "All he gets is a hundred bucks for the motel room and a piece of your ass."

Sally's partner got into the car and cranked the engine without speaking, guiding the rain-spotted Maxima to a room at the far end of the one-level motel.

Sally exhaled and watched the windshield wipers sweep away the drizzle. Her propositioner slumped lower in the backseat.

It was rapidly becoming too late to back out.

The man sank into a chair facing the bed as Sally and her partner stood idly by. Did he have to be so close? Must he breathe down her neck while she performed for him? But she said nothing, by now almost too nervous to speak. It was as if she were caught up in a whirlwind, and though she knew that what she was about to do was wrong, there was no way to stop now. She was about to enter the downhill side of a roller coaster, and the ride would soon be over.

Reaching inside his jacket, the man pulled out a pair of black nylon blindfolds. "Put these on before you take off your clothes," he said to both of them. "Then take as much time as you like. The longer, the better. Just do anything you feel comfortable with, until I suggest something different."

Sally removed her eyeglasses and placed them on the nightstand. The blindfold firmly in place, she shucked her clothes and sprawled across the bed, intent on getting the act over with as quickly as possible. She felt as if she were about to be examined by a gynecologist, that what she was about to experience would be purely mechanical in nature, with no sexual context at all; her feet might as well be in stirrups. She listened for the frictioned movement of her partner's clothes being removed and felt the bed sink as his weight was added to hers on the mattress. "Let me feel . . . the condom," she muttered. "I want to know for sure that it's on." She could smell the lubricant but wanted assurance that the condom was actually in use.

A phantom hand guided her fingers to a semierect penis. A loosely fitted condom was, indeed, in place. Laughter erupted from the room next door. A car door slammed outside.

"No more talking," the man said from somewhere to the side of the bed. His breath smelled of garlic and liquor.

Sally swallowed hard and tried to relax, though it was practically impossible. Her nipples were erect, but only from the cold. She stopped herself short of asking the man to turn up the heat—he had ordered her not to say anything else—and besides, she would soon feel the warmth of her partner.

A pair of masculine hands explored her body in the artificial darkness, squeezing her breasts, then massaging her thighs, the fingers eventually clearing a path through her pubic hair. But there was nothing erotic about it, at least not for Sally. She was dry and would need lubrication before intercourse. She couldn't imagine herself actually becoming aroused. Not like the man, who was probably getting his rocks off already, masturbating at the sight of her blind seduction.

But then the realization struck Sally that her partner and the man might have switched roles. Could it be that the person running his tongue between her legs wasn't the partner she had selected? This was all a game to the man. Maybe role-switching was the true reason for the blindfold. Perhaps her chosen partner was actually sitting in the chair watching the man explore her body.

But did it really matter at this point? For some reason, she had to know for sure, if for no other reason than sheer curiosity.

Sally nervously reached down to run her fingers through the hair of the head between her legs. Both men wore their hair approximately the same length, but her partner sported a mustache. She bent over slightly to extend her fingers farther down the cheeks of the person's face whose tongue would normally be driving her to heights of pleasure by now. She felt a blindfold first—and there! A mustache! It was the right man after all, and for a moment she felt relieved, as if she could relax and derive at least minimal enjoyment from the experience.

But then another fear surfaced: Does the man have a camera? Would he use photographs to blackmail her out of what little money she had available to live on? Or could this have been a setup orchestrated by her ex-husband in an attempt to frame her and gain custody of her son? She held her breath to listen. There was no click of a shutter, and even a silent-operating camcorder couldn't have been concealed inside the man's tightly fitting clothing. Neither could he have hidden any equipment in the room in advance, because she herself had selected the motel, and her partner had secured the room. Sally listened again and heard no movement at all other than the pumping fist of her propositioner and the steady tongue-lapping between her legs. Her partner seemed to be enjoying himself, and the sound of the man whacking off confirmed that voyeurism had been his true motive after all.

Sally relaxed against the mattress. She had gone too far to punish herself with fear, and it was too late to do anything about it now. Perhaps her best alternative would be simply to clear her mind of any further suspicions and let her partner finish. She didn't have to enjoy herself, but neither should she scare herself to death over such a foolish predicament.

Sally closed her eyes despite the blindfold, gritted her teeth, and agonized through the slow passage of time. A pool of trapped tears accumulated inside the confined space of the blindfold. Her refusal to perform oral sex on her partner met with little objection from the man, and as full intercourse commenced, she noticed the contrasting sounds of heavy breathing from both above her and to her side. She felt filthy, and she punished herself by enduring the discomfort of dry sex. It would soon be over, and she would wipe this evening from her memory faster than her weekly paycheck cleared the bank. She couldn't wait to hold John Jr. in her arms again and put this nightmare behind her.

"Sir?" the man's voice interrupted. "Please rise to your knees and spread her legs far apart while she lies flat on her back. Cup your hands under her ass. I'd like to watch the actual penetration."

Her partner's breath was heavy as he complied, stretching her legs uncomfortably far apart as the bedsprings squealed with disapproval. Still Sally refused to complain, taking her punishment boldly. The thrusts seemed to stab deeper from this position, and from the sound of her partner's moans of passion, she knew he couldn't last much longer.

"At the point of orgasm, please pull out, remove the condom, and ejaculate on her stomach," the man directed.

Before Sally could object, the pace quickened. Heavy breathing seemed to descend upon her from both directions. And as her partner moaned and awkwardly withdrew, Sally resigned herself to the final act of degradation. Warm fluid splashed across her abdomen and her partner collapsed heavily on top of her, pinning her momentarily against the mattress. His moans contrasted sharply with those of the man at her side as a second surge of wetness soaked her shoulder from that direction.

But then Sally noticed that the gush of warm liquid from her partner had not ceased. This is impossible, she knew. No one could ejaculate continuously. She struggled to free an arm to remove the blindfold, regardless of the man's instructions, and as she wrestled against the dead weight of her partner, she turned her head to avoid his harsh gasps for air at her ear. She grabbed the elastic band of the blindfold and carefully slipped it off, an accumulation of tears spilling down her cheeks.

The room was a soft blur. Sally reached for her eyeglasses on the nightstand, then surveyed the scene. For a moment she could barely breathe. Blood poured from a gaping wound in her partner's side, the lower half of her own body covered with a crimson sheen. The smell of blood mixed with semen hit her like an odorous wave of raw sewage. She pulled her legs from beneath the victim and retched, closing her eyes quickly, then opening them again to focus on the man, who was now slipping off a pair of rubber gloves as he prepared to leave.

"A word of advice," the man cautioned with a cocky air. "When the police arrive, don't even try to tell them what actually happened here. They'll never believe you." He leaned over and snatched the blindfold from her fingertips, then snapped the other one from the face of the dying man now curled into a quivering fetal position at the foot of the bed. "This poor fool checked you into the motel, and he's the one you were seen approaching at the party while I waited in the hall. I doubt that anyone saw the three of us leave together, but even if someone did, you haven't got a shred of evidence. You'll just appear to be covering your own ass, like any common criminal." He paused, obviously enjoying one last look before fleeing the scene.

Her partner gagged, blood foaming from his mouth, and the man lifted his right foot over the mattress and shoved the mortally wounded man to the floor with a dull thud. Then he kneeled at the bloody carpet and watched his victim die.

"You fucked this man to death!" the man exclaimed, proudly staring at Sally with the first sign of an expression since they'd met: a look of cheerfulness, of accomplishment. But his face suddenly went blank and he stared across the room in a psychotic daze. "There's nothing like the look on someone's face who dies at the point of orgasm," he said. "It's the ultimate turn-on." He glared at her coldly, his eyes vacant, his chin held high. "It could have been you, you know," he hissed. "I kill the one who's most easily within reach, and this time the guy happened to be in the most convenient position."

Sally pleaded with her eyes. "Y-y-you can't do this to me! You can't leave me here like this!"

"Oh, but I can," he answered, her voice jerking him back to reality. The man's lips formed a wicked smile as his eyes dropped to a bloody letter-opener on the floor. "If I had killed you, I would've used a screwdriver," he said as he patted an inside pocket. "That would've seemed more like a man's weapon."

Sally didn't know what to say. The man stopped at the door and scowled at her one last time. "Think about me while your ass rots in jail, you cheap whore," he hissed. The man turned the doorknob with a handful of rubber glove and whisked outside.

As the door clicked shut, Sally tried to calm herself. Panic at this point would accomplish nothing. She reached for the bedside telephone and jabbed a shaking finger at the *O* button. When the front desk answered, she pleaded, *"Please call an ambulance to Room 110. And get the police, too."*

Trying carefully not to disturb the evidence, she hung up the phone and slid from the bed, her bare feet almost stepping on the murder weapon on the floor. A stream of blood and semen ran down her stomach and tickled her inner thigh. She grabbed a towel in the bathroom to clean herself, then went to a nearby closet and found two spare flannel blankets, wrapping one around herself, then kneeling beside her immobile partner on the floor.

"Can you hear me?" she whispered.

His lips were blue; there was no response at all. She placed an ear against his nose and detected no sign of breathing.

"Help is on the way," she told him, as if he could hear—as if it really mattered. Gently, she covered him with the other blanket to his neck and stared into the stillness of his face, at his glazed, unblinking green eyes. Although he was a stranger, he had made love to her, and, to his credit, he had been a thoughtful, considerate lover. Even amid the horror of the scene, a sense of loss prevailed.

Then the man's last words echoed through her mind: *You cheap whore.* Sally took a deep breath and returned to the bed, searching for the wallet where she had dropped it on the carpet near the nightstand. If the man had been legitimate, if all had gone as planned and he had reached for his wallet to give her the money he had promised, she would have led him to believe the wallet had simply fallen from his hip pocket. She looked inside and found a driver's license with the man's photo staring back at her: Jeremy K. Slatts. A shiver ran through her body, and Sally slammed the wallet against the top of the nightstand to await the police. She recalled the arrogance in the man's voice, so confident that he had committed the perfect crime.

Sally forced a smile. You won't get very far this time, Jeremy Slatts, she thought.

Former pickpockets make lousy scapegoats.

SEX OBJECT

Graham Masterton

She sat against the foggy afternoon light, perched straight-backed on the black Swedish chair, her ankles crossed. She wore a perfectly tailored Karl Lagerfeld suit and a black straw hat and her legs were perfect, too.

Dr. Arcolio couldn't see her face clearly because of the light behind her. But her voice was enough to tell him that she was desperate, in the way that only the wives of very, very rich men are capable of being desperate.

The wives of ordinary men would never think about such things, let alone get desperate about them.

She said, "My hairdresser told me that you were the best."

Dr. Arcolio steepled his hands. He was bald, dark, and swarthy, and his hands were very hairy. "Your hairdresser?" he echoed.

"John Sant'Angelo . . . he has a friend who wanted to make the change."

"I see."

She was nervy, vibrant, like an expensive racehorse. "The thing was . . . he said that you could do it very differently from all the rest . . . that you could make it real. He said that you could make it *feel* real. With real responses, everything."

Dr. Arcolio thought about that and then nodded. "This is absolutely true. But then I'm dealing with *transplants,* you

113

understand, rather than modifications of existing tissue. It's just like heart or kidney surgery . . . We have to find a donor part and then insert that donor part and hope that there's no rejection."

"But if you found a donor . . . you could do it for me?"

Dr. Arcolio stood up and paced slowly around his office. He was a very short man, not more than five-foot-five, but he had a calmness and a presence that made him both fascinating to watch and impressive to listen to. He was dressed very formally, in a three-piece chalkstripe suit, with a white carnation in the buttonhole and very highly polished oxfords.

He crossed to the window and drew back the curtains and stood for a long while staring down at Brookline Place. It hadn't rained for nearly seven weeks now, and the sky over Boston was an odd bronze color.

"You realize that what you're asking me to do is very questionable, both medically and morally."

"Why?" she retorted. "It's something I want. It's something I *need.*"

"But Mrs. Ellis, the operations I perform are normally to correct a physical situation that is chronically out of tune with my patients' emotional state. I deal with transsexuals, Mrs. Ellis, men who have penises and testes but who are psychologically women. When I remove their male genitalia and give them female genitalia instead . . . I am simply changing their bodies in line with their minds. In *your* case, however—"

"In my case, Doctor, I'm thirty-one years old, I have a husband who is wealthier than anybody in the entire state of Massachusetts, and if I don't have this operation then I will probably lose both him and everything I've ever dreamed of. Don't you think that falls into exactly the same category as your transsexuals? In fact, don't you think my need is greater than some of your men who want to turn into women simply because they like to wear high heels and garter belts and panties by Frederick's of Hollywood?"

Dr. Arcolio smiled. "Mrs. Ellis . . . I'm a surgeon. I perform operations to rescue people from deep psychological misery. I have to abide by certain strictly defined ethics."

"Dr. Arcolio, *I* am suffering from deep psychological misery. My husband is showing every sign of being bored with me in bed, and since I'm his fifth wife I think the odds of him divorcing me are growing steadily by the minute, don't you?"

"But what you're asking—it's so radical. It's *more* than radical. And permanent, too. And have you considered that it will disfigure you, as a woman?"

Mrs. Ellis opened her black alligator pocketbook and took out a black cigarette, which she lit with a black enameled Dunhill lighter. She pecked, sucked, blew smoke. "Do you want me to be totally candid with you?" she asked.

"I think I *insist* on your being totally candid with me."

"In that case, you ought to know that Bradley has a real thing for group sex . . . for inviting his pals to make love to me, too. Last week, after that charity ballet at Great Woods, he invited seven of them back to the house. Seven well-oiled Back Bay plutocrats! He told me to go get undressed while they had martinis in the library. Then afterward they came upstairs, all seven of them."

Dr. Arcolio was examining his framed certificate from Brigham and Women's Hospital as if he had never seen it before. His heart was beating quickly; he didn't know why. Wolff-Parkinson-White syndrome? Or atrial fibrillation? Or maybe fear, with a subtle seasoning of sexual arousal? He said, as flatly as he could manage, "When I said candid . . . well, you don't have to tell me any of this. If I *do* decide to go ahead with such an operation, it will only be on the independent recommendations of your family doctor and your psychiatrist."

Mrs. Ellis carried on with her narrative regardless. "They climbed on top of me and all around me, all seven of them. I felt like I was suffocating in sweaty male flesh. Bradley penetrated me from behind; George Cartin penetrated me from the front. Two of them pushed themselves into my mouth, until I felt that I was choking. Two forced their penises into my ears. The other two rubbed themselves on my breasts.

"They got themselves a rhythm going like an Ivy League rowing team. They were roaring with every stroke. *Roaring.* I was like nothing at all, in the middle of all this roaring and rowing. Then the two of them climaxed into my mouth, and the other two into my ears, and the next two over my breasts. Bradley was the last. But when he was finished, and pulled himself out of me, I was dripping with semen, all over me, dripping; and it was then that I knew that Bradley wanted an object—not a wife, not even a lover. An *object.*

Dr. Arcolio said nothing. He glanced at Mrs. Ellis, but Mrs. Ellis's face was concealed behind a sloping eddy of cigarette smoke.

"Bradley wants a sex object, so I've decided that if he wants a sex object I'll *be* a sex object. What difference will it make? Except that Bradley will be happy with me and life will stay the same." She gave a laugh like a breaking champagne glass. "Rich, pampered, secure. And nobody needs to *know.*"

Dr. Arcolio said, "I can't do it. It's out of the question."

"Yes," Mrs. Ellis replied. "I knew you'd say that. I came prepared."

"Prepared?" Dr. Arcolio frowned.

"Prepared with evidence of three genital transplants that you performed without the permission of the donors' executors. Jane Kestenbaum, August 12th, 1987; Lydia Zerbey, February 9th, 1988; Catherine Stimmell, June 7th, 1988. All three had agreed to be liver, kidney, heart, eye, and lung donors. Not one of them had agreed to have their genitalia removed.

She coughed. "I have all of the particulars, all of the records. You carried out the first two operations at the Brookline Clinic, under the pretense of treating testicular cancer, and the third operation at Lowell Medical Center, on the pretext of correcting a double hernia."

"Well, well," said Dr. Arcolio. "This must be the first time that a patient has *blackmailed* me into carrying out an operation."

Mrs. Ellis stood up. The light suddenly suffused her face. She was spectacularly beautiful, with high Garboesque cheekbones, a straight nose, and a mouth that looked as if it were just about to kiss somebody. Her eyes were blue as sapphires, crushed underfoot. To think that a woman who looked like this was begging him to operate on her, *bullying* him into operating on her, was something that Dr. Arcolio found incredible, even frightening.

"I can't do it," he repeated.

"Oh, no, Dr. Arcolio. You *will* do it. Because if you don't, all of the details of your nefarious operations will go directly to the district attorney's office, and then you will go directly to jail. And with you locked up, think of all those transsexual men who are going to languish in deep psychological misery, burdened with a body that is so chronically out of tune with their minds."

"Mrs. Ellis—"

She stepped forward. She was threateningly graceful, and nearly five inches taller than he was, in her gray high heels. She smelled of cigarettes and Chanel No. 5. She was long-legged, and surprisingly large-breasted, although her suit was cut so well that her bosom didn't seem out of proportion. Her earrings were platinum, by Guerdier.

"Doctor," she said, and for the first time he detected the slight Nebraska drawl in her undertones, "I need this life. In order to keep this life, I need this operation. If you don't do it for me, then so help me, I'll ruin you, I promise."

Dr. Arcolio looked down at his desk diary. It told him, in his own neat writing, that Mrs. Helen Ellis had an appointment at 3:45. God, how he wished that he hadn't accepted it.

He said, quietly, "You'll have to make three guarantees. One is that you're available to come to my clinic on Kirkland Street in Cambridge at an hour's notice. The second is that you tell absolutely nobody apart from your husband who undertook the surgery for you."

"And the third?"

"The third is that you pay me a half-million dollars in negotiable bonds as soon as possible, and a further half-million when the operation is successfully completed."

Mrs. Ellis nodded the slightest of nods.

Dr. Arcolio said, "That's agreed, then. Christ. I don't know who's the crazier, you or me."

In the dead of February, Helen Ellis was lunching at Jasper's on Commercial Street with her friend Nancy Pettigrew when the maitre d' came over and murmured in her ear that there was a telephone call for her.

She had just been served a plateful of nine Wellfleet littlenecks with radish-chili salsa and a glass of chilled champagne.

"Oh . . . whoever it is, tell them I'll call back after lunch, would you?"

"Your caller said it was very urgent, Mrs. Ellis."

Nancy laughed. "It isn't your secret lover, is it, Helen?"

The maitre d' said, soberly, "The gentleman said that time was of the essence."

Helen slowly lowered her fork.

Nancy frowned at her and said, "Helen? Are you all *right?* You've gone white as a sheet."

The maitre d' pulled out Helen's chair for her and escorted her across the restaurant to the phone booth. Helen picked up the receiver and said, "Helen Ellis here," in a voice as transparent as mineral water.

"I have a donor," said Dr. Arcolio. *"The tissue match is spot-on. Do you still want to go through with it?"*

Helen swallowed. "Yes. I still want to go through with it."

"In that case, come immediately to Cambridge. Have you eaten anything or drunk anything?"

"I was just about to have lunch. I ate a little bread."

"Don't eat or drink anymore. Come at once. The sooner you get here, the greater the chance of success."

"All right," Helen agreed. Then, "Who was she?"

"Who was who?"

"The donor. Who was she? How did she die?"

"It's not important for you to know that. In fact it's better psychologically if you don't."

"Very well," said Helen. "I can be there in twenty minutes."

She returned to her table. "Nancy, I'm so sorry . . . I have to leave right now."

"When we're just about to start lunch? What's happened?"

"I can't tell you, I'm sorry."

"I knew it," said Nancy, tossing down her napkin. "It *is* a lover."

"Let me explain what I have been able to do," said Dr. Arcolio.

It was nearly two months later, the first week in April. Helen was sitting in the white-tiled conservatory of their Dedham-style mansion on the Charles River, on a white wickerwork daybed heaped with embroidered cushions. The conservatory was crowded with daffodils. Outside, however, it was still very cold. The sky above the glass cupola was the color of rainwashed writing ink, and there was a parallelogram of white frost on the lawns where the sun had not yet appeared around the side of the house.

"In your usual run-of-the-mill transsexual operation, the testes are removed, and also the erectile tissue of the penis. The external skin of the penis is then folded back into the body cavity in a kind of rolled-up tube, creating an artificial vagina. But of course it *is* artificial, and very unsatisfactory in many ways, particularly in its lack of full erotic response.

"What *I* can do is give my patients a *real* vagina. I can remove from a donor body the entire vulva, including the muscles and erectile tissue that surround it, as well as the vaginal barrel. I can then transplant them onto and *into* the recipient patient.

"Then, by using microsurgery techniques which I helped to develop at MIT, all of the major nerve fibers can be 'wired into' the recipient patient's central nervous system . . . so that the vagina and clitoris are just as capable of erotic arousal as they were within the body of the donor."

"I've been too sore to feel any arousal," said Helen, with a tight, slanted smile.

"I know. But it won't be long. You're making excellent progress."

"Do you think I'm really crazy?" asked Helen.

"I don't know. It depends what your goals are."

"My goals are to keep this lifestyle which you see all around you."

"Well . . ." said Dr. Arcolio, "I think you'll probably succeed. From what he's been saying, your husband can't wait for you to be fit for lovemaking again."

Helen said, "I'm sorry I made you betray your ethics."

Dr. Arcolio shrugged. "It's a little late for that. And I have to admit that I'm really quite proud of what I've been able to achieve."

Helen rang the small silver bell on the table beside her. "You'll have some champagne, then, Baron Frankenstein?"

On the second Friday in May she came into the gloomy, high-ceilinged library where Bradley was working and posed in the center of the room. It was the first time that she had ever walked into the library without knocking first. She wore a long scarlet silk robe, trimmed with scarlet lace, and scarlet stiletto shoes. Her hair was softly curled and tied up with a scarlet ribbon.

She stood there with her blue eyes just a little misted and the faintest of smiles on her lips, her left hand on her hip in a subtle parody of a hooker waiting for a curb-crawler.

"Well?" she asked. "It's four o'clock. Way past your bedtime."

Of course Bradley had known all along that she was standing there, and even though he was frowning intently at the land-possession documents in his hands, he wasn't able to decipher a single word. At last he looked up, tried to speak, coughed, cleared his throat.

"Is it ready?" he managed to ask, at last.

"It?" she queried. She had a new-found confidence. For the first time in a long time, she had something that Bradley seriously desired.

"I mean, are *you* ready?" he corrected himself. He stood up. He was a very heavily built, broad-shouldered man of fifty-five. He was silver-haired, with a leonine head that would have looked handsome as a piece of garden statuary. He was one of the original Boston Ellises—shipping magnates, landowners, newspaper publishers—and now the largest single broker of laser technology in the Western world.

He slowly approached her. He wore a blue-and-white-striped cotton shirt, pleated blue slacks, and fancy maroon suspenders. It was a look that the Ellises cherished: the look of a hands-on newspaper publisher, or a wheeler and dealer in smoke-filled rooms. It was dated, but it had its own special Bostonian charisma.

"Show me," he said. He spoke in a low, soft rumble. Helen *felt* what he said, rather than heard it. It was like distant thunder approaching.

"In the bedroom," she said. "Not here."

He looked around the library with its shelves of antique leatherbound books and its gloomy paintings of Ellis ancestors. In one corner of the library, close to the window, stood the same flatbed printing press that Bradley's great-great-grandfather had used to print the first editions of the *Beacon Hill Messenger*.

"What better place than here?" he wanted to know. She may have had something that he seriously desired, but his wish was still her command.

She let the scarlet silk robe slip from her shoulders and whisper to the floor, where it lay like a shining pool of sudden blood. Underneath, she wore a scarlet quarter-cup bra that lifted and divided her large white breasts but didn't cover them. Her nipples wrinkled as dark pink as raspberries.

But it was the scarlet silk triangle between her legs that kept Bradley's attention riveted. He tugged his necktie loose and opened his collar, and his breathing came harsh and shallow.

"Show me," he repeated.

"You're not frightened?" she asked him. Somehow she sensed that he might be.

He fixed her with a quick, black-eyed stare. "Frightened? What the fuck are you talking about? You may have been the one who suggested it, but I'm the one who paid for it. Show me."

She tugged loose the scarlet string of her panties, and they fell to the floor around her left ankle, a token shackle of discarded silk.

"Jesus," whispered Bradley. "It's fantastic."

Helen had bared her pale, plump-lipped, immaculately waxed sex. But immediately above her own sex was another, just as plump, just as inviting, just as moist. Only an oval scar showed where Dr. Arcolio had sewn it into her lower abdomen, a scar no more disfiguring than a mild first-degree burn.

Eyes wide, speechless, Bradley knelt on the carpet in front of her and placed the palms of his hands against her thighs. He stared at her twin vulvas in ferocious delight.

"It's fantastic. It's *fantastic!* It's the most incredible thing I've ever seen."

He paused and looked up at her, suddenly little-boyish. "Can I touch it? Does it feel just like the other one?"

"Of course you can touch it," said Helen. "You paid for it. It's yours."

Trembling, Bradley stroked the smooth lips of her new sex. "You can feel that? You can really feel it?"

"Of course. It feels good."

He touched her second clitoris, until it began to stiffen. Then he slipped his middle finger into the warm, moist depths of her second vagina.

"It's fantastic. It feels just the same. It's incredible. Jesus! It's incredible!"

He strode to the library door, kicked it shut, and then turned the key. He strode back to the middle of the room, snapping off his suspenders, tearing off his shirt, stumbling out of his pants. By the time he had reached Helen he was naked except for his large striped shorts. He pulled those off, revealing a massive crimson erection.

He pushed her onto the carpet and he thrust himself

furiously into her, no preliminaries, no foreplay, just raging, explosive lust. First he pushed himself into her new vagina, then into her own vagina, then into her bottom. He went from one to the other like a starving man who can't choose between meat, bread, and candy.

Frightened at first, taken aback by the fury of his sexual attack, Helen didn't feel anything but friction and spasm. But as Bradley thrust and thrust and grunted with exertion, she began to experience a sensation between her legs that was quite unlike anything that she had ever felt before: a sensation that was doubled in intensity, trebled. A sensation so overwhelming that she gripped the rug with both hands, unsure if the pleasure wasn't going to be too great for her mind to be able to accept. As Bradley plunged into her second vagina again and again, she felt as if she were going to go mad, or die.

Then, like a woman caught swimming in a warm black tropical swell, she was carried away.

She opened her eyes to hear Bradley on the telephone. He was still naked, his heavy body white and hairy, his penis hanging down like a plum in a sock.

"George? Listen, George, you have to get up here. You have to get up here *now!* It's the most fantastic thing you ever experienced in your life. George, don't argue, just drop everything and get your ass up here as fast as you can. And don't forget your toothbrush: You won't be going home tonight, I promise you!"

Just before dawn, she opened her eyes. She was lying naked in the middle of the emperor-sized bed. On her right side, Bradley was pressed up close to her, snoring heavily, his hand possessively cupping her second sex. On her left side, George Carlin was snoring in a different key, as if he were dreaming, and *his* hand was cupping her original sex. Her bottom felt sore and stretched, and her mouth was dry with that unmistakeable arid taste of swallowed semen.

She felt strange; almost as if she were more than one

woman. Her second vagina had brought her a curious duality of personality, as well as a duality of body. But she felt more secure. Bradley had told her over and over that she was wonderful, that she was spectacular, that he would never think of leaving her, ever.

Dr. Arcolio, she thought, you would be proud of me.

Winter again. She met Dr. Arcolio at Hamersley's. Dr. Arcolio had put on a little weight. Helen was thinner, almost gaunt, and she had lost weight off her breasts.

She toyed with a plate of sautéed skate. There were shadows under her eyes the same color as the brown butter.

"What's wrong?" he asked her. He had ordered smoked and grilled game hen with peach chutney and was eating at a furious speed. "You've had no rejection, everything's great."

She put down her fork. "It's not enough," she said, and he heard the same dull note of despair that he had heard when she first consulted him.

"You have two vaginas and it's not enough?" he hissed at her. A bearded man at the next table turned and stared at him in astonishment.

Helen said, "It was wonderful to start with. We made love five or six times a day. He adored it. He made me walk around naked for days on end, so that he could stare at me and put his fingers up me whenever he felt like it. I gave him shows, like erotic performances, with candles and vibrators, and once I did it with his two Great Danes."

Dr. Arcolio swallowed his mouthful with difficulty. "Wow," was all he could say.

There were tears hovering on the edge of Helen's eyes. "I did all of that but it wasn't enough. It just wasn't enough. Now he scarcely bothers anymore. He says we've done everything that we could possibly do. We had an argument last week and he called me a freak."

Dr. Arcolio laid his hand on top of hers, trying to be comforting. "I had a feeling this might happen. I talked to a sex-therapist friend of mine a little while ago. She said that once you start going down this road with human sexuality— once you get into sadomasochism or you start nipple-piercing or labia-piercing or tattooing or any other kind of heavyweight perversion—it becomes an obsession, and you never get satisfied. You start chasing a mirage of ultimate excitement that doesn't exist. Good sex is being exciting with what you've got."

He sat back and fastidiously wiped his mouth with his napkin. "I can have you in for corrective surgery early next week. Fifty thousand in advance, fifty thousand on completion, scarcely any scar."

Helen frowned. "You can get donors that quick?"

"I'm sorry?" said Dr. Arcolio. "You won't need any more donors. We'll simply take out the second vagina and close up."

"Doctor, I believe we're talking at cross-purposes here," Helen told him. "I don't want this second vagina removed. I want two more."

There was a very long silence. Dr. Arcolio licked his lips, and then drank a glass of water, and then licked his lips again. "You want *what,* did you say?"

"Two more. You can do it, can't you? One in the lower half of each breast. Bradley will adore it. Then I can have one man in each breast, and three inside, and two in my mouth, and Bradley will adore it."

"You want me to transplant vaginas into your *breasts?* Helen, for God's sake, what I've done already is advanced enough. Not to mention ethically appalling and totally illegal. This time, Helen, no. No way. You can send all of your incriminating particulars about my transsexual surgery to the D.A. or wherever you damn well like. But no. I'm not doing it. Absolutely not."

Bradley's Christmas treat that year was to invite six of his friends for a stag supper. They ate flame-grilled steak, and drank four jugs of dry martinis between them, and then they roared and laughed and tilted into the bedroom, where Helen was waiting for them, naked, not moving.

They took one look at her and they stopped roaring. They approached her in disbelief, and stared at her, and she remained quite still, with everything exposed.

In drunken wide-eyed wonder, two of them clambered astride her. One of them was the president of a Boston savings bank. Helen didn't know the other one, but he had a ginger mustache and ginger hair on his thighs. They took hold of her nipples between finger and thumb and lifted up her heavy breasts, as if they were lifting up dish covers at an expensive restaurant.

"My God," said the president of the savings bank. "It's true. It's fucking true."

With gradually mounting grunts of excitement, the two men pushed their reddened erections deep into the slippery apertures that had opened up beneath Helen's nipples.

They forced themselves deep into her breasts, deep into soft warm tissue, and twisted her nipples until she winced with pain.

Two more crammed themselves into her mouth, so that she could scarcely breathe. But what did it matter? Bradley was whooping with delight, Bradley loved her, Bradley wanted her. Bradley would never grow tired of her now, not after this. And even if he did, she could always find new ways to please him.

He didn't grow tired of her. But then he didn't have very much longer to live. On September 12, two years later, Helen woke up to find that Bradley was lying dead, his cold hand cupping her original vulva.

Bradley was buried in the grounds of the Dedham-style house overlooking the Charles River, in accordance with that strange pretense that the dead can still see, or even care where they are.

Dr. Arcolio came to the house and drank champagne and ate little bits of fish and artichoke and messy little barbe-cued ribs. Everybody spoke in very hushed voices. Helen Ellis had kept to herself throughout the funeral and had been heavily veiled in black. Now she had retreated to her private apartments and left Bradley's family and business friends and political henchmen to enjoy his wake without her participation.

After a while, however, Dr. Arcolio climbed the echoing marble stairs and tiptoed along to her room. He tapped three times on the door before he heard her say, indistinctly, "Who is it? Go away."

"It's Eugene Arcolio. Can I talk to you?"

There was no reply, but after a very long time, the doors were opened, and left open, and Dr. Arcolio assumed that this must be an invitation for him to go inside.

Cautiously, he entered. Helen was sitting by the window on a stiff upright chair. She was still veiled.

"What do *you* want?" she asked him. Her voice was muffled, distorted.

He shrugged. "I just came by to say congratulations."

"Congratulations?"

"Sure . . . you got what you wanted, didn't you? The house, the money. Everything."

Helen turned her head toward him and then lifted her veil. He wasn't shocked. He knew what to expect. After all, he had undertaken all of the surgery himself.

In each of her cheeks, a vulva gaped. Each vulva was pouting and moist, a surrealistic parody of a *Rustler* center-spread. A barely comprehensible collage of livid flesh and composed beauty and absolute horror.

It had been Helen's last act of complete subservience, to sacrifice her looks, so that Bradley and his friends had been able to penetrate not only her body but her face.

Dr. Arcolio had pleaded with her not to do it, but she had threatened suicide, and then murder, and then she had threatened to tell the media what he had done to her already.

"It's reversible," he had reassured himself as he meticulously sewed vaginal muscles into the linings of her cheeks. "It's totally reversible."

Helen looked up at him. "You think I got what I wanted?" Every time she spoke, the vaginal lips parted slightly.

He had to turn away. The sight of what he had done to her was more than he could bear.

"I didn't get what I wanted," she said, and tears began to slide down her cheeks, and drip from the curved pink labia minora. "I wanted vaginas everywhere, all over me, so that Bradley could have twenty friends for the night, a hundred of them all at once, in my face, in my thighs, in my stomach, under my arms. He wanted a sex object, Eugene, and I would have been happy, you know, being his sex object."

Dr. Arcolio said, "I'm sorry. I think this was my fault, as much as yours. In fact, I think it was *all* my fault."

That afternoon he went back to his office overlooking Brookline Square where Helen Ellis had first consulted him. He stood by the window for a long time.

Was it right to give people what they wanted, if what they wanted was perverse and self-sacrificial, and it flew in the face of God's creation?

Was it right to mutilate a beautiful woman, even if she craved mutilation?

How far did his responsibilities go? Was he a butcher, or was he a saint? Was he close to Heaven; or dancing on the manhole cover of Hell? Or was he nothing more than a surgical parody of Ann Landers, solving marital problems with a scalpel, instead of sensible suggestions?

He lit the first cigarette he had smoked in almost a month and sat at his desk in the gathering gloom. Then, when it was almost dark, his secretary, Esther, knocked on the door, opened it, and said, "Doctor?"

"What is it, Esther? I'm busy."

"Mr. Pierce and Mr. De Scenza. They came for their six o'clock appointment."

Dr. Arcolio crushed out his cigarette and waved the smoke away. "Oh, shit. All right. Show them in."

John Pierce and Philip De Scenza came into his office and stood in front of his desk like two schoolboys summoned to report to the principal. John Pierce was young and blond and wore an unstructured Italian suit with rolled-up sleeves. Philip De Scenza was older and heavier and darker, in a hand-knitted plum-colored sweater and baggy brown slacks.

Dr. Arcolio reached across his desk and shook their hands. "How are you? Sorry . . . I've been a little preoccupied this afternoon."

"Oh . . . we understand," said Philip De Scenza. "We've been pretty busy ourselves."

"How are things coming along?" asked Dr. Arcolio. "Have you experienced any problems? Any pain?"

John Pierce shyly shook his head. Philip De Scenza made a circle with his finger and his thumb and said, "Perfect, Doctor. Two thousand percent perfect. Fucking-A, if you don't mind my saying so!"

Dr. Arcolio stood up and cleared his throat. "You'd better let me take a look, then. Do you want a screen?"

"A *screen?*" John Pierce giggled.

Philip De Scenza dismissively flapped his hand. "We don't need a screen."

While Dr. Arcolio waited, John Pierce unbuckled his belt, tugged down his zipper, and wriggled out of his toothpaste-striped boxer shorts.

"Would you bend over, please?" asked Dr. Arcolio. John Pierce gave a little cough and did as he was told.

Dr. Arcolio spread his muscular bottom to reveal two perfect crimson anuses, both tightly wincing, one above the other. Around the upper anus there was a star-shaped pattern of more than ninety stitches, but they had all healed perfectly, and there were only the faintest diagonal scars across his buttocks.

"Good," said Dr. Arcolio, "that's fine. You can pull up your pants again now."

He turned to Philip De Scenza, and all he had to do was raise an eyebrow. Philip De Scenza lifted his sweater, dropped his pants, and stood proudly brandishing his improved equipment: one dark penis, like a heavy fruit, surmounted by yet another dark penis; and four hairy testicles hanging at the sides.

"Any difficulties?" asked Dr. Arcolio, lifting both penises with professional detachment and examining them carefully. Both began to stiffen a little.

"Timing, that's all." Philip De Scenza shrugged, with a sideways smile at his friend. "I still haven't managed a simultaneous climax. By the time I've finished, poor John's usually getting quite sore."

"General comfort?" asked Dr. Arcolio tightly.

"Oh, *fine* . . . just so long as I don't wear my pants too tailored."

"Okay," said Dr. Arcolio dully. "You can zip yourself up again now."

"Over so soon?" Philip De Scenza flirted. "That's not very good value, Doctor. A hundred dollars for two seconds' fondle. You should be ashamed of yourself."

That evening, John Pierce and Philip De Scenza went to Le Bellecour on Muzzey Street for dinner. They held hands all the way through the meal.

Dr. Arcolio picked up a few groceries and then drove home in his metallic-blue Rolls-Royce, listening to *La Boheme* on the stereo. He glanced in the rearview mirror from time to time and thought he was looking tired. Traffic was heavy and slow on the turnpike, and he felt thirsty, so he took an apple out of the bag beside him and took a bite.

He thought about Helen; and he thought about John Pierce and Philip De Scenza; and he thought about all of the other men and women whose bodies he had skillfully changed into living incarnations of their own sexual fantasies.

Something that Philip De Scenza had said kept nagging him. *You should be ashamed of yourself.* Although Philip De Scenza had been joking, Dr. Arcolio suddenly understood that, yes, he should be ashamed of what he had done. In fact, he *was* ashamed of what he had done. Ashamed that he had used his surgical genius to create such erotic aberrations. Ashamed that he had mutilated so many beautiful bodies.

But as well as being painful, this surge of shame was liberating, too. Because men and women were more than God had made them. Men and women were able to reinvent themselves, and to derive strange new pleasures from pain and humiliation and self-distortion. Who was to say that it was right or that it was wrong? Who could define the perfect human being? If it was wrong to give a woman a second vagina, was it also wrong to repair a baby's harelip?

He felt chastened; but also uplifted. He finished his apple

and tossed the core out onto the highway. Ahead of him he could see nothing but a Walpurgis Night procession of red brakelights.

In her house, alone, Helen wept salt tears of grief and sweet tears of sex, which mingled and dropped on her hands, so that they sparkled like diamond engagement rings.

BOX 69

Rex Miller

*H*e picked her up in a bar just off one of the big noisy casinos on the strip. Had to be a showgirl. A real killer pony with legs that never stopped and a beautiful face—or so it appeared in the hotel-bar lighting. He'd picked up cocktail waitresses who looked like a million bucks until you got them under some strong light. The Pfeifferesque mouth would turn out to be mostly lipstick and very little lip. Or they'd have bad teeth—whatever.

Her long blond hair was off the forehead. That was the first thing he looked for. He hated those frizzy fucking bangs, and so many women wore their hair in that style now, with a wispy fringe of hairs combed down in their eyes. She had a good, strong face with bold features and the cheek-bones of a model or television actress—very fine-looking stuff.

A smoothie about ten years younger than himself, in a brown suede shirt, with hair almost as long as hers, tried to hit on her. She iced him with a couple of words and he moved on. Clean. This was some clean trim.

"WHOOOOOA!" somebody screamed. The two of them made eye contact, laughing.

"Another satisfied customer," he said, and she nodded.

"Sounds like it." She had beautiful teeth. Had to be caps.

BOX 69

For a moment he wondered if she was a pro, but a pro who looked that good would be working off a phone somewhere, she wouldn't be sitting in a casino bar. The girl named Barrie who usually worked this station during the early evening shifts was waitressing, he was pleased to note. She knew what she was supposed to do when a loose chick was around.

He felt Barrie come up behind him and get his old glass, exchanging it for a new drink but making it a Marilyn production, her weight against him the whole time, looking good in the short toga-thing the hotel made the girls wear, rubbing herself up against him, doing it well, selling it, asking him if he wanted anything else in this breathy whisper. Barrie had a nice chest and it was turning him on to get the full treatment—even if he paid for it.

He didn't even bother to say no—just gave an imperceptible, frosty shake of the head. No smile. Nothing. Chilled the bitch to the bone, so it appeared. He saw the woman observing the encounter, rather speculatively, he thought.

The man was very careful that the looker would not see him push the folded fifty under his cocktail napkin. He was happy to pay for it when it made him look good. But unless it got him over on somebody he couldn't groove with it. That was his action. That was why he counted cards instead of making his bucks the old-fashioned way. He liked to scam. It was a buzz.

If he had to straight-up pay for it and didn't sting some poor schlub in the bargain, it was no deal. You'd not find him up in his room with the *Sun,* the paper open to the classified PERSONALS:

NATASHA IS A 42-D ! Exotic, Sensuous Brunette. I love to party all nite long, and I mean long and hard. I am not a service.

24-YEAR-OLD BLONDE would like to meet you personally. Attractive, liberated, and into YOUR fantasies. I'm not an agency.

SIDESADDLE OUTCALL specializes in double-bills. We have classy, well-built escorts who love to get down with you. Adrianna and Lisa are beautiful, dumb, and 21. When's the last time YOU hit 21?

. . . Pasadena.

He watched her slide her hands along the sides of her knees. A sort of nervous mannerism. He studied things like that. She noticed him looking at her, his dark eyes fixed on the lovely dancer's legs in spike heels, the skirt short to begin with but really hiked up the way it will when a person sits down.

She tried to pull her skirt down a bit but didn't succeed. He made sure he was making full eye contact and asked her if she'd permit him to buy her a drink.

"No thanks," she said, simply. It wasn't a full turn-down. Or even an "I don't think so—not today" thing that she wanted to be talked out of. Just a frank, simple answer. No. But thanks anyway.

"Would you like some company while we finish our drinks?" He kept his face smiling and serene.

"Sure." She smiled and gave a shrug to let him know she didn't care one way or the other. It was up to him now, he thought. He had one of his size twelves in the door and he could find out whether this one liked his line or not. He got his drink and moved over, sitting with his back to the table where he was and blocking that part of the room off. He was pleased to see Barrie move over to clean the table. Always good to work with a pro.

"Are you here on a visit?" he asked. Everybody in Vegas asked you if you were from someplace else, even some of the locals. If there was a transient spot on the globe, it was Las Vegas, Nevada.

"Yes. I'm here on business. Just be here a couple of nights and back home." She was "with an advertising concern."

Home, it developed, was San Francisco. Her name was Robyn Arné, Robyn with a *Y*, Ar-*nay*. She had a voice like a

BOX 69

call-in hooker service, or maybe he was just hor-nay. ("CALL CANDY FOR SOME HOT CONVERSATION! I LIKE WHAT *YOU* LIKE!") She was cultured, sophisticated, a complete turn-on for him.

They talked current affairs. They had a lot in common: Both of them thought all hostages should be released; serial killers were scary; the vice-president was a dork; abortion was a controversial, touchy issue; the cost of medical care in the U.S. was too high; and time passed too quickly.

"Well," she said, "I enjoyed this."

"So did I," he told her.

"I should get to bed early," she said, and took her right hand and made that move on her knee, sliding it back, touching the short skirt and sliding it—he was sure—way up her thigh. He couldn't exactly see it, but he sensed it. He was convinced this was the sexiest woman he'd ever seen in his life. She was making him crazy.

"Please," he said. For once in his life he was tongue-tied. He wanted her so badly it had rendered him stupid. Where was that old silver tongue when he needed it? "I don't want to say goodbye. Is that too dumb?"

"No. It's very sweet, in fact," she told him with her eyes as well, which were a deep, remarkable violet. Everything about her was that color—from her high-heeled sandals to the dress she was almost wearing. Ultraviolet all the way. He felt the heat, that much was for certain.

He was cooking. Perspiration trickled down his back. His mouth was dry as cotton and he felt like a hundred-and-ten-year-old loser instead of the forty-one he was, so fearful was he of blowing it.

"Please. Could we spend some more time together?"

She blinked the violet at him. Let a half-second tick by as she scanned the depressing vista of the casino bar as if to say—why?

"Not here. We could go—anywhere you say?" He shrugged. "My room?" He blurted it out like a kid.

"Okay." She smiled and his heart melted. Ya-HA! He wanted to shout—like the satisfied screamer at the craps table layout. Oh, baby, don't screw it up now. Not when you're this close to some gen-u-wine movie star stuff. Talk about clean! Mercy.

In the elevator they touched hands and it was as if he'd grabbed a hot wire with his feet in a pool of water. The shock waves went up his arm and shot straight for the groin. He'd never wanted a woman so desperately as he wanted Robyn-with-a-hot-Y Ar-nay, as hot as Texas Chile con Car-nay.

The long walk down the hallway to his room took forever. If the key jammed he silently vowed to take her right there in the hall. The maids and room-service people could just wheel around them.

Inside he swallowed, wondering if he should pour them a drink or what—but she was no tease, and she initiated it herself, stripping for him.

Had to be a dancer, this Robyn. You couldn't move that gracefully without training, and the lady had the moves. She took it off slowly, in stages, humming a soft little tune as she slid out of the clinging thing. She was violet underneath, too—what else? Damn! She was something to see— standing there posing in high-heeled nothing, just a lacy G-string-type deal and half-cups, the underbra what-chamacallits pushing those nice breasts up. She was fucking gorgeous.

He didn't remember shedding his clothes, he was so wrapped up in her—completely engrossed by this perfor-mance. When she bent over, keeping her legs real straight, to remove her shoes, it was such a fabulously sexy move he had to concentrate not to go off in his jockey shorts.

Still she wouldn't touch him—teasing him with peach fuzz of tanned arm, deep hollow of throat, soft, and long as a Modigliani, hand slowly reaching down and caressing her-self, getting hot and wet for herself, cocktease-type parody in sideview, having fun with it, turning and giving him her calendar-girl–class ass, long, shapely Hollywood legs, turn of the curvaceous upper bod and erect nipples, back around with high half-moons of cheeky derriere stuck into his face, flirtatious bodacious wiggle of silky hip, and he was *gone,* at

BOX 69

her, on her, kissing, gobbling, pawing, touching, eating, squeezing, going after her like a big dog in heat.

The first time it was over he thought he was gone for good, but she played on him and revived the dead man.

"I'm out of it. I'm dead." He tried to beg off. He felt as if he'd been hit by a truck.

"Think so, darling?" she whispered. "Think again." She moved away from him and he watched her stand still, bend over the table beside the bed, slowly, those legs back in the high heels now, and with her ass nude and shoes on, her legs were about ten feet long. She had almost no tummy, and she was sort of posing with her back and ass up and out, her butt in the air, and it was too much for him again. He was wetting her in back and ramming it in the back door. He had to get some fudge, judge, that's all there was to that.

This time, when he was through, he . . . was . . . through. End of story. Don't slam the door on your way out. It's been real but I gotta catch an early jet. Huh-uh. She wanted her fun. She started kissing him, and if there was anything that could make him hot it was a kissing bandito, and this honey was a clean smoocher make no mistake. What a talented tongue. Again with the erection. He felt twenty.

She stopped.

"What's wrong?"

"Nothing."

"Hey! Tell me. I must have done something. What did I do?"

"It's me, doll. I'm weird."

"How so?"

"I can't get off like—you know—a guy can. I'm kinda kinky. I have to have things a certain way," she purred.

"What way? Hell, I'm kinky too, baby. Tell me what makes your sub dive—I'll do my best to please."

"Nah."

"Come on."

"I have little fantasies." She colored. She was either a hell of an actress or she felt ashamed.

"What kind of fantasies?"

"Rape—you know. I like to play like I rape the guy—you know?"

"So play. I'll play."

"I have to tie you up. Most guys don't get off when they're tied."

"What would you tie me with?"

"I don't know. I never get to do it. It's just a fantasy." She laughed.

"Let's do it. Use my tie. We'll find something. Wait a minute." He was so into pleasing her he took his pocket knife and cut the telephone cord. So he'd pay for a new phone tomorrow. He wanted this honey happy. "Tie me up. I'll play your kinky game."

"Really?" She seemed shy about it.

"Do it. Tie me. Rape me. If that's what you want." She was so fucking beautiful.

"I get hot thinking about it, but then I feel so ashamed. Women don't rape men."

"Do it. Fantasies are good. It's therapeutic." He convinced her and she bound him, rather tenderly, to the bed.

"Tighter," he told her. "The way you're doing it I'm not even tied. Tie me up, baby. Rape my cock."

"Yeah! Okay." It was turning her on, too. He could tell. He watched the lovely woman secure him spreadeagled to the bed.

"You want me, baby?"

"Yeah." She was ready.

"Do it."

It happened too fast. All of it. The tape was over his mouth and done professionally, as a nurse might do it. Carefully. She wasn't trying to hurt him—whatever else she was into—so at least it wasn't that. No pain. Surgical tape. Adhesive tape—whatever. ZZZIP over his mouth, gently tearing it off, trying not to get it in his hair. He of course trying to get loose now, wanting to tell the great-looking cunt to GET THE FUCKING TAPE OFF HIS MOUTH and saying it through the tape, the mean juices filling up behind his eyes.

"No—no, honey." She soothed him. "Your lover doesn't

BOX 69

want you to scream. I'm not going to hurt you but you said to do the rape thing, and let me have my fun. You're bound and gagged—get it?" Okay. He calmed down. All right. But she should have warned him about the tape over his mouth and GOOD GODDAMN SHE HAD A FUCKING RAZOR BLADE OH, NO! He knew now he'd been scammed. He'd been set up. A fucking sadist. She was going to do a j-o-b with the damn blade. Oh, God. No. He begged her with his eyes.

"Really, sugar. You said fantasize. I'm not going to do anything to hurt you. This isn't for you," she said. Naked and glistening with a sheen of perspiration. "This is for me." What the fuck what the fuck what the fuck—it was stuck like a broken disc caught on a stylus. Get out of this somehow—think!

She didn't make a big deal about it. She just made the cut, a long incision across her beautiful belly. Blood welled up in a line, surprisingly little blood for the length of the cut, then it started dripping. "See, baby?" she said. And she got on him like a freaky pony, mounted his cock, soft, it mooshed out and she didn't care, she was on top and made a little funny face and ZZZIP again, another horizontal slash with the razor and this guy who hadn't prayed for thirty years you had best believe was doing some big-time Heavenly Father action now, begging to keep his masculinity down there, but that wasn't where she cut him. She gave him a cut to match hers, a line across the belly, and he was almost relieved. Then she worked the cuts open a bit with her fingers, mashing the two of their bods together. Kissing him once on the mouth, leaving a big red kiss on the white tape.

Off him now and all business. A different Robyn, this. Dressing hurriedly after she zipped a big piece of tape across her tummy and his, blotted off on the hotel towels, made sure no blood was showing on her dress or shoes. Checked her hair and makeup. He was trying to groan through the tape.

"Sure. I know, baby. You've got a few questions. Let me hip you to the scene, as they used to say back in your day. My name's not Robyn Arné, although it is a pretty name.

She gave me the name—it's her name." Her name? Whose name?

"Remember Nora? Nora Byrne?" Nora—fuck. Some cunt he'd known a zillion years ago. She watched his shoulders sag in recognition. "This is Nora's present. She said you dumped on her real bad once—I didn't need details. Said you were a total prick with women—a real asshole who needed some punishing. So." She turned and checked herself in the mirror. Gave the hair a few pats and got a list out of her purse. Read it over, as if it were a checklist. Okay—*what?* What's the fucking schtick, chick?

"Robyn Arné—pretty cool—that's Nora Byrne jumbled up. Her little joke, I guess. You must have really fucked this lady over, eh? Well—whatever. I've had a couple of guys do it to me real good, too, in my day. That's why I was willing. That and the big bucks. She said not to take a dime from you—that you'd be loaded with dough, but to leave it. That was important. All she wanted was"—the gorgeous woman looked at her list—"saliva, sperm, and blood." She looked at him with her violet contacts. "The body juices—right? So you'd have my particular slow poison. She said it was a perfect way for you to go, slooow and tough toward the end—so you'd have lots of time to worry and think about the pain that was coming. She said it would bother you to know you were dying the same death as any gay or any junkie. You thought you were so fucking special—such hot shit."

He pulled at the phone cord. But he'd picked her up, made her tie him. She read his thoughts, it seemed.

"I'm an actress and a damned good one. Case you're wondering. She flipped out when she saw my picture." He could see why. She still looked so good—even now—the sleekly edible thighs under the violet mini, the gentle convexity of the flat, sexy tummy, and that mouth. If only nasty things would stop spilling from it. "I'm not really from San Francisco, but that was one of the three cities where she had these ads and cards distributed among the counterculture. She wanted anybody who'd had the Bad News to see it. So . . . you've got a lot to think about, sport.

BOX 69

Time to repent . . . and who knows? Any day they could come up with something. Oh—last thing—here's my report."

She showed him a medical report with the name and address blanked. It looked official. Someone had tested positive for HIV virus. So—big deal. What the fuck did this have to do with him?

"You made her lose her baby, she said to me on the phone. The one thing she wanted most in the world. You knew that, but you took her to some fool that cut her up. Left her unable to walk, let alone have any future kids. Then you walked out on her. That's pretty fucking low.

"It was all I could do not to scream, you know? It was like letting a snake go inside me. I guess I wanted this almost as much as she did."

He was there in the Vegas strip air-conditioning long after she left, working at the cord and reading the ad she'd left propped on the pillow beside him:

IF YOU HAVE TESTED POSITIVE AND WANT TO PERFORM A COURAGEOUS ACT, FOR WHICH YOU WILL BE HANDSOMELY PAID, CONTACT ME WITH TOTAL CONFIDENCE. IF YOU HAVE THE COURAGE AND THE VIRUS, I HAVE THE MONEY AND THE TARGET. WRITE LAS VEGAS, BOX 69.

PRIZED POSSESSION

Jeff Gelb

*T*hey sized each other up through the small glass window of the ranch home's front door, like two prizefighters about to do battle. Inside, Berton Randolph, tall, blond-haired, and wiry, opened the door an inch.

"Crawford?"

"You were expecting maybe Jamie Gillis?"

"Anyone with you?"

"Like who—the FBI? Cut the shit. You know I wouldn't bring anyone."

"What took you so long?"

"Fuck, this place is twice as far out of town as you said on the phone. I got lost. There's not exactly any neighbors to ask directions from. I only stumbled on the road by mistake."

Randolph shrugged. "I like my privacy." He looked beyond Crawford at the peaceful, rolling hills of rural upstate New York. "So where's the stuff?"

"In the car." John Crawford, dark, bearded, and stocky, pointed to the station wagon parked in the dirt driveway. Its side and rear windows were obscured by darkened glass.

"You could fit it all in there?" Randolph sneered.

"Hey, it ain't the size, it's the quality," Crawford retorted. "We gonna get on with this or what?"

Randolph scowled. "I made the offer, you accepted. You feel like backing out, now's the time."

Crawford said nothing, his face betraying his hatred for the man in front of him. Finally, Crawford strode back to his car, turning off the burglar alarm and unlocking the doors with a keychain control.

Randolph joined Crawford at the car and hoisted several large acid-free cardboard containers out of the stuffed trunk. He whistled. "There's more in here than I thought."

"Of course," Crawford said. "No one in the world has more than I do."

"Until today," Randolph jeered.

Ten minutes later, they'd emptied the car of its load, piling twenty-seven boxes of various sizes outside a locked room in the back of the house.

Crawford looked around. "Anyone else here?"

Randolph shook his head.

The two eyed each other suspiciously.

"You know I can't let you in till I search you," Randolph said defensively.

"Well," said Crawford with a sigh, "let's get on with it, then."

Randolph patted Crawford from head to toe, back and front, and then stood up while Crawford mirrored his movements. When both were satisfied that neither was hiding a weapon, Randolph turned away from Crawford, hiding his movements as he fingered the lock of the door. It clicked, was removed, and Randolph swung open the door.

Crawford had to smile as he looked inside. The twelve-by-twelve room was even better than he could have imagined—it was a virtual shrine. Floor-to-ceiling shelves were bulging with magazine-sized boxes, videotapes, and other memorabilia. The sight nearly brought tears to his eyes. It was, in bulk anyway, seemingly an even better collection than his own.

"Stacey Tracey," he whispered. It sounded like a prayer.

"No one but," breathed Randolph. "The porn queen of all time."

Crawford nodded, his mouth agape at the sight of a life-sized stand-up of Tracey. Randolph noticed the stare and smiled. "One of only twenty-five made. It's from her last film, *Tracey Takes on All Cummers.*"

"I know that," Crawford hissed.

"I have stand-ups from three of her films," Randolph crowed, obviously enjoying watching Crawford squirm. "But you didn't come to see my collection. You came to sell me yours."

Crawford walked slowly around the room. His fingers traced the stacks of skin mags. He picked up a batch and flipped through it, recognizing many of the titles from his own collection. He gazed at row after row of videos, all pristine in their original box-cover art.

"All ninety-six films," Randolph said, the scorn evident in his voice. "Including the one she made before she was eighteen."

Crawford ignored him, continuing to look around the room. One wall was covered with posters and photos. Crawford counted seven with her autograph.

"All genuine," Randolph said, as if reading Crawford's mind.

"Shit," Crawford muttered. There was no doubt about it: Randolph's collection eclipsed his own. "How'd you score them? She never signed autographs."

"I don't take no for an answer, that's how. Unlike you, Crawford. I met her at the adult video awards two years ago and I made her an offer she couldn't refuse."

"Shit." Crawford sulked. He'd always thought he owned the most obscure Tracey memorabilia around, but he was way out of his league here.

Crawford had first learned of Tracey from a fellow bank teller who'd just rented one of her earliest adult films, back in the last dying days of 35mm adult features. She had reminded Crawford of a girl he'd had a crush on throughout high school but had never spoken with, let alone seen naked, legs spread, breasts upthrust. Except in his dreams.

Always a collector at heart, Crawford had gone around the

bend in his efforts to amass the world's largest hoard of Tracey memorabilia. His obsession ate up all his time, distracting him at work, until even the co-worker who'd turned him on to Tracey had refused to speak with him, branding him "weird." Well, what did he—or any of them—know?

He could still remember the moment he'd heard she was quitting the business. She was supposedly marrying a retired millionaire to live on his yacht, cruising the world, getting the ultimate tan all over that ultimate body.

Once she'd dropped out of circulation, it had become next to impossible for Crawford to find anything new of hers to collect, until he'd learned of Randolph, who had come out of nowhere and supposedly built up an even larger stash of Tracey stuff than his own. Randolph immediately became Crawford's archrival, and his new obsession.

Crawford continued his inspection of the room. There was the spiked collar from *Give the Dog a Boner*. The ivory dildo from *Jungle Lust*. He picked it up gingerly, sniffed it, hoping for some trace scent of her. It smelled like lilac soap.

"Time's wasting, Crawford. You gonna show me what you got or what?"

Crawford turned his attention back to Randolph, who stood against a mannequin dressed in the same nightie, stockings, and heels that Tracey had worn in her most famous role, *Old Loves Die Hard*. In the dummy's hand was the whip Tracey had used in *Whipped Cream and Other Sexual Delights*.

Randolph smirked. "I also have the heels she wore in *Spike Jones*, the costume from *Superbitch*, the—"

"I get the picture," Crawford hissed. "If you've got all this stuff, why buy my collection? You probably have everything I have."

Randolph shrugged. "I'll admit it: You stumbled over some good shit along the way. It bothers me that anyone else has Tracey stuff I don't have."

"So why not just buy the stuff you need?"

Randolph shrugged. "I'm a collector. I don't like the

competition. If I buy you out, it'll give me by far the biggest collection of her material. You might say it's the culmination of my collecting career.

"And," he finished, "it puts you out of business."

"Yeah, but I'll be rich."

Randolph snorted. "It won't matter, Crawford. Lots of people have money. Only one person will have the ultimate Stacey Tracey collection. And it won't be you."

Randolph turned his attention to the first of the boxes they'd dragged in from Crawford's car, examining and inventorying its contents. Crawford turned away. It was almost unbearable to see Randolph fingering the photos, videos, magazines, and ephemera Crawford had spent the last five years and thousands of dollars accumulating.

"I'll bet you were shocked when I called," Randolph said.

Crawford shrugged.

"So why'd you decide to sell?" Randolph asked as he sifted through boxes stuffed with still shots from each of her films, plus reams of candid shots and outtakes from various adult-mag photo shoots.

"That's my business," Crawford snarled as he continued his visual search of Randolph's collection. There were all four yearbooks from Tracey's high-school days; the two Tracey calendars that had instantly sold out.

Randolph nodded, continuing the work at hand: sorting, writing, calculating conditions and prices. Finally, he looked up again, wiping his tired eyes. "Twenty thousand cash, right now."

Crawford grimaced. "You haven't even opened the last box." He pointed to his feet, where a small box had been partially obscured by a Tracey stand-up.

Randolph shrugged. "I don't need to. To tell you the truth, I'm disappointed in your collection, Crawford. I guess the rumors I've heard weren't true. Your collection is shit, but it makes me feel good to take you out of circulation. Twenty grand."

"It's worth twice that much easy and you know it."

Randolph shrugged. "Fine. Go sell it. Maybe a classified

in the *New York Times?* Do you really want junkies or cops clawing over your stuff?"

"Thirty."

"My price is firm and it goes down in ten minutes. Think about it."

You shit. You don't deserve to be Tracey's biggest fan.

"Maybe you'll change your mind when you see what's in this box," Crawford said as he reached down and carefully tore tape off the sides and center of the box lid. He put a hand inside and came out with a .38 Special, which he pointed at Randolph.

Randolph blinked, then laughed nervously. "What is it, a prop from *Tracey's Dick?*

Crawford pulled the trigger and a deafening shot rang out. Across the room, the ivory dildo exploded into shards. "Oops," Crawford said, smiling wickedly.

Randolph literally jumped to his feet. "Hey, I was just kidding. I think I can go thirty thousand. Just put the gun down."

Crawford laughed humorlessly. "Oh, I'll take your thirty thousand *and* your collection, asshole. I never planned to sell my stuff to you. And you'll never live to enjoy mine."

Randolph's eyes darted from Crawford to the door and back. "You're going to . . ."

"It doesn't take a genius, dickhead. There's only room in this world for one man to be Tracey's biggest fan, and that's going to be me."

Randolph bolted for the open door and was felled by an immediate shot from Crawford's gun that struck him in the shoulder. Randolph cursed as he fell to the floor. "Oh, shit," he grunted through clenched teeth. "Please don't shoot again. I'll do anything. I'll give you anything."

Crawford cocked an eyebrow. "Like what?" There was no telling what other Stacey stuff Randolph might have stashed away somewhere else, stuff even better than what was in this room, Crawford thought. Might as well help myself to it all.

Randolph crawled over to a framed painting of Tracey, lifted it off the wall, and twisted the dials on a hidden safe. It opened, and Randolph grabbed three unmarked videotape boxes from its depths. He carefully loaded one of the tapes into a Super VHS machine and turned on a high-resolution thirty-inch TV monitor.

Onscreen was a crystal-clear image of Tracey, writhing on the concrete floor of an empty room. She was nude, legs spread, fingering herself. A masked man entered the scene, grabbed Tracey by her long dyed-blond hair, and impaled her face on his dick. She lapped at it with wild abandon, as if it were manna from heaven. In less than a minute, the man squirted a creamy load onto her balloonlike, uptilted breasts.

Crawford nodded. "I'm impressed. I don't remember this scene in any of her movies. And she looks . . . different, somehow. Thinner, or something."

Randolph whispered, "This is private stock." Even in pain, his voice had an air of superiority.

"Where'd you . . . ?" Crawford was unable to finish his question, as the man on film began doing things to Tracey that were at best degrading. "I can't believe she would do this stuff," Crawford sputtered, unable to look away from the video.

Randolph's hand jerked back into the safe and brought out a gun. He fired a bullet that whizzed past Crawford's forehead and into the life-sized breast of the Tracey stand-up.

Weak from his wound, Randolph wiped at his eyes to regain clear vision. Crawford fired. Randolph gasped and fell against a bookshelf, dislodging hundreds of magazines and videotape boxes, then the bookshelf itself, which fell in a heavy metallic heap atop him. He groaned as blood gushed out of his mouth and a hole in his chest.

"Help me," he whispered. "Get me to a hospital."

"Fuck you, Randolph." Crawford laughed. "You probably meant to kill me all along." He pointed the weapon at Randolph's head.

"No, wait. I'll . . . give you something else. Something better. My . . . most prized possession," Randolph sputtered through bloody lips.

Crawford laughed. "What's that? An Uzi you have hidden somewhere?"

Randolph reached a shaking hand to touch a switch behind the filing cabinet.

"No you don't," Crawford said as he fired again. Randolph's hand blew apart as a bookshelf against the opposite wall moved sideways to reveal a door that popped open.

Stacey Tracey, bound, gagged, nude, writhed against the chains that held her to the far wall of the empty room.

"Ohmigod," Crawford muttered.

"Yours," Randolph gasped, the blood from his mouth now just a trickle. "Just call the . . ." His head hit the carpet and bounced once, then was still.

Crawford's attention was diverted by Stacey's cries, muffled by the rubber ball in her mouth, held in place by leather straps around her face.

He ran to her side, untying her bonds. "It's okay," he said, attempting to calm her. "Everything's going to be all right now. I'll get you out of here. The guy was obviously a fucking maniac, keeping you here like this."

She fell into his arms. He was actually holding Stacey Tracey! He could feel the fullness of her breasts heaving against his chest, the roundness of her hips grinding against his groin, the long fingers reaching for his hand and grabbing the gun away from him before he even knew it.

And pulling the trigger once, twice, three times, the sound deafening. He gasped, more in surprise than pain, falling against the wall and then dropping to the floor like a marionette severed from its strings.

Crawford fruitlessly tried to cover the three bullet holes with his hands. He was starting to feel the pain now, but beyond the agony there was the ecstasy of Stacey Tracey, kneeling before him, looking exactly like she did in the video he'd just watched. The video, Crawford realized woozily, she'd obviously been forced to make with Randolph, her captor.

"I . . . don't understand. I tried to save you," he lied. It wasn't too late, he figured, to play her knight in shining armor.

"Save me from what?" she screamed, her voice sounding to his dying ears like a bad connection on a long-distance call. As he faded from consciousness, he heard her say, "You stupid shit! Berton Randolph was the only one who knew how to please me—he was my *husband!*"

MR. RIGHT

Chris Lacher

*R*uss put his psychology book aside and rubbed his eyes. The clock on the nightstand read six P.M. He picked up the copy of *Gent* he'd bought with lunch at the liquor store and flipped it open. The first pictorial displayed a homely black teen with fifty-inch tits and a chunky ass—which would've been okay if her face were a little easier on the eyes. Nonetheless, Russ started to get a boner.

He sighed and looked out the bedroom window. Across the street, volunteers for the Catholic church were preparing for their annual fiesta. Big rigs had been arriving since yesterday morning, dumping small cranes, rides, booths, and other carnival equipment onto the fields normally reserved for the youth baseball leagues. Russ had a unique view of the goings-on from his upstairs window, as if he were watching from a misplaced Ferris wheel or something. He'd asked Vicki before she left for work that morning if she wanted to go over tonight, but she hadn't really answered.

Just then, the phone rang. He picked up the receiver. "Hello?"

"Hi," Vicki said cheerfully, "what's up?"

"Nothin' much. What's up with you, babe?"

"Got a big collar. Some dickhead dope dealer led us to a whole buncha drugs, plus a coupla other dealers. I'll try t'get outta here by nine or so."

"Oh. Okay, no problem. I'll be here."

"Good." She sounded as cheery as when he'd first answered. "We'll go over to the carnival tomorrow, okay?"

Russ said fine, told her to be careful, then hung up and went back to his magazine. He didn't like to think about her work too much—it scared him, naturally. She was a tough girl—she could get into *Gent* with no problem, he thought, or at least she could've before she lost all that weight—but anything could happen nowadays. All those assholes runnin' around with Uzis and shit.

He sighed again. He was definitely not in the mood to study, and the magazine wasn't as good as he'd hoped. He dug the church bulletin out from under a stack of papers on his desk and found out that the fiesta started at seven. He checked his watch, took a quick shower, and headed across the street.

The carnies had done a pretty remarkable job in such a short amount of time. There were ten or twelve food and game booths spread over the baseball fields, and there was actually a midway to walk down. The rides loomed over the far end of the lot like gigantic eyes on metal stalks. None of them—a Ferris wheel, a Hammerhead, circular swings, something called Cyclone, and a bunch of smaller rides for the kids—looked safe enough to justify the ticket price. The Hammerhead seemed to be constructed of metal, even though it was decayed and weakened by rust, but the Cyclone had a wooden base. There were long lines in front of all of them, though; people were having fun, kicking up dust and dirt—which would be murder later for his hay fever—so Russ decided to stick to the booths.

As he went from booth to booth, losing his money at dime toss and at other games, Russ became less and less impressed. The tents were made of moldy canvas, and some horrid country-western music was piped into crackling loudspeakers. There was an annoying trilevel siren on the Cyclone ride, which creaked painfully as it turned; a maniacal *hee*-ing giggle taunted him from the House of Mystery.

He bought a small pizza, tossed a pocketful of dimes at some Budweiser glasses, then decided to leave. Rather than cross the busy parking lot, he headed for a break between two tents that led to the street.

Next to the Mystery tent sat a small stage. The words "Live Freaks" were printed in small letters on the curtain off to the side. The entrance was marked with a small sign that read "$2."

Russ stood undecided. Across from him, one of the metallic tentacles from the Cyclone viciously clawed the air. The siren squealed. Smoke swirled off the chugging gears— souls of past riders, possibly.

He fished inside his pocket and pulled out a five-dollar bill. He wasn't too thrilled at the prospect of seeing living deformities, but it'd certainly be more interesting than the rip-offs out here. Anyway, how bad could a freak tent at a church carnival be? He unfolded his money and pushed back the flap.

It was dark and stuffy inside; Russ saw a light bulb overhead, but it was so grimy he couldn't even tell if it was lit. Someone stood in the gloom up ahead; dust swirled in a jagged beam of light across its feet. Russ stepped forward.

Eyes adjusted to the darkness, Russ stared open-mouthed at the creature before him. It was obscenely thin, as seemingly malnourished as the kids in those "Feed the Children" spots on TV, but what astounded Russ most was its height: It had to stoop to fit under the tent's ridgepole. Even more disconcerting was the way it tottered forward, like a giraffe before a tall tree. Dressed in a black body stocking, it wore a straw hat and white mime's cuffs around tube-thin wrists. The creature looked rubbery, boneless, like a hollow puppet-kite from a Mardi Gras parade.

"Goin' in, dude?" Breath on his neck from behind. Russ held out his money.

The thing swooned forward, bobbing on the fawn-weak support from its legs. Instinctively, Russ leaned back, afraid it might fall over. Instead, it took his money, then counted off three singles into Russ's palm. "Three back," it said, then it turned to pull back the stained flap to the main tent area.

Quickly, Russ stepped through.

Just ahead, two large specimen jars sat atop a metal folding table. A human infant had been canned in one of the jars. Suspended in the other was a two-headed fetus Russ couldn't identify. He bent down to peer at it more closely, but he still wasn't sure what it was; its eyes were open, though. A chill clawing him, Russ moved away.

In the rear of the tent, reclining on a sofa perched atop a rickety plywood stage, was the fattest woman Russ had ever seen. She must've weighed half a ton, literally. She wore a blue, floral-print muumuu, and her knotted black hair stretched like soggy licorice sticks all the way to her waist. She had a bullfrog's throat, cheeks the size of softballs, and her bare feet, supported by a peeling Ottoman, were so monstrously oversized they nearly swallowed her toes. Russ thought of that joke: He didn't know where the tits ended and the belly began. Flesh hung off her upper arms like bleached saddlebags, and even the muumuu couldn't hide the triangular outline of fat drooping down between her thighs. She munched on potato chips and watched an *I Love Lucy* rerun on a portable black-and-white TV.

Russ was repulsed by the sight of her—he hadn't realized until now that his upper lip and nose were crunched slightly in disgust—but he couldn't stop himself from taking a few steps closer to the stage. He gagged slightly on the odors of moldy upholstery, stinking feet, and the body odor indigenous only to the grossly obese, yet he almost didn't care. She was gross, but she was the ultimate fat model, even if no one would dare print nude pictures of her. Weird.

Two boys with skateboards stepped up beside him. Russ glanced down at them, then over to the pancake-sized calluses on the fat woman's feet; then, her face.

She was staring right at him.

Russ couldn't look away.

Peripherally, he saw the boys with the skateboards turn to peer at him.

Slit eyes in the doughy face. Red clown cheeks.

He was immobilized.

Still eyeing him, she leaned forward on the couch and said, "Now the real show starts, honey." Her voice was thick and husky, in some way mutated.

Without moving his head, Russ glanced down. The boys were gone.

Movement on the stage brought his eyes forward again. A girl, apparently normal except for the absence of her legs—she had feet and ankles but they seemed soldered to her torso—had made her way up onstage. She duck-walked over to the couch, a shiny black vibrator clutched firmly in her hands, big brown eyes fixed on Russ's. After the fat thing had hiked up her muumuu, she took the vibrator from the girl's outstretched hand.

She stuck the tip of it in her mouth to moisten it, then turned it on. Shifting her weight to the edge of the couch, she lifted the caul of flesh between her thighs and slowly inserted the vibrator into her vagina. She moaned; the legless girl, glowing with excitement, clapped her hands together; the vibrator purred.

"No hands," she stuttered at Russ, exposing rotted teeth. The visible end of the vibrator resembled a bruised, thickly overgrown clitoris.

Russ was able, finally, to pull himself away. He crashed into the rubber freak on the way out but didn't slow down. Once outside the tent, he experienced a severe attack of ground vertigo and threw up in the cotton-candy booth.

Russ showered for nearly half an hour when he got home, but neither the Lava nor the scalding water did much good. Sticky disgust filled his pores like tar.

He couldn't figure out why she'd *do* something like that. It was a *church* carnival, for Chrissakes. Was she doing that for *every*-body who paid their two bucks? It was downright perverse. *Fuckin' carnies—what a dirty buncha scum.* Leering at everything in a skirt, blind and deaf to everything else. What had that cow Russ had worked with last summer in the student store said to him once? "I'm sorry you hate your job." Exactly. Fuckin' scum.

He was fixing a microwave pizza when Vicki finally got home. He offered her half, but she scrunched up her nose in disgust, then kissed him deeply. "I guess that's a no," he said, as they went upstairs. While she took off her khakis and T-shirt in the bathroom, Russ munched on the pizza.

She doesn't even look like herself, Russ thought, staring at Vicki as she brushed her teeth. He felt a twinge of guilt, thinking something so odd, but when she stood in just her bra and panties, her weight loss was plainly evident. She weighed a mere one-thirty now, sixty pounds less than a few months ago, and now, for the first time since she'd begun dieting and working out, Russ wasn't sure he liked her so thin. He had always liked girls with a little meat on their bones—he'd even liked the ones who were a bit *more* than simply meaty—but he was the one who had told Vicki that he thought she was getting a little thick, which was as magnanimous as he could be. She had agreed, surprisingly enough, and it had felt really good for Russ to think that he was part of the reason she was dieting. But he never really expected her to drop so much weight so quickly. Of course, he couldn't say anything after urging her into the whole thing, but he didn't like her like this, and he had never really admitted it to himself before tonight.

Good goin', you dick.

Vicki moved to his desk. "I see you were busy," she said with mock sarcasm, leafing through his plumper magazine.

"All work and no play, y'know." Russ was still looking her over.

"Um-hm." She put the magazine down and climbed into bed, put the plate with the half-eaten pizza on the nightstand, and kissed him. She burrowed her crotch into his; then she ran her tongue over his lips; finally, she sucked his dick, but even that garnered scarcely a half-decent response.

"Not in the mood, I guess." She stuffed everything back into his underwear.

"My stomach doesn't feel too good."

She lay down next to him and he held her. "Probably the pizza, dip."

"Probably," he said. Then she turned on her side.

After a few moments of silence, Vicki was asleep. Eyes closed, Russ listened to the noises from across the street. In his head, he saw the obese thing lift the apron of flab from between her legs. He heard the vibrator buzz.

His penis began to stiffen.

"Fuck," he grumbled, then rolled out of bed. He hurried downstairs—always effective in ridding oneself of unwanted boners—and grabbed a Coke from the refrigerator. He drank half of it, then headed back upstairs. After thoughtfully maneuvering Vicki beneath the covers, he stepped over to the window.

The fiesta was still going strong. Lights were blinking, flashing, rides were grinding, the music was faint but distinct. He even heard dimes clinking on the glasses in the dime-toss booth.

He realized suddenly that he was holding his breath. His heart beat as loud and fast as automatic-weapon fire.

With a shaky hand, he wrote a quick note, in case Vicki awoke, and put it on his side of the bed. Russ got dressed.

It was nearly ten-thirty when he awoke the next morning. Vicki's side of the bed was empty, of course.

Russ showered, dressed, and crossed the street. He told one of the priests milling about that he'd like to help out if he could, so the priest gladly led him to the hall where some Knights of Columbus members were setting up for bingo.

Russ helped an older, balding man set up chairs while two more older, balding men set up and arranged metal tables. One of them was talking passionately about something, but Russ only caught bits and pieces of the conversation. "Nobody really knows why anybody does anything," he said, as Russ hefted another metal chair off the nearby flatbed, unfolded it, and shoved it into place. "A lotta people *think* they know why he did it, but nobody'll ever *really* know."

"What're you two talking about?" the man assisting Russ

inquired, sounding peeved, since he seemed to have barely enough air to work and breathe, let alone gab.

"That freak who shot all those people," the other man said. "Over in L.A."

"Oh."

The mention of freaks made Russ's stomach lurch. Excusing himself for a moment, he stepped outside. Why was he back here again, anyway? He couldn't really answer himself. Maybe that guy was right. Maybe nobody knew why anybody did anything, Russ thought, looking past the booths to the freak tent. Maybe he should just go home and forget about it. Take Vicki to dinner tonight, come over with her, and lose some dimes, forget all about it.

Maybe that's what he should do.

Fuck it. Russ headed back into the hall. When he was finished setting up for bingo, he walked toward the freak tent.

When he'd come over alone last night, heart still firing, he'd noticed only a few small groups of people hanging around the booths and rides. A gang of dirty carnies was gathered outside the freak tent. One lifted something shiny up to his nose, then passed it to one of his greasy buddies. Russ shook his head slightly, then went home.

But that was last night; now, the day was sunny. He knew there was nothing to be afraid of, dark or light, but satisfying his curiosity—going in for another look, whatever—felt much better with the warmth of the sun on his shoulders.

Russ palmed his two dollars and stepped inside the tent. A stool squatted beside the main entrance, but the rubber man wasn't there. Rather than pocket his money, Russ left it on the seat. He pressed through the next flap.

The stage was empty. The table was set up, but the fetus jars were missing.

Russ checked his watch. Officially, the fiesta had been open for twenty minutes. He took a last glance around and turned to leave.

Peripherally, a flash of something hideous and malformed

appeared from behind the tent flap, near the stage. Quickly, though, it disappeared. Russ turned again, bent, peered into the knee-high gloom, and saw only the dull glow of *eyes* staring back at him. He was about to ask if it was all right, when something beside it moved—then something beside *that*, and something beside *that*. "Finally," one of them uttered with what sounded like relief.

Russ straightened. His panicky heart ballooned in his throat. *They* had been thinking about him, too! They were fucking waiting for him to come back. He spun on his heels to break for the exit.

Russ tore the tent flap aside. A thin triangle of sunlight outlined the exit flap ahead. He smiled welcomingly.

But a strip of darkness gracelessly stepped forward and collided with him. Before he could even look up, it seized his throat in a python-grip.

As Russ struggled to break free, he was dragged bodily away from the sunlight—away from *home*—back into the main tent area. The grip on his throat tightened mercilessly. Sunspots speckled his fading vision.

Suddenly, he was slammed down onto the stage, and everything came soaring back into focus. Russ craned his head to see who or what was holding him.

Towering above him was the skinny giant he'd glimpsed the other night. It had a normal-sized head, but the skin stretched over the bald skull was as thin and transparent as cellophane. Still dressed in the black body stocking and white cuffs, it looked like a psychotic mime, stretched and altered by the rack. It released Russ's neck but coiled its reed-thin arms around Russ's chest, heaving the air from his lungs, then lifted him upright. A scream boiled on Russ's lips.

"Come on," the giant hissed, kicking dirt under the stage to arouse them. Effortlessly, it folded Russ to his knees.

The two deformed creatures that waddled out of the gloom were identical to the legless girl who carried the vibrator. *Twin freaks*, Russ thought madly. They were both naked, with tiny breasts, hairless gashes, and blond ponytails tied with red ribbons. They hauled Russ into a sitting position while the giant increased the pressure on Russ's neck.

"Angela," it hissed again. *Calling.* One more creature emerged from the darkness under the stage.

Russ finally screamed, only loud enough for the thing restraining him to hear, however.

Some kind of larva with a human head slithered forward on uncanny hands, palms slapping the dirt like seal fins. Promptly, it wedged itself between Russ's legs. Bobbing unsteadily at a height above his waist, it unzipped his pants and plunged its moist hand inside his underwear. Cold slime gripped Russ's penis. Gleeful hunger shone in the larvoid eyes.

Once Russ's dick was extracted, the larva bent forward and began to suck him. The giant pulled Russ back to his elbows. The twin legless girls spread his legs open, to be helpful.

Russ shuddered again and again. Its lips and mouth were hot and greasy, lubricated with drool. He tried to deny the stimulation. Eyelids clamped shut, he concentrated on swallowing the bile lurching into his throat, but his body denied his mind's plea. He bit his tongue until he tasted blood; he shrieked; he snapped at air, kicking and twisting, but his penis continued to stiffen.

A few seconds later, Russ felt *air* on his erect dick.

He held his breath—he didn't dare open his eyes.

Stench assaulted him like high tide on a polluted beach. His eyes jerked open involuntarily.

She was bending over him. Smiling, mumbling something unintelligible, lifting her muumuu, tit-bellies sparkling with sweat. She sank with a thud to her knees and skewered him. Her eclipsing vagina was waxy, coal-hot.

As she began to rock, the giant holding Russ in place slavered in its arousal; drool spilled into Russ's ear while the fat thing worked. Finally, he ejaculated, felt it draining out of him, along with his will to fight, like water from a dribble glass.

They helped her off him. Russ deflated onto his side,

curled into a ball. He was only remotely conscious when they dragged him behind the stage and out the back of the tent to a nearby trailer.

As they were leaving, one of the legless girls—the one who had carried the dildo—stopped to kiss the tip of Russ's nose.

Feverish from shock, Russ thought: Vicki? *Vicki's* here?

The tiny girl's face danced before his like meat on a hook. "You rest here for a while, then you can go home," she said. Tears began to well up in Russ's eyes. "Oh, don't be sad. We'll be back next year," she confided cheerfully. "Just think: It'll be *three months old* by then." She smiled and put her lips to Russ's ear, whispering, "I hope it looks like me'r my sister. Some of the others are, well, such freaks . . ."

AT THE COUNT
OF THREE

Michael Garrett

---

*T*he chill of a cool autumn night brought goose bumps to
Eric Gentry's flesh as he slid from beneath a thick cotton
blanket in the middle of the night to go to the bathroom.
The hallway of the small river cabin was heated at this
hour by only the dying embers of the fireplace in the living
room, and Eric's feet were numbed by the touch of the cold
floor.

He stopped in the hallway at the sound of heavy breathing.

The door to the second bedroom stood a few inches ajar,
the steady hum of a small electric heater near the closet
having masked the sound of his approach. Inside, Eric saw
moonbeams filtered through frosted windows and lace
curtains, illuminating the amorous activities of his weekend
guests, Jake Edwards and Wendy Stevens.

Eric hurried back to his own bedroom to retrieve his
eyeglasses, then quickly returned to the scene. Jake's head
was jammed between Wendy's legs, his nose almost lost in a
thick tuft of pubic hair. He was braced on both sides of
Wendy with his palms planted firmly against the mattress,
the veins of his muscular arms bulging from the pressure.
Wendy's golden hair fanned across the pillow behind her
head like the tail of a peacock. Her eyes were closed, and her
exposed breasts rolled softly with the motion of her thrust-

ing hips. Her nipples were hard and her face contorted in waves of ecstasy. Eric felt himself growing quickly aroused as he watched. He swallowed hard and eased a step closer to the doorway for a better look. As the pace increased, Jake shifted his weight to the support of only one arm and stroked her inner thighs with his fingertips. Wendy's creamy white skin answered with involuntary spasms.

Eric's eyes were riveted to the display—he couldn't pull himself away. Wendy moaned softly, her breath suddenly quickening. Then, as her pleasure peaked, she tossed her head wildly from side to side against the pillow and sucked the sweet night air through her clenched teeth. The fury of her response increased as Wendy reached with both hands and grasped Jake's long curly hair, pulling his face closer against her. She tensed, her arms stiffening as her grip tightened, then she exhaled and relaxed her weight against the ruffled covers.

Eric wiped beads of perspiration from his forehead. For over two years now he had lusted after Jake's girlfriend, his crush on Wendy obsessive almost from the beginning. He couldn't get her off his mind. At football games, he watched the cheerleaders—and saw Wendy. Every reasonably attractive waitress at every restaurant was Wendy. And as his fixation over her deepened, Eric's jealousy of Jake skyrocketed until it infringed upon their relationship. Just once he would love to nail Wendy in bed—friendship be damned. But, unfortunately, she was crazy about Jake, and despite a number of serious arguments and near breakups, Jake and Wendy always managed to stay together.

Eric leaned against the cool cedar paneling of the hallway, oblivious to the cold and hidden from view of the two lovers. He had frequently double-dated with them, but the frustrations of watching them together were becoming unbearable.

Especially now.

Shaking his head, Eric fingered his mustache as he peeked into the bedroom again. Jake was on top of her now, and it was almost more than Eric could stand. He wanted Wendy more than anything else in the world.

And somehow he would find a way to get her.

At the bar of the Thirsty Rhino Saloon, Eric waved the bartender away as he held his cousin Ray's attention with his story. "It was great to see her naked," he concluded, "but I hated watching her with him." He stopped to slurp away the remains of a draft beer, then continued. "And the worst part of all was how much she enjoyed it. Wendy would do anything for that asshole." A ceiling fan blew stray locks of stringy unkempt hair against Eric's neck, tickling him in the process.

"So what did you do? You had a date, too, didn't you?" Ray asked.

"Yeah, but Mandy's nothing special." Eric pursed his lips and shrugged. "I woke her up and fucked her from one end of the bed to the other. She loved it, but it was no good for me. I kept seeing Wendy in my mind, and I knew what she was doing next door." Eric shook his head. "That son of a bitch Jake doesn't know how lucky he is. I wish to hell I knew what Wendy sees in him."

"Forget her!" Ray suggested. "Give Mandy a chance. What's so bad about her, anyway?"

Eric rolled his eyes and shifted his skinny buttocks on the hard barstool, ignoring the question. Instead he leaned closer to his cousin. "I've got to have her, Ray," he whispered, "and that's why I called you. I want to hypnotize Wendy."

Ray laughed. "If it was that easy to get laid, I wouldn't be here with you." He paused for a sip of beer. "Hypnosis wouldn't help you get her into the sack, but she might tell you what it is subconsciously that attracts her to Jake. You might learn what really turns her on."

"Come on, Ray, that's not good enough," Eric answered.

Ray checked his appearance in a mirror behind the bar, rearranged his hair, and stared back at Eric. "It won't work. You can't make a subject do something against her will," he repeated. "Would I lie to you?"

Eric lowered his empty mug to the countertop, swiveled on his barstool, and flashed a disbelieving grin at Ray, then grabbed his cousin's arm and pulled Ray back to the bar when Ray abruptly stood to leave.

"Hey, take it easy on the arm," Ray growled. "I've got a date to play tennis tomorrow."

Eric sulked as Ray returned to his seat. "If the clinic you work for can make people quit smoking through hypnosis, then I don't see why it can't help me get Wendy in bed," Eric hissed.

"Yeah, but my clients *want* to stop smoking," Ray replied. "Wendy doesn't want to fuck you. Like I said, it would be against her will."

Eric stubbornly shook his head and reached for a nearby bowl of popcorn. "I still say there's a way to do it, and I want to learn how."

Ray expelled a burst of beery breath in disgust. He glanced around the room and spotted an empty table in a dark corner. Then he turned to Eric. "Do you want proof?" He sighed, then, with a nod, added, "Call that waitress over here."

Moments later, the two had offered a twenty-dollar tip to Angie, an attractive but tired cocktail waitress, to serve as Ray's subject.

"Now, keep this quiet," Ray warned the weary brunette. "I'm not doing any grandstand performance here. I only want to prove a point to my hardheaded cousin."

Eric grinned as Ray nodded in his direction.

Groaning in exhaustion, Angie pulled up a chair. The rough evening shift had obviously taken its toll: Her hair was slightly mussed and her face looked tired. But Eric focused only on her ample cleavage below the plunging neckline of her skintight outfit.

"Let's make it quick, guys," Angie said, "before a customer calls me."

Eric smiled and pulled his chair closer to the table. Angie's brown eyes glittered from the reflection of a flickering candle on the table. "Aren't you nervous about being hypnotized?" he asked.

"Why should I be?" she countered. "I can take a joke. Besides, I can use the money."

Eric listened intently as Ray's monotone voice caught Angie's attention. Surprisingly, Eric was about to succumb to the chant himself, but he somehow managed to snap out of it before it was too late. Angie fell promptly under Ray's spell and sat motionless, her eyes closed, her breath slow and steady.

"Angie, at the count of three you will awaken feeling alive and refreshed," Ray began. "My voice is the only one you will hear. Do you understand?"

Angie nodded, her eyes still tightly closed.

"You will find yourself seated at a corner table of the Thirsty Rhino Saloon. On the floor is a twenty-dollar bill. When you reach to pick it up, you will find it is stuck. While no one is looking, you will carefully attempt to peel the money away from the floor. Do you understand?"

". . . Yes . . ."

"All right—one . . . two . . . *three!*"

Angie slowly opened her eyes and surveyed her surroundings. Her gaze immediately became glued to the floor. Tactfully, she stooped to her knees and lightly tugged at the imaginary bill.

Eric was genuinely amazed, but his attention was riveted on Angie's neckline. As she yanked at the floor near Eric's feet, he could see the pink circles around her nipples. The soft, silky curve of her breasts squeezed over her neckline with the movement of her arm—she obviously didn't realize he was watching. Eric bent over behind her for a view of her ass. Her nylon-covered cheeks were evenly divided by the tight dark crotch of her outfit.

"Angie, you will now return to your seat," Ray commanded.

Eric stared squarely into her face as she settled back into her chair. The waitress hardly blinked, as if there were nothing before her but smoke-filled air. "She's like a zombie," Eric said. Then, after flashing a flirtatious wink at her, he added, "How about a blowjob, Angie?"

Ray hooted with laughter. "She can't hear you," he said. "She's blocking out everyone but me."

Eric wasn't about to stop. "Then tell her to give *you* a blowjob."

Ray hesitated. "I shouldn't do this," he said. "It can be traumatic for the subject. But I know you won't believe it until you see it can't be done, and since I'm about as much of a jerk as you are, I'll do it this one time."

Ray stared deeply into Angie's eyes. "Angie," he said softly. "There is no one in this room but you and me. You will get down on your knees, crawl under the table, and give me the best blowjob of my life."

Lines of stress streaked the waitress's forehead. She looked as if she might drop beneath the table and do it, but every time she started, she held back and returned to her seat before her knees touched the floor.

"She's struggling," Ray said. "I've got to bring her out."

"Wait a minute!" Eric complained. "Let's try something else."

"Look, it's getting late and I need to stop by the clinic to pick up some papers before I go home," Ray growled through gritted teeth. Then he turned his attention back to Angie. "At the count of three, you will awaken and remember nothing that has taken place at this table," he said.

Eric folded his arms in disgust and pouted as Angie concentrated on the hypnotic count.

When she opened her eyes, Angie flashed an impatient expression at both guys. "Look, I haven't got all night," she complained. "Let's get this over with fast, or else count me out!"

The cousins shared a laugh, and Eric squeezed a crumpled twenty-dollar bill into Angie's hand while planting a quick kiss on her cheek. Ray grabbed his wrinkled lab coat from a nearby chair, and the two chuckled as they walked to the door.

"Did it take long for you to learn how to do that?" Eric asked.

Ray stopped to straighten his younger cousin's necktie.

"It's not very difficult," he said. "Like anything else, it takes a lot of patience and practice, that's all."

Eric's eyes widened with anticipation. "Will you teach me how to do it?"

"Why should I teach you?" hedged Ray. "I could lose my license. And besides, it's like I said: You can't make a broad do anything against her will. You just saw it for yourself."

"Hell, I don't care," Eric argued. "I could be the life of the party if I knew how to do that!"

"What's in it for me?" Ray countered.

Eric eased closer to his cousin. "I always repay my debts," he whispered.

After Eric swore that he would never reveal the source of his instruction, Ray finally gave in. "All right," he began, "the secret is in controlling the immediate environment of your subject. You've got to put yourself in command, so that your subject sees and hears nothing but you. Eliminate all distractions."

When Eric first attempted the simple chant under Ray's direction, he seemed a natural. The tone of his voice and his expressionless face proved invaluable in repeating the trance-rendering phrases. In closing, Ray cast a serious look at his eager cousin.

"If you want to be successful, you've got to practice," he said. "And I don't mean with subjects. I mean at home, alone. Listen to yourself as you chant. You'll get the hang of it."

"Hell, I'll practice night and day," Eric gleamed. "This is fuckin' great!"

"But remember," cautioned Ray, "you saw it for yourself. You can't command a subject to do anything she wouldn't ordinarily do. Otherwise I'd be one happy camper and would be a fool to share the secret with anyone."

"I know, I know. I've heard all that mumbo jumbo," said Eric.

But maybe he could think of a way to get around it.

For weeks Eric concentrated on the tone variations and ·oice inflections of the hypnotic chant. He prepared himself for the perfect opportunity, which finally came when Jake suddenly went out of town on business.

When Eric called Wendy, her phone rang a number of times before she finally answered. Her voice sounded weak and distressed—probably missing Jake, Eric thought.

"Wendy?" he began. "It's Eric." He paused for effect, then added, "I need someone to talk to."

"Eric, what's wrong?" she answered, and by the tone of her voice, he knew she'd been fooled.

Eric hesitated briefly, hoping to sound even more upset, as he told Wendy that he and Mandy were having problems, that he was lonely and would like to get a woman's perspective on the situation so that maybe he could gain a better understanding of Mandy.

"Well, let's talk," she said agreeably. "I'm all ears."

"I'd rather see you in person, if you don't mind. I don't want to be alone right now. Will you come over to my place for a short visit?" he asked.

"Well, why don't you just come over here?"

"Uh," he stalled, remembering the importance of controlling her environment as he searched for an excuse. There could be too many distractions in her own apartment. What if her telephone rang? Here, he could have the phone unplugged before she arrived. "That's part of my problem," he finally said. "I sprained my ankle and can't get around very well."

"Hmmm." Wendy mulled over the proposition. "Sounds all right to me. And I'm sorry to hear about your accident."

Eric prepared a dark corner of his living room for the encounter. Everything was in place when she knocked at the door, but this time Wendy wasn't as stunning as usual. Eric was disappointed that she hadn't thought highly enough of him to make herself more presentable, but even without makeup, Wendy looked great. A tight blue sweater hugged her ample breasts, and her thick lips formed a sultry pout, but her eyes were red and swollen.

How does that asshole do it? Eric wondered. How does

Jake maintain such control over this gorgeous woman that she cries her eyes out whenever he's away?

Eric smiled and escorted Wendy to the sofa, remembering at the last moment to limp. "Would you like a drink?" he offered as she settled herself.

"No, thanks," she replied, pressing her forehead against an open palm. "I'm not feeling well. I suppose I really shouldn't have come, but I guess I needed someone to talk to, too."

"Well, let's not cry on each other's shoulders. We need to cheer each other up," he began. "You probably didn't know this, Wendy, but I've been studying hypnotism. I'm pretty damn good at it, too."

She raised her head attentively. "You've been studying *what?*" she asked.

"Hypnotism. Let me show you."

Eric reached for her hand, but she cautiously pulled away.

"You've got to be kidding," Wendy said.

"It's true," he answered. "Hypnosis is great for calming your nerves. I use self-hypnosis all the time now."

"You're *serious!*" she exclaimed with a forced giggle. "I had no idea—but I still don't believe you."

Eric smirked.

"Besides," Wendy continued, "if you can relax yourself with self-hypnosis, why did you need to talk to someone tonight?"

Eric cleared his throat and gave her the best shit-eating grin he could muster. "Because nothing can take the place of human companionship," he whispered. "Nothing." He knew it sounded corny, but it seemed to have worked.

Wendy stifled a laugh and shook her head. "I still don't buy it," she said.

"Then let me prove it."

Reluctantly, she accepted his extended hand. Eric led Wendy to the corner chair, then sat on a stool facing her. The mood of their conversation shifted as she turned with a nervous twist, clutching her purse tightly in her lap.

"I'm not sure that I'm ready for this," she said. "Is it for real? Are you sure it's safe?"

"Certainly. It'll only take a minute, and you won't remember a thing. Besides, it'll make you feel better."

"Yeah, but if I won't remember, then how will I know I've been hypnotized?" she asked.

Good point, he thought. One he hadn't considered.

"I'll record the whole thing on my tape recorder," Eric said. "Then you can hear exactly what went on."

She was hooked.

Eric switched on a nearby microcassette recorder and chuckled to himself. He would turn the machine off as soon as she was under and later pretend the batteries had gone dead.

"Well, all right," she said in a reluctant tone. "But if I decide to back out, I want you to stop, okay?"

"Of course," he agreed. "Now, are you ready? Comfortable?"

"Yes."

Eric dimmed the lights and instructed her to breathe deeply and concentrate on his voice. Then he began the monotone chant.

"You're going deeper and deeper to sleep . . . relaxed and free . . . deeper and deeper . . ."

She was fighting it, he could tell. He spoke to her softly, reassuring her and putting her mind at ease. Then he tried again.

"Deeper and deeper to sleep . . ."

Her eyelids slowly closed.

"Relaxed and free . . ."

She was on her way now.

"Deeper and deeper . . ."

Her facial muscles relaxed and her head gradually drifted forward. She was under! Eric switched off the tape recorder.

"When I count to three, Wendy, you will awaken. You will be sitting face to face with Jake Edwards, who has returned early from his business trip. For days you've waited for this moment, planning a special private welcome for Jake. The two of you will be completely alone, and you will greet him in a way that only he deserves."

She sat motionless, like a vulnerable child.

"One . . ."

Eric had been careful not to command Wendy to fuck. This way, it would be *her* decision.

"Two . . ."

And while she would never knowingly fuck Eric, if she subconsciously saw him as *Jake,* she just might do it. Hell, it was certainly worth a try!

"Three . . ."

As Wendy slowly opened her eyes, her face became instantly flushed. Tears flowed down both cheeks and her lower lip quivered. Eric couldn't believe the transformation: Jake's control over his girlfriend was uncanny—eerie, almost.

Wendy cleared her throat and wiped her eyes. "Oh . . . when did you get home?" she asked, her voice strangely subdued. And she hadn't leaped into his arms, as Eric expected. But at least she saw him as Jake. It was a damn good sign.

"Hey!" Eric chirped. "You don't seem very pleased to see me."

Wendy stared at him in silence. She's at a loss for words, Eric thought. But just wait until she unwinds.

"Jake, I'm surprised that you . . ." she sobbed.

She called him by Jake's name! Eric leaned forward and stroked her golden hair. "I'll tell you about the trip later," he said softly. "Right now, *let's party!*" It was Jake's favorite expression. Eric knew it would make his role sound more convincing.

Wendy raised her head, sniffled, and forced a smile. "That's what you always want," she said. "I should have known."

Eric's eyes widened as Wendy pulled her sweater over her head, unbuttoned her blouse, and loosened her bra. Her tits sprang forward, straight and proud. They looked delicious!

"You seem upset," Eric cooed tenderly. "This will make you feel better."

Her expression remained unchanged as Eric licked and sucked her breasts. His arousal became so intense, he could hardly stand it. But she continued to sit motionless, keeping her arms to herself, until, without warning, Wendy hit him hard against the side of his head with her purse. Eric tumbled off-balance to the floor and scrambled to locate his dislodged eyeglasses as she fumbled inside her handbag.

"You son of a bitch!" she screamed. "I told you I'd never forgive you, and *I meant it!*"

"But Wendy"—Eric looked up with a puzzled expression—"I don't understand—"

But now the barrel of a .38 Special was pointed directly at his forehead.

"You couldn't control yourself, could you?" Wendy screamed. "You're such a stud, you just had to make it with my sister! Right under my nose!" She sobbed and wiped a new stream of tears from her cheeks. "You didn't think she'd tell, did you, smart ass!"

"But wait, Wendy, it's me, Eric—"

"Let's party!" she mocked in a crazed, high-pitched tone. Then she jammed the cold steel barrel against the bridge of his nose. "Party with *this,* you two-timing bastard."

The gun wavered in her grasp. She's gonna do it, Eric realized. She's gonna fuckin' shoot me!

Beads of sweat dampened Eric's cheeks. A warm stream of urine ran down his leg. Got to break the trance, he thought. Got to stay calm.

"Wait a minute, Wendy," he muttered breathlessly, as calmly as possible. He swallowed hard and wiped perspiration from his brow. "At the count of three—"

"That's right, you son of a bitch," she interrupted as she got ready to squeeze the trigger. *"At the count of three . . ."*

GENDERELLA

Ron Dee

*I*t wasn't fair.

Tom held his chin in his palms, sitting on the bed. He *was* attractive, wasn't he?

He smiled at his long but gently defined face in the mirror across the bedroom. The reflection hung on the wall beside his closet door that was filled with the brightest clothes he could pick out. They looked good on him.

Because he was attractive!

Even without eyeshadow and blush.

But he wasn't going to the prom.

Because he was different.

In his makeup, he looked better than any of the girls who were going, and they all had dates. Good-looking dates, too. Ones he'd had his eyes on all year. But no matter how sweetly he talked to them or how accessible he made himself, the hunks ignored him completely.

Grant was the one he really wanted. Grant, with his suave manner and wondrously hairy chest, and muscles that made him look like he was wearing shoulder pads even when he wasn't. Tom often batted his eyes at Grant the way that Candy, the cheerleader, did.

But Grant barely smiled.

Tom stood and stared at his slim, naked body in the

mirror, imagining Grant there with him, imagining himself in Grant's arms at the prom.

Imagining himself in the backseat of Grant's car after the prom.

The problem was, Grant was straight and too embarrassed to be seen talking to him. When they had been younger and more naive, it hadn't made a difference. Grant and Tom had spent the night in the same bed when they slept over on weekends. Sometimes they'd walked together holding hands. Like most girls, Tom had an earlier awakening into his sexual identity than his male friends, and he cherished those moments of his youth, even though they meant little to Grant.

But in middle school, Grant had grown aware of sex, too. His eyes were riveted to the opposite gender, and he spent less and less time with Tom. Tom missed him, and he started hanging around with another guy who was more like himself. Before long, everyone was talking about Tom and Donnie. About the *queer boys*. The *faggots*. Then Donnie moved away and left him alone.

Tom blinked back a tear. Grant had deserted him, too. He had called Grant then and tried to talk to him.

"I can't talk to you," Grant had said. *"I don't want to be called a pansy, too. I like girls!"*

But Tom didn't believe him. He wanted to be with Grant, especially tonight. Because despite those denials, Tom knew Grant was like he was, deep inside. He knew the sensations he'd had for Grant all his life were real and that, secretly, Grant really felt the same toward him.

One summer, when they were fifteen, they had each been invited to Candy Wadd's sixteenth birthday party. Candy's parents had left the house to their daughter and her friends until midnight. The party turned into a free-for-all, and Candy took advantage of it. She went up to her room and invited the boys to form a line at the door, to initiate her into womanhood.

Grant, in a state of unrequited love for Candy, had taken it badly. Fueled by the alcohol he'd imbibed, Grant wandered off by himself into Candy's dark back yard to sit on the swing set. Grant had been teary-eyed when Tom followed to see what was wrong. Tom felt sorry for him, but he rejoiced at the opportunity nonetheless.

Tom put his arm around Grant and led him to the bushes surrounding the back fence. "You don't want to let the guys see you crying," he'd explained.

That made Grant wail louder, and Tom suddenly clutched him tightly in a secure hug, then planted his lips squarely on Grant's.

Grant had opened his mouth, maybe in surprise, but Tom didn't care. He jumped at the chance to dive his tongue inside.

For a moment, the boys had wrestled inside each other's mouths. Tom felt the surge of true love, and though Grant pushed him away a moment later, he knew Grant felt it, too.

"Hey—don't you dare do that anymore!" Grant had blustered, punching Tom in the face and backing off. *"I'm not a queer like you!"*

The pain inflicted by Grant's fist had made his mouth sore for days, but the harsh words had badgered Tom for years. They hurt, but all the more because Tom knew they weren't true. Instead of quelling his feelings for Grant, his love for the husky boy increased. Tom knew Grant had enjoyed their closeness, too, somewhere deep within his subconscious. Hadn't Grant hesitated before pulling away and striking him? Tom just hoped Grant would someday overcome the fear of ridicule and make his hidden love for Tom known— *publicly.* Tom had harbored the desperate hope that Grant would even take him to tonight's prom.

But Grant was taking a bitch instead. Not Candy, but another cheerleader. Her name was Ginger, and she was prettier than Candy. Bigger tits, too, but just as much of a slut. Tom had seen her sucking off the coach after practice.

"I wish I could be a girl—one of those bitches—for just one night," Tom murmured to himself.

He had no sooner said it than the air seemed to grow sharper, electric. Tom stared into the mirror at the yellow pastel walls of his room as they grew dim, fogged.

"That's not all you want," said a loud voice. "Methinks you want a lot more."

Tom's eyes grew huge at the glare taking shape in the room's center: a woman in a tight blue dress, her sleek blond hair flowing madly around her face to her wide shoulders. Tom blinked.

"I'm Selina, your fairy godmother," the woman said. But as he stared, Tom knew it wasn't a woman, but a man. One of the sexiest men he'd ever seen.

"Don't get any ideas," said the glowing transvestite, holding out a limp wrist to keep Tom back. "I'm not a wish come true, okay? I'm only here to make your true wish come true."

Tom grinned, moving closer.

The wildly dressed man waved a gaudy wand with a star at its end, and a solid, invisible force field rose up between them. Tom touched the dense air disbelievingly.

"I'm magic. I'm your fairy godmother—get it?" The man whistled with giddy laughter. "No drugs, no fake. I'm *real.*"

"You're very pretty," Tom said with a smile, disappointed that he couldn't touch his strange visitor.

"Ease up, Tom. I'm here to give you your wish for a night as a girl, okay? Flat stomach, nice hips, big boobs, snatch instead of tools. You know the rules." He laughed at his rhyme. "You can do whatever you want as long as you're home by midnight. The clock strikes, and you're a fag dressed like a bitch, got it?"

"This is full of shit."

"So what? Enjoy yourself."

Poof.

The brightness of the room faded. Selina disappeared, and Tom was staring dazedly at himself in the mirror. He gasped at the way his hair suddenly blossomed into long auburn curls that reached down to expanding, firm breasts; how his legs grew supple, and curly hair spread between them, replacing his dissolving anatomy. He saw his sweet face, covered in perfect makeup, with red, luscious lips.

"Wow."

Poof.

A second later, his new nakedness blurred, and he was clothed in a white satin dress wrapped tight about his delicate hips. The low-cut top with opaque ruffles almost exposed the protruding nipples of his newborn breasts.

"I don't fucking believe this!"

Poof.

Tom's ears popped. An unexpected gust of wind whipped his dress. He was standing in the high-school parking lot. He opened his mouth wide and held down the fabric as voices cut in, then blinked and sniffed the air with astonishment. Despite the stink of car exhaust, the night smelled of fresh spring weather. Bright overhead lights illuminated rows of parked cars and guys in tuxes escorting their gown-clad dates to the doors. Tom stared blankly, trembling.

It was real.

Someone whistled.

It's real, Tom thought. He pinched his dainty arm with misgiving but was still in the parking lot as teenagers ushered past him on either side.

"Looking good," whispered a voice in his ear.

Tom swung around to see Jim Turtle, the asshole from geometry who always made the "queer" jokes.

"Too good for you," Tom sniffed, coming to grips with his transformation.

Jim backed up and bowed his head. "I didn't mean anything by it," he explained. "It was a compliment."

The squeaky snivel in Jim's voice made Tom chuckle— except it came out as a giggle.

"M-maybe a dance inside?" Jim asked.

Tom frowned as more classmates passed by. He giggled again and looked into the forlorn face of the boy who had tormented him for years. He couldn't bring himself to feel sorry for Jim, and he had to hold in the laughter. Revenge was sweet. "Want to escort me inside?"

Jim dropped his jaw and nodded quickly, taking Tom's arm. Tom giggled again, almost wishing he could change back into his true form at that moment so he could see the expression on Jim's face.

But there was no time for that. He wanted to dance, and more—with Grant.

Jim's sweaty palm held Tom's elbow tightly as they stepped to the glass doors with the other students. The three-story school building loomed high above, reaching toward a clear sky full of stars. Tom's heart soared to the heavens, to pinpricks of twinkling light, and he smiled as several of the other boys glanced his way, uttering murmurs of approval.

Inside, Jim clasped Tom's hand tightly as they joined the crowd climbing the stairs to the second-floor lobby. The big, open space was decked out with banners and balloons colored with the blue and gray school colors and ribbons and posters celebrating graduation. The loud music of a live band rumbled down the locker-lined halls. The local rock group was almost hidden from Tom's sight by the dozens of couples gyrating back and forth over the lobby's checkered tile floor. Chaperoning teachers drank Cokes and watched with boredom from the sidelines.

And then Tom saw Grant, already dancing with Ginger.

"Wanna dance?" begged Jim.

Tom smiled, pursing his lips. "Not now, little boy." He walked carefully in his high heels to the center of the room, giggling his new tones at Jim's disintegrating grin. But there was no time for a colder vengeance. Tom eyed a wall clock that displayed 8:45 and strolled with careful balance to Grant and Ginger, swaying together on the dance floor.

The song ended.

"That was great, Grant," Ginger said, crushing her corsage and stiff pink gown against him.

Tom stepped forward and stared at Grant. The square-jawed football player was more handsome than ever in the white tux and ruffled shirt. The lines of his body were strong and perfect. He was too good for Ginger, with her reputation of being hot to trot. Tom hated seeing them together. Grant deserved better.

Grant deserved *him!*

"Hi," Grant spoke uncertainly, as though Tom seemed familiar.

Little did he know.

"Hi," replied Tom delicately. "Are you Grant?"

Grant's lips tightened as he nodded, and Tom thought of all the things he'd always wanted to say to him.

"And you are?"

Tom batted the long lashes. "Tom . . . uh . . . *Tommie.*"

Ginger was making a face. Grant took Tom's slender hand cautiously, and the touch of those strong, smooth fingers sent a chill through his new body. "Pleased to make your acquaintance," Grant said, smiling.

"I'm pleased to make yours. I've heard a lot about you."

"Really?" Grant's face turned pink.

"Really," replied Tom, licking his lips and moving nearer. His heart exploded as he felt Grant's hot breath lick his forehead. They were just an inch apart. Grant's attention was focused on him so entirely.

"Are you here with a date?" asked Grant, again drawing Ginger's frown.

Tom thought fast. "Uh . . . my cousin Tom brought me, but he wasn't feeling good and left as soon as we got here. He pointed you out and said, uh, that, uh, you'd take care of me. He said you two used to be good friends."

A slow frown crept over Grant's face. He glanced at Ginger quickly. "That was a long time ago."

Tom pouted.

"Still, I'll keep you company for old times' sake. What was wrong with Tom?"

"I just don't think he could go through with it, you know? Being here with a girl, I mean."

The band started playing again. Couples began to drift from the tables of munchies and punch toward the center of the dance floor. Ginger tried to lead Grant away.

"Come on, Grant. Let's dance."

Tom looked at Ginger, then back at Grant. "Won't you dance with me this time?" he asked in a high voice, pouty again. "Maybe you could let me have one dance and then I'll go. I just hate to think I dressed up for nothing at all."

Grant returned Tom's stare with growing interest, gulped,

and faced Ginger. "I'll give this one dance to Tommie, okay?"

"Instead of *me?*"

Tom put his small hand into Grant's, and their fingers intertwined. "Just one dance," Grant said.

Ginger's face twisted, and she looked around the room. "Maybe you can dance with me later, then. Maybe." Ginger walked to one of the food tables and tapped a burly jock, Ralph Mahoney, on his shoulder. Ralph turned around, looking like an overweight undertaker in his black tux, then smiled happily. Ginger's hand went into his, and Ralph nodded with excitement when she spoke inaudibly.

"Looks like I messed up your date. Sorry."

Grant rubbed Tom's fingers gently. "Maybe you just made yourself my date."

Tom blushed, for real. "Don't tease me."

Grant put his other hand on Tom's waist, pressing their bodies together and letting loose a fire in Tom that grew intense. "I'm not teasing," Grant whispered.

They danced slow, and Tom laid his head on Grant's shoulder, smelling the football player's manhood through his sea-water cologne. The second dance was slow, too, but their hips ground together faster and faster. The third was a speedier tune, but they stepped out of rhythm, still close and touching.

Grant kissed Tom's full red lips, gently and shyly, but Tom kissed back with pent-up lust, his excitement growing as Grant's hands dropped down to Tom's ass and pulled their sexes even closer together. Tom smiled as Grant's bulge rubbed against him.

When they broke, the next dance was midway through, and rather than try to catch up and take part, they walked together to the rail beside the stairs. Grant leaned against it, and Tom supported himself against the muscular body he'd wanted for so long.

"I feel somehow like I've known you before," whispered Grant. His face stretched between an honest confusion and a smile. "That's not a line, either. I mean it."

Tom pressed against the tall, husky boy and looked up into his eyes. "I feel like I know you, too, Grant."

The music stopped.

"Do you want to dance again?"

An urgency surrounded them, reminding Tom that his time in female form was limited. He turned to the wall clock and cringed. It was already ten o'clock. Fighting disappointment, he squeezed Grant's hand. "What do you want to do, Grant?"

Grant blushed this time. He looked at the clock, too. "What time do you have to get back?"

Tom wanted to say never. "Midnight," he purred softly.

"That's awful early."

Tom pouted again.

"Are you staying with your cousin?"

Tom nodded slowly.

"How about if we take a drive before I bring you back there, then? Get out of this noise and crowd."

Tom's heart leapt. *This was too good to be true!* But he refused to let himself doubt that it was happening. He only prayed that nothing would mess up this golden opportunity. Happily, he saw Ginger across the floor in Ralph's arms as the big jock's hands kneaded her firm ass. Grant saw, too.

"I'd love to," Tom breathed.

Grant was still glaring at Ginger. "Let's go."

Without a word, they turned from the dance floor and started down the steps, hand in hand. Tom's heart was beating fast as he pressed against Grant, feeling Grant's heart pounding in rhythm, too.

In the parking lot, Grant led Tom to the passenger side of his big blue Pontiac Grand Prix. He opened the door and helped Tom in like a gentleman. Tom fluttered his lashes once more and licked his lips when Grant squeezed into the driver's seat.

"Where do you want to go?" asked Grant sheepishly, starting the car.

Tom closed his eyes and stuck a long nail in his mouth delicately. It was now or never. Tom's wristwatch read 10:05. "How about the lake?" he asked.

Grant laughed lightly, backing up the car. "You can even read my mind."

They kissed for several minutes in the front seat, then Tom winked at Grant and got out of the car, entering the backseat and lying down, the dress pulled above his beautifully formed knees. Grant blinked, hesitated, then followed.

"I can't believe this is happening," Grant said happily, crawling over Tom carefully. He trembled as Tom guided his hand under the long gown.

"Me neither," whispered Tom. "I've dreamed of this moment . . ." Tom loosened Grant's tie as Grant straddled above him, then unbuttoned Grant's shirt. If only time would stop.

"It's like we've been waiting for each other to meet, that we already knew each other in some kind of way," gasped Grant as Tom licked his hairy chest.

"We do," Tom sighed, unbuckling Grant's belt and then sliding the slacks down muscled thighs. "We're meant for each other."

"Tommie," Grant moaned as Tom threw the clothing to the front seat, bending over to kiss him and lick him. "Oh, God, *Tommie* . . ."

Tom giggled, shivering as Grant's hands reached around him to unhook his soft dress. Grant carefully lifted it up, bringing it over Tom's head and dropping it onto the front seat with the discarded tux. Grant unhooked and removed the sexy lace coverings underneath and tossed them aside, too, until they were both naked and close. Very close. Grant was redfaced and hard. Tom was wet and ready, fighting the desire to just pull Grant down quickly and be finished with this long, long torment of waiting, to feel the length he'd desired and dreamed of for untold nights.

Grant sucked Tom's breasts, licked at his pubis, and touched wet lips to his. Their tongues wrestled again as their bodies moved into position, and then the object of Tom's desire entered Tom's new pleasure center with a stunning hugeness that made him climax immediately. And even as

Ron Dee

the vibrations of ecstasy shook him, Tom felt Grant shaking in kind, sharing in instant gratification.

Grant lay on top of Tom, their sweat mingling, joining with the sweet scent of their love.

"I always knew it would be like this," Tom whimpered, tears of joy flooding his eyes and cheeks. "I knew you loved me."

Grant looked at him curiously in the shadows but nodded in agreement. "I feel that way, too. It's funny, isn't it?"

Tom saw moonlight flicker across Grant's watch face: *11:30.* His stomach trembled and he felt tears again, of sadness this time. Of futility that this once-in-a-lifetime experience was almost over.

He wanted *more!*

But he knew it couldn't be. In half an hour, he would be Tom, not Tommie, and if he didn't conceal this secret from Grant . . .

Grant might be so shocked and infuriated by the trickery that Tom might never be able to even speak to Grant again.

"I need to go home." Tom forced himself to say the words.

Grant groaned. The pain and desire was heavy in his eyes and leaked from every pore of his face.

Maybe . . .

Tom shivered, wanting Grant more than ever.

Maybe . . . maybe Grant would understand. Maybe Grant would still want and love him despite the deception.

They kissed. A long, deep kiss, both of them sighing as they pulled away.

"You do want me, don't you?" whispered Tom.

"Yes. You know I do."

"I love you. It may sound funny so sudden like this, but it's not sudden at all. Not really. *I really do love you.*"

Nodding, Grant dropped his face to an erect nipple and sucked tenderly. "I love you, too."

"Promise me that tonight won't be the end—that you'll be with me again."

"You got that."

"I mean it, Grant. *I love you.* Promise me that even if I'm

184

not exactly what you think I am that you'll love me anyway."

Grant's lips dropped past Tom's sex-soaked pubic hair. Tom wriggled at the way Grant used his tongue, knowing it would feel just as luscious running up and down Tom's usual equipment.

If Grant weren't lying.

"Tell me truly. Tell me that nothing will ever make any difference to our love. Tell me that you want me, no matter how much I change or how different I may become . . ."

"You make it sound like you're a werewolf," Grant said, gurgling among Tom's lower juices. "But everybody changes. I'll be bald with a potbelly someday." His tongue moved deftly between sentences.

Grant's voice was reassuring and smooth, but Tom knew it wasn't a full guarantee. His eyes flipped down to the watch. It was 11:45. No time to get home before the transformation. In minutes he would know whether or not Grant truly loved him for himself, or if . . .

But now that they had been a part of each other, Tom couldn't bear the thought of losing him. And when Grant understood what had happened, that he'd given up Ginger for Tom, Tom still worried that he might lose Grant *forever*.

Their lips touched. Tom tasted himself and Grant simultaneously with the greatest satisfaction he'd ever known. Contentment he had only dreamed of.

"Please," Grant implored, pressing his resurrected virility against Tom's bush, trying to nudge inside. *"Please.* I want you, Tommie. I *need* you. Something about you—I need you. I need to make love to you tonight at least once more."

Tom didn't move, though desire exploded inside him, too, warping his thoughts, making him want Grant more than just for tonight, for more than just the nine remaining minutes.

"Please, I love you, Tommie! I promise—*I'll never leave you!*"

Tom began to move more slowly. "Is that what you really want? To be with me?"

"Yes," answered the husky tremble of Grant's moan.

He opened the sleek, padded thighs of his body, exhaling loudly as Grant filled him again, plunging deeper. "Oh, yes. *Yes!* Slow, Grant. Slow this time, okay? *Make it last . . ."*

"Forever," Grant mumbled as he slipped his tongue inside Tom's mouth once more. Their bellies pressed tightly together, shimmering in ecstasy that grew stronger by the minute.

"Hold on," gasped Tom, greeting Grant's steady pumping with a rhythm of his own and loving each movement as though he'd never known pleasure before. His eyes blurred, and the watch face blurred, too.

Sweat glistened across their bodies and faces. They moved faster and faster. Minutes passed impossibly fast, but Tom still tried to slow the pace, to stretch the moment forever. "Not yet," he whispered. *"Not yet . . ."*

Grant was too excited to slow down. Tom could tell by his quickened pace, by the tight mold of Grant's ass cheeks. And now Tom could no longer hold out, abandoning all hope of stretching out their union for the ultimate joy.

Midnight.

"I'm coming!" shrieked Tom as the big hand reached twelve.

"Me too!" cried Grant.

And on cue, the magic spell of the fairy godmother ended. Tom's penis sprang forward without warning, replacing the vagina it had earlier become, growing around Grant's penis like a groping umbilical cord as the throes of their orgasm exploded again and again. Their mouths parted, and Tom's firm breasts became mere nipples beneath Grant's fingertips.

But as the acute pleasure ebbed, their unity stood firm. As Tom had hoped, their last moment of intercourse would continue forever. He cried with glee as his flesh mixed with Grant's, binding them together like Siamese twins, making them more truly one than any wedding vow between man and bitch.

But in the dimness, Tom looked down Grant's muscular

chest and taut stomach to where their sexes connected—
forever.

Forever.

Tom pulled back gently and winced at the pain. He
reached down and, as though awakening from a wild dream,
he suddenly understood.

Forever. Till death do you part.

And then Grant noticed that Tom's body was no longer
soft and supple, that the hair on his head was now short and
coarse.

Grant stared ahead blankly, making gurgling noises in the
darkness. His luminous watch hands read 12:01.

Tom was breathing hard again, but this time it wasn't with
excitement. Grant was still inside him, and he could feel
Grant's hatred.

Inside him.

Even that emotion of disgust was a part of him, would
always be part of him now.

Grant shook his head, choking as his hands flattened
against the wiry hair scattered over Tom's hard chest. His
fingers stretched down to their melding and flew back
warily, then back down. A low bellow of agony burst out of
Grant's lungs, becoming furious, uncomprehending wails
and tears. "Oh . . . oh, my God! *Tommie!*"

Grant's hand squeezed their sharing, crushing Tom's
fingers. They both tried to jerk away, and now Tom's cry was
as loud as Grant's. "No!" he whined.

"No—*NO! Tommie! What have you done to me!*"

Tom was sobbing, then laughing insanely, missing the
high giggle and knowing that this wasn't what he wanted. He
had a sudden overpowering urge to urinate.

And soon, Grant would have that need, too.

SAFE AT HOME

Steve and Melanie Tem

Mindy.
"Touch me. Here. Like this.
"You like to touch me, don't you?
"That's a good girl. Oh, that's right."

Charlie was incredulous. "You want me to take you to another horror movie? But you hate that stuff."

"The monster in this one has long sticky tentacles that come up out of a dark pool." Melinda squinted at the newspaper ad and gave a short, brittle laugh.

"Let me guess: It has a particular affinity for pretty young women." Charlie's laugh was easier, fuller than hers.

"Don't they all?" she said.

Charlie took her to the movie because she wanted to go, and also because he knew there was a good possibility of sex afterward. She didn't begrudge him that. Charlie was a good guy, and Melinda felt bad about using his baser instincts to get what she wanted. But it worked. It had always worked.

She didn't love Charlie, not yet. And he didn't love her. She hoped he didn't love her.

"I love you, Mindy. You're my favorite niece, did you know that?

"You want to make your uncle Pat happy, don't you? Let me show you how to make me happy.

"Oh, you are such a good girl."

Charlie was a tender, considerate lover. He went slow. He'd never hurt her. She knew he thought what they did together in bed was beautiful.

It made her want to throw up.

Monsters made it possible for her to throw up. Monsters in horror movies especially, with sticky appendages or gaping maws or formless bodies that oozed from everywhere and never went away.

At some point during every show she'd get up and hurry to the ladies' room, hoping there wouldn't be a line. She'd crouch over a toilet and vomit for a long time. If she'd been able to force herself to eat any popcorn or candy, it would come out of her in recognizable chunks, but everything else being expelled from her body was whitish and viscous, like semen. For a while then—sometimes minutes, sometimes the rest of the night—she wouldn't be sick to her stomach.

"Oh, no, Mindy, this isn't wrong. We love each other, so how could anything we do together be wrong?

"Show me that you love me, Mindy.

"That's right. That's my girl."

She hated having to chew and swallow in front of people. Sometimes she caught herself imagining that if she opened her mouth too wide a sticky, sinewy monster would slide out and wriggle into the darkness under the house, under the streets, under the world.

She watched Charlie eat. She wanted to see what his teeth did to the food, how his tongue rolled and humped to get the food down. Sometimes in the middle of a meal she'd reach over and very lightly rest her fingertips on the hinge of his jaw, where she could feel the bones and muscles, sinews and tendons, all working together in one building rhythm.

"You're weird," Charlie said the first time she was brave

enough to do that. Mouth full of spaghetti, he leaned across the table and kissed her.

Melinda had thought he was going to say he loved her. He'd had that tender, passionate, self-absorbed look on his face that had nothing to do with her. Relieved that he'd said something else, she didn't pull away.

She tried hard not to imagine the spaghetti in his mouth. For some reason it scared her.

Then she gave up and set herself to imagining it as vividly as she could. Whitish sticky tendrils, viscous sauce. Charlie's mouth caressing it, taking everything from it, the inside of a kiss.

"Sweet," Charlie said, still looking at her more intently than she liked. "And very beautiful. But definitely weird."

"Your mommy and daddy didn't mean *me*. I'm your daddy's brother.

"They asked me to babysit this weekend, remember? They asked me to take care of you while they were gone. Don't you think they must trust me a lot to let me take care of their precious little girl?

"So you can trust me, too.

"Come here, Mindy. Come to Uncle Pat."

After the movie they often rode the bus across town to Charlie's house. When she rode the bus alone, Melinda watched all the men waiting for her, in the other seats, at stops, on street corners, on billboards, and on movie posters. During heavy rains there were so many people in doorways that she couldn't tell which ones were waiting for just her, and in the wet shadows she usually couldn't see their hands. There ought to be a law requiring men to keep their hands exposed at all times in the presence of females. Especially girls. Especially little girls.

A man with a narrow face, or maybe with only a penis for a face, stared at her from a narrow passageway when the bus stopped for a light. His long pale tongue slid out of the shadows and down his coat, down one leg and across the sidewalk, leaving a slick, steaming trail. The tongue was wiggling its way toward her when the bus pulled into the intersection. Charlie hugged her and whispered a soft alien language into her ear.

In Charlie's bedroom she took off her clothes, forcing herself to move slowly, holding her breath, hoping the bile in her stomach wouldn't rise into her throat. Charlie watched her adoringly. "You are so beautiful," he kept saying, and Melinda flinched that he would say such a thing out loud. "You are so beautiful."

Melinda could barely let herself hear such nice things about her body, but she liked hearing them, was relieved each time that he didn't say how ugly she was, how pale, how skinny or how fat, how wormlike smooth or how hairy. If she didn't trim her bikini line her pubic hair would just keep growing, would spill out of her crotch and rise above the waistband of her shorts, would wrap itself like monkey tails up and down her limbs.

A woman was never safe. Like all women, Melinda had a wet, hairy hole in the middle of her body. A hole in the middle of her life. Where awful things might enter.

Charlie invited her to stay the night. Melinda said no, she wasn't ready, and Charlie didn't push. He insisted on accompanying her on the bus all the way home. He was so sweet. Gratefully, she kissed him goodbye at her door, although she really didn't want to touch him anymore. She didn't ask him in.

Alone in her apartment, she sat naked in the dark, all the bedclothes pushed well away from her. Cloth would burn her; her bare flesh was already aching with nothing touching it at all. It hurt her to be exposed like this; it would hurt more to try to cover herself up.

Then she waited until she was too tired to wait anymore. She waited, as she did every night, for something to break her door down or to seep in under it. For something to drag her or coax her into the sticky dark outside.

Safe. Safe at home.

"Mindy, Mindy, you are so beautiful."

* * *

That July the annual invasion of miller moths was the worst anybody could remember. They bred somewhere in the South and would go up into the mountains to die, Melinda read, or maybe it was the other way around; when she was afraid of something she tried to find out as much about it as she could, but often she had trouble keeping her facts straight, and that just made her more afraid. It didn't matter anyway; the truth was, they came from everywhere, bred everywhere, and they would never die.

Miller moths were monsters, and she was terrified of them. They swarmed so thickly around the lamp on her bedside stand or the hoodlight on her stove that they looked like clots of curly hair. They got stuck in her food, drowned in her coffee. They flew into her face, into her mouth, into the hole in the middle of her body, leaving everywhere the dust from their wings. The dust from their wings was poisonous. It was also what enabled them to breed.

They were in her bed. When Charlie wasn't there she felt them all night long, flicking against the back of her neck, kissing the insides of her thighs, crawling into her vagina.

Finally, after three virtually sleepless nights, Melinda danced around her bedroom in a frenzy, with a rolled-up newspaper in one hand and a flyswatter in the other. She smashed every moth she saw or thought she saw, until the paper was tattered and the flyswatter was covered with pulpy wing dust and she was faint with exertion and fear. But in the end she was helpless against them. There were miller moths everywhere.

And they would get their revenge. They would pass stories on from one generation to the next about what she'd done to their family, or tried to do, and someday when she thought she was safe at home—in the winter, say, when there weren't supposed to be any moths—one or a dozen or a million of them would lay their eggs inside her.

Monsters were everywhere. Great hairy things with eyes and teeth, miller moths with poisonous wings, squirmy creatures with tentacles that caught and held. All the monsters communicated with all the other monsters—the moths with the beasts, the caterpillars with the men. They spoke a language Melinda frequently understood but could not quite use herself. They talked about her. They watched her every minute of every day and night.

Everything was a monster, monstrous and magical. Everything was family but her. Everything talked.

"If you tell, they won't understand."

"If you tell, they'll be mad at me. And at you."

"If you tell, you'll get us both in big trouble."

"If you tell, you'll tear our family apart."

"If you tell, Mindy, I'll go to jail, and then I won't love you anymore."

Charlie lay back in her arms. He was so sweet, so patient and good to her.

He was watching her. He watched her all the time. Even when they made love he didn't close his eyes; she'd open hers during a long, breathtaking kiss and find him looking at her, his eyes so close they didn't look like eyes anymore but like dark pools out of which anything might rise. Even when she let him spend the night (at her place, at home, never at his, where she wouldn't know where the monsters had bred in the night) and she woke up from her habitually fitful sleep, she knew he was watching her in his dreams. Every minute of every day and night.

"Sometimes you're such a little girl," he observed. "Like when we go to horror shows and you get so scared you have to run to the bathroom and throw up."

Melinda hadn't realized he knew about that. She felt her face and neck go hot.

"And other times," he persisted, "you're like a beautiful, wise old woman. No, not old—ageless. Like you've been alive forever. That's how you seem when we make love."

"Sex is older than we are," Melinda said. "It's older than anybody. It's so old and so powerful it's like a god, or a monster. People will do anything, tell themselves anything, to make what they do all right, just so they can hold onto it for a split second."

She saw Charlie's eyes widen, heard him catch his breath,

saw an appendage with a searching eye and clinging membranes slither toward her as he started to say, "Love's like that, too, you know."

She stopped him with a kiss. The tentacle went into her mouth, into her throat. She sucked. The hole in the middle of her body filled up with viscous whitish fluid, and she ran to the bathroom to vomit it away.

"You're growing up now. You're becoming a woman.

"Why do you treat me like this? Why do you hate me?

"I don't understand why you want to hurt me. We've been so close.

"I don't understand.

"I love you."

Charlie sneaked up on her. They were in her bed and she was relaxing in his arms, feeling pleasantly hungry, thinking that even if that furry shadow in the corner of the ceiling was a moth it wouldn't hurt her, that it was as afraid of her as she was of it, when Charlie said before she saw it coming, "I love you."

She was going to throw up. She struggled to get up, to free herself of him, but he wouldn't let her go.

"Melinda, wait. Please don't go. I *love* you."

The miller moth elongated and swelled and inserted itself into her mouth. Its poisonous dust was making her choke. It pushed its way down through her body; she felt it circling her heart, winding among her intestines, nudging the inside of her vagina, but it didn't come out.

"I know you're afraid. I know somebody has hurt you. But I won't hurt you. *I love you.*"

The monster was godlike; the god was monstrous. It had a single wet eye and a bifurcated heart. She would do anything she had to do to keep it away from her, anything to make it forever her own.

But not now. She wasn't ready now.

"Mindy. I love you."

"No no no!" She pulled away from his wet tongue, his

hairy hands, his single eye. She sprang from the bed and ran, the monster who loved her stumbling after her.

She ran down the hall, painfully aware of her nakedness, of the hairy, wounded hole in the middle of her body that wanted to be filled, that wanted to be protected from the crawling, slimy vermin that filled the world. Even as she ran she frantically considered what she might use to plug it up.

She ran into the bathroom and slammed the door, locking it. Outside the monster panted, out of breath. "Mindy, Mindy . . . love . . ." And then it fell silent.

She crouched on the cool tile in the corner, her head pressed against cold porcelain. It was too late to vomit. Too late to escape. Under the edge of the door, black hair was spreading toward her.

Melinda tried to pull herself into the hole in the middle of her body, the hole in the middle of her life, the hole she had become. She knew she wouldn't die there, although sometimes that's what she wanted. She hoped she wouldn't have to eat there, that nothing would have to enter her body ever again.

There she knew she could be the monster who never needed to love. She could be the god.

Safe. Safe at home.

HOW DEEP THE TASTE OF LOVE

John Shirley

Sid Drexel was just totally into it. He was so fucking happy it stank from him. Just coincidentally, his wife was dead.

He was sitting in the bar of Tuffy's, the "Hottest Little Singles Bar in the Bay Area," and the place was jiggly with women. Some already had men talking to them, but there were women sitting in twos and threes who were only marking time with each other while they waited for a Sid Drexel to make his move.

Drexel could barely keep himself glued to his barstool. He bobbed his head to the MTV stuff coming from the hidden speakers near the big-screen TV, he chewed handfuls of twiglike pretzel sticks, and he made rude noises with his straw in the soupy dregs of his second strawberry daiquiri. He had to talk to somebody. He tried the bartender, an almost unnaturally good-looking guy with a golden tan, wearing an odd, sleeveless tuxedo. The bartender had pumped-up arms, and he moved with no wasted motion as he poured things, shook things, gave things, accepted things, wiped things; Drexel admired the way one smooth action became another.

"Tom Cruise's got nothing on you," Drexel said.

The bartender glanced at him as he opened a glass-washing machine. The look seemed to ask if Drexel was in the wrong kind of bar.

"I mean," Drexel hastened to explain, "that movie *Cocktail*—Tom Cruise played this slick bartender—"

"Oh. Yeah. Thanks." The bartender did a sort of glissade to the Jack Daniels bottle, sweeping it off its rack and pouring, all in the same motion.

"My wife's dead," Drexel announced, beaming at him. "I mean, it's a shame and all. But, tell you the truth—"

"Oh, I understand," the bartender said. He took someone's money for the Jack Daniels. There was a small tattoo of a star inside a toothy mouth on the bartender's tanned forearm, Drexel saw.

"You understand? You know what I mean? Twenty-one and a half years, my friend. You know what else?" But Drexel decided not to say it: that he had once considered killing Helen. Not too long ago, either. But it was risky. And divorce? Jeez, with his contracting business and California's community-property laws, she'd take him for half of everything. But *this* way . . . Boom! A car accident! And none of his doing! It was so sweet that the cops had checked her car to see he hadn't messed with the brakes or something. But he hadn't, he really hadn't; he'd just been lucky. And he still felt lucky.

"Maybe it's the dance training," the bartender said, with narcissism glazing his eyes. He looked at Drexel. "The reason I can do the Tom Cruise behind the bar."

"You're a dancer?"

"Why you think so many ladies are here? To see you?" A crooked grin said he meant no offense. He nodded toward the small, circular, tinsel-curtained stage. "Male dancers for the ladies. My bar shift ends in twenty minutes. Five dancers in all."

"Oh." Thud. There it was. The ladies were here to see guys undulating their muscle tone on the stage. "And I got to leave?"

"In twenty minutes it becomes ladies only. But come back after showtime." He winked. "At eleven." He drifted over to talk to a tall, busty blond woman with skin that looked faintly blue in this light. The bartender looked directly at Drexel, then back at the blonde.

Eleven, he'd said. Eleven? Drexel'd be half in the bag by then, or half asleep. He had to get something *going* with someone. Helen was in the ground a month now, he had given himself a week's vacation, he had plenty of money, he had that pricey Mercedes convertible that Helen had bitched about, and he had his looks. Okay, sure, his face was sagging around the edges, and he had that pattern-baldness thing, but he was still a good-looking guy . . . Maybe he should have had his teeth cleaned.

Don't worry about it, he told himself. Just—*go for it*. Life is short. And Helen had been very particular. Everything had to be just so when she did it. Except for a couple of whores watching the clock the whole time, and Billy Jane Dotts in her parents' garage, Helen had a corner on Drexel's sexual experience. And Helen was not into . . . exploring. You read those magazines—*Forum*, things like that; people wrote in all kinds of letters about every damn kinky thing in the book. Like there was nothing weird about it, in particular. Like it was okay. But Helen wouldn't even talk about it, let alone . . .

"Excuse me. Is this seat taken?" It was the blonde.

No, came the reply in Drexel's head, is yours? But he was savvy enough to say, instead, "Nope. Have a seat." She was damn good-looking. Smooth skin—still looking blue-black —beautifully Asiatic eyes, the shape of her face maybe Hispanic, some kind of foxy crossbreed. The hair looked like a wig, but so what? And those *tits*. God. She sat with her shoulders thrown back, chest jutting in her tight cream-colored sweater. It was sewn with black beads in an odd pattern he almost recognized but knew he'd never seen. He didn't spend much time looking at the beads. Her breasts were almost too magnificent to be real. Then, too, she had that wig. And she was tall. Maybe . . .

He looked at her closer. Some kind of transsexual?

He looked at her neck, her lips, her cheekbones. No way: This was a woman.

She looked frankly back at him. "Aren't you going to offer? I mean, here's the first guy I've met all night I'd like to buy me a drink, and he's the only one not offering."

"Oh—well, shit, I mean—yeah! Bartender! Hey, pal, anything this lady wants . . . I'll have another . . . right."

She said her name was Sindra. She had some kind of slight accent he couldn't place, maybe Middle Eastern. She sat very quietly, but he had a feeling she was just bursting with something inside, like him. *We're two of a kind.*

He prided himself on his sense of humor, so he tried telling her a joke. The bartender listened in, wiping the bar. The only one that'd come to mind was: "So this guy comes into a bar with a frog growing out of his forehead! A whole, live frog! And the bartender says, 'Hey buddy, how'd the hell that happen?' And *the frog* says, 'I dunno, it started out as a wart on my butt.'" She stared at him for a moment; he seemed to have startled her, somehow. She and the bartender exchanged looks.

Then she laughed politely. "Do you believe in omens, Sid?"

"Hm?" Drexel shrugged. "Sure. I hope it's a lucky omen, whatever it is. Say, pal, can I get another? Right."

He got only halfway through the daiquiri before an amplified voice interrupted the MTV T&A to announce that the men had to leave in five minutes for the ladies only show. The ladies clapped and whooped.

"Well hell. I guess you're waiting for the show, huh, Sindra?" Drexel asked. He thought that was a pretty smooth segue.

"Actually, no," Sindra said, adding gravely, "no, I'm . . . waiting for you, I think. I need someone to live out some dreams with. Tonight."

He felt his groin churn with blood. "Yeah? Man, I've been waiting for someone like you for . . ." And it all came tumbling out. She listened, nodding, as they put on their coats and—without ever having to discuss it—walked out to the parking lot to his car. On the way out, Drexel absently noticed the bartender up onstage, half nude, throwing his muscles suggestively around, and she didn't even glance at the guy, *not once,* and the bartender gave them a long look that might have been a kind of resentment.

"I understand exactly what you've been going through," she told Drexel, holding his gaze with hers as they stood by the white convertible, in the monoxide velvet of the warm Indian summer night.

He hadn't noticed, in the bar, how golden her eyes were. Golden—or almost lemon-colored.

"I was in the same position—in more ways than one— with my husband of many years," Sindra said. "He would try nothing new. And sex is like a continent. A tropical continent. It must be explored to be appreciated. Don't you agree?"

"Hey, listen, I . . . okay, maybe it sounds like one of those things that's just . . . that everyone . . . that's . . . what's the word?"

"Trite? Cliché?"

"Right! Trite, like, but Sindra, I couldn't agree more. I am just totally there with you."

He hadn't gotten to his forties without knowing when something was too good to be true. If some guy wanted to pay you three times the rate to build something that was too easy to build, it was always too good to be true. The mob was covering up something, or there was some other hassle behind it.

And he knew Sindra was too good to be true. Women like her just didn't come at you this easily.

"Don't they?" Sindra said.

"What?" He did a double take.

"I can see it in your expression. You don't trust me. 'People don't do this sort of thing.' There are some one-night stands, but women who . . . well . . ."

"Women as good-looking as you don't offer to, you know, uh . . ."

"Fulfill a man's every fantasy within minutes of meeting him?" She smiled. "I didn't offer that."

"Oh. Right. I, uh—"

"But you're right: I was going to. I still am."

"Uh, is there, I mean—"

"No charge. Unless *you* cost something."

He laughed. "Hey—for you, it's free."

They both enjoyed that. He was having one motherfucker of a good time. He really was.

"How would you know if things like this never happen?" Sindra asked. "Living with your Helen, you'd be out of circulation. But you must have heard about it happening to other people." She was slightly hunched down in her seat to keep her wig out of the wind streaming over the open top of the convertible.

They were tooling down the 580 toward the turn-off that'd take them into the Berkeley Hills, where Sindra lived. Drexel replied, "I've heard of people having encounters like that, but you always figure those stories are bullshit."

"No. It's simply . . . rare. Rare that it comes true. See, it only comes true for special people, who are into special things. And those people are rare. They're *select*. A kind of sexual elite. And they're carefully selected."

"You *selected* me? Like you've been watching me?"

She hesitated. "No. No, but—I have a special instinct for these things. That's why they send me."

His hands got sweaty on the steering wheel. "They?"

"Here's the exit . . ."

He took it, mechanically. "You said *they?*"

"Perhaps I should have said *we.* You did say you wanted to experiment. To really live. Go into some new directions. Why don't we talk about it frankly? You can tell me: What sorts of things did you want to try?"

"Uh . . . well . . ." Could he really tell her?

"Tell you what: I'll go first. Turn right at the next light. Best get in the right lane. That's it. I'm into being tied up with my own panties, given golden showers, then covered in fragrant oil and gang-fucked. Among other things."

If he'd been in a cartoon, his lower jaw would have bounced on his lap. Which would have been kinky itself, considering his hard-on.

"Jesus," he said, shaking his head in admiration.

"'Among other things'? I really—I admire that. How you can just come out and talk about that and . . . and not only talk about it. This is great. I always wanted to . . . well, lots of stuff. Two girls. And being . . . being spanked by two girls. And they make me do things. Then I spank them. And make them do things."

"Turn right again. Up the hill here. Turn left at the corner."

"Up near the big burn-out, huh?" They were driving through the hills charred by the Berkeley-Oakland fire of '91. The black ash had seeped away in the rains, except along the concrete foundation lines of the burned houses; most of the ground was gray and muddy and erosion-raked. Chimneys jutted here and there like those termite towers you see in pictures of arid African plains.

He drove onto her cul-de-sac. The fire had been a windfall for Drexel's contracting business, but he hadn't been on this particular street. All the houses were burned away except one, with thick brush around it. Brush that should have burned, he would have thought.

"Yes, we were lucky in the fire. The neighbors were crowding us." She smiled distantly. "'Make people do things,' you said. What sort of things? In your fantasies?"

"Hm? Oh, God."

"Come on. I told you mine."

"Right. Chewing on people. Chewing on feet. Clean feet, of course. Chewing on private parts. Not . . . not hurting anything but . . . sucking and chewing on fingers and toes and nipples, really *chewing* . . . God, it feels good to just . . ." He shifted in his seat. He hadn't been this hard since his teens.

He parked in front of her house. Drexel had flirted with architecture in his one year of community college; he recognized the house as an old Maybeck, heavy on the dark wood, the intricate levels, the big windows. The yard was overgrown; he didn't recognize most of the plants. There were pines encircling the place and more pine and fir, singed survivors of the fire, marching down the hill behind it. The Bay, Berkeley, much of Oakland would be visible on the other side of the house, maybe even San Francisco.

They went up the mossy flagstones; brown pine needles fringed the stones, and stiff silvery-green brush pressed in from both sides of the winding path. Sindra stepped over something on the porch—something that made Drexel backpedal a few steps. A large gray tarantula. It made tentative, feathery movements, like the fingers of an anxious piano player, and slipped into the succulents lining the porch. "It's that time of year in the East Bay hills," Sindra said, noticing his reaction. "It gets warm and they come out and mate."

She unlocked the door and they went in. It was cool and moist here and smelled of mildew. They passed along a dim hallway to a living room. There were picture windows that should have looked down on Berkeley and the Bay—but they were covered with red cellophane. There were large, shapeless cushions on the hardwood floor. Nothing else to sit on.

He stood awkwardly in the flushed light by the window as Sindra went to the built-in bar. There were paintings on the walls, but standing here he couldn't quite make them out.

Sindra knelt beside a small refrigerator—the movement tightened the skirt around her ass. She took out a Mason jar of dark liquid and poured some into two cups with a little cola. "I make a mind-fuck of a cocktail," she said. "I keep it premixed."

She brought the glasses back to him, and they each drank. The stuff was both sweet and acrid. He couldn't quite . . .

"What is it?"

"Tarantula venom, partly," she said, as he began to twitch.

Even in his toxic delirium, he thought passingly: They must be silicone. Too perfect, too firm.

She was on her back, nude, legs spread, her whole body beckoning. Her breasts looked violet in this light, with purple-brown nipples. They were vast, jutting, round, perfect, and just impossible.

But they weren't silicone. One of the whores had been silicone-enhanced that time. Kneeling between her legs, exploring with his hands, he knew: This wasn't the same. This was . . .

They were meaty. They were *big* breasts, not like enhanced pectorals, and she had a real pussy; it wasn't as if she were some kind of transsexual, no. But these things were filled, he assumed, with muscle. Which was impossible, wasn't it?

He thought about all of this for maybe two and a half drugged seconds. Then the convulsions hit him.

After a while he stopped noticing. The convulsions stopped scaring him. And not long after that they stopped entirely.

It was all the same to Drexel: He had gone through the panic and sickness stage, and now, with the psychedelic effects of the high-dose venom, he was riding waves of psychotic exultation through a storm of light. The storm's colors were sultry shades of the primaries, and neon variants of violet and emerald and gold, whipping past him in arching, interweaving wires, like lasers gone rubbery. The wires of light dove into him and careened down his spine, each color a different sensation; other lights arched over him like the buttresses of some infinitely refined cathedral, where even the building stones were of stained glass. And occupying completely the floor of the cathedral was the naked Sindra and her impossibly perfect breasts.

He'd twitched his clothes off, and his cock was hard as teak. She took him immediately, all in one embrace, cock into yielding, slick pussy, his face into her cleavage.

There was a delightful scent off her that was like venison and gardenias with just a touch of frying trout. It translated into taste as he thrust his tongue into her meaty cleavage; he rocked back from her a little with the intensity of the feeling, a sexual sensation as palpable as the heat waves you felt rolling off the tarmac when you stepped off a plane in hot-season Florida. "Jezzusya . . . Jezzusya . . ." His heart felt like a molten lump. He couldn't quite talk. "Jezzusya fuggincredibuh . . . Yuh incredibuh . . ."

"Why thank you, Sid," she said quite clearly, her voice chiming against the incandescent glass of the air.

He shoved up into her and he seemed to go farther than physically possible—as if the cleft of her kept parting, wider and wider; as if he were wading into her, as a man might wade into a swamp.

And her nipple in his mouth—it moved, the nipple *probed* in his mouth. . . .

"Bite it, sweetheart," she said, sweetly and lucidly.

"Yuh ruhlly wahmuh?"

"I really do. Bite it hard."

He bit down, and forty years of frustration came rollicking out of him, singing. A lifelong weight he'd taken for granted simply curtsied and left him. This was *way* better than he'd hoped for.

"Bite harder, much harder. Yes. Now harder still." Her voice was quite clear and insistent, there was no mistaking it, but it was hard to believe she wanted . . .

"Harder."

"Yuh sure?"

"Oh yes."

He bit down as hard as he could, and if he hadn't been in unspeakable ecstasy he would have screamed in revulsion as her skin parted under his teeth. As his teeth sank into the meat of her.

"Now chew it up."

Oh no. But he could no more spit it out than a two-year-old boy could spit out his first taste of real candy. Maybe he'd be sorry later, maybe he'd be explaining it to the police and the *National Star* and specialists in criminal psychiatry, but right now was Right Now more than it ever had been, and this was the most delicious bite he'd ever taken; it was the most satisfying oral sensation he'd ever felt. Her flesh was drugged. It was cocaine and heroin and quaaludes, oozing velvety fingers of electric delight into his brain. As he chewed, he waited, rather abstractedly, for her to scream and push him away. But after he swallowed—that itself a deeply satisfying act, awakening unheard-of erogenous zones in his esophagus—she demanded, *"Take another bite. A big one."* When he hesitated, she said, "Bite and chew it up and swallow! It *doesn't hurt me!"*

He ate most of her right breast and was working on the left before he began to feel full. And even then he could feel the bitten-off breast *melting* in his stomach . . . dissolving into him, more rapidly than with anything so banal as digestion. The taste was of meat, almost a sausage but more delicately flavored, and some sort of exotic fruit pie, and just a *faint* touch of blood, hardly any at all, and a faint underflavor of something he'd had at a Japanese restaurant. Roe? Sea-urchin eggs?

And the texture: wonderfully creamy, but with just the right meaty resistance to his mastication.

He could hardly breathe, with his sticky face thrust deeply into the rind of her left breast. But he couldn't get enough; he was infinitely hungry, endlessly consumed by lust. His hips thrusting, cock working almost incidentally in her pussy (orgasm was not an issue, so to speak—he was far beyond that), he devoured the pulpy wet blue-violet glory, working his way greedily down into the breast, down to a sort of root . . . Like the little nubbin one finds at the inside bottom of a pumpkin, a kind of internal stalk. He gnawed at the stalk, sucking away the last of the drugged flesh around it—and she said, "That's about right, I'd say."

The stalk opened and took hold of his tongue.

Someone in the background said, "Are you in full contact?" A man's voice.

"Yes," she said. "I have his tongue and his cock."

He tried to pull free, of course; both extensions of him were pinned, and pain warned him not to try again. The pain was as intense as the pleasure. It commanded him to stillness.

He was still drunk on her; the high had programmed a profoundly somatic trust in him. He was hers.

A man squatted behind Drexel and thrust something in Drexel's ass.

But he knew from the shape of it—it hadn't been a penis. It was a rounder, more truncated shape. It dissolved, like the stuff in his stomach, and seeped into him.

He saw someone else out of the corner of his eye— another man, kneeling by Sindra's head. Bending, thrusting his hips toward her face.

She bit off the man's penis and chewed it up, her smile droopy with euphoria.

The man arched his back, but not in pain. This wasn't something masochistic. There was no blood at the bitten-off root of the man's cock. Only the same bluish pulp at the stub.

Drexel couldn't see the man's face clearly from this awkward angle. But he recognized the tattoo on the muscular arm: the bartender.

He felt something flush into him through his tongue; tingling, interpenetrating. Something else warmly *hissing into* his trapped cock, like a backward ejaculation. Some secretion, entering him, from her. He sensed that the seeming cock that Sindra had bitten off, the flesh of the bartender, had been *processed through her* somehow and was now entering Drexel, fertilizing the meaty secrets he'd swallowed.

Most of the time he would lie passively in the low, bowl-shaped bed. Squirming only occasionally, when the internal sensations unsettled him. Now he reposed dreamily, listening to her soothings. Sindra was standing over him, telling him a few things just to keep him quiet, so it would all seem natural. So he wouldn't struggle, though there was little struggle left in him. His limbs had merged arm into arm, leg to leg. There wasn't much he could do. The inhabited flesh he'd swallowed, with the secretions that she and the men of her peculiar species had mixed into it, were changing him; were guiding him, on a cellular level, along some metamorphic byway of synergenesis.

She remained nude when she was in the house; so did the "bartender." So did the others: the women with the slightly blue skin; their heads, when they'd removed their wigs, furred with the faintly waving blue polyps; the men had golden polyps on their craniums, and their skin was softly gold. It was not a tan.

The bartender's cock was growing back.

As Sindra stood beside Drexel, gazing at his changing body, smiling beatifically, he could see that her breasts were already rapidly growing back as well; the little stalks were covered over, the rinds of the old breasts fallen neatly away. At this rate she'd be back up to size in a week.

A little boy came to the incubator bed; a boy of about five, nude and golden-skinned but without the quivery polyps on his scalp the others had. More than once he'd come to look at Drexel with some unspoken personal fascination.

Sindra shooed the boy away with a murmur, then turned to the bed, reached in, and stroked Drexel as she spoke. "It's all a cycle, a natural, beautiful cycle, Sidney. We have a pact with them—we call them the Guests. They are the brethren of the Akishra. Their world intertwines ours, in places; we've always had a sort of overlapping ecology with it, with their dimension. A lot of the old Nature gods were just people altered by the Guests, Siddy." She cocked her head thoughtfully, looking for the most calming way to explain it. "Some of us are suitable to be hosts to the Guests—and others are to be incubators, for their young. It's to do with your DNA, I suppose, and your spiritual type. It's something we can sense. Carl and I sensed you were perfect incubator material—and so you are! Not everyone is suitable, so it's fortunate the Guests only need to lay once or twice a year. The Guests use us as hosts—people like me, and Carl, your 'bartender'—and they change us and give us life. A very, very long life with many pleasures. They pass through us to you incubators, and we feel no pain, and our lives are sweet and varied." She paused to stroke his swelling belly.

"They've passed fully into you, Sidney; *you* brought the layings of the Guests in, hungrily, and willingly. I used the venom of our pets to make it faster. And because I enjoy it. But we didn't really need the drug. *You wanted me that way, Sidney*—and now you're fulfilled!"

She crouched beside the incubator bed, letting him try out his feeble protest, which came out as unintelligible mutterings. She stroked him, and pinched one of her own nascent nipples thoughtfully, as she went on.

"Hush, hush and lay still, Sid. The real miracle is still to come. We fertilized that which you devoured from me; from my breasts; it's growing in you. You won't be one of us; they need you differently. But you'll have your own rewards . . ."

She bent near him with a sponge of nutrients, sweet and syrup-thick, blowing kisses at his muted lips.

At the Feedtime, the time of reconfiguration, they no longer had to soothe him. The unneeded part of him was gone. It was displaced when the one who'd grown in his belly moved up, through the passages within, and entered his skull for its first feeding.

Sindra and Carl and the boy and the others knelt beside the incubation bed. Hugging one another in excitement, they watched as the transformation achieved its penultimate stage.

The Guest had moved into Drexel's head like a hermit crab into a seashell. Now the onlookers gasped in wonder and joy, like anyone privileged to watch a birth, as Drexel's head detached itself from his neck and crawled—*the head crawled*—on its gastropodic underside, down the length of Drexel's body. It began to graze contentedly, nourishing itself on his flesh. It would fill itself thus until the Growtime should come, and then the bonding with a host: the little boy who watched eagerly and happily beside his parents, Carl and Sindra. The boy had been instructed in what to expect; he would not become an incubator like Drexel—he would become a carrier for a Guest, like Carl and Sindra, immortal and perfect. He watched rapturously as the Guest in Drexel's head fed on the body it had quit; he watched in a glow of anticipation, eager for the day the Guest should be ready to join with him, to bring him into the manhood of his people . . .

HARD EVIDENCE

John Edward Ames

They say you never hear the shot that kills you," re-marked Dez Lofley.

The forensics lab chief raised his eyes from a 9mm bullet under the scanning electron microscope in front of him. It was one of several instruments lining a long, zinc-topped counter. Behind him another lab tech was heating up a fiber sample in a quartz tube.

Lofley wore a pullover that proclaimed KARMA OWES ME, DUDE. His seamed face broke into a triumphant grin when he looked at Reno Morgan, the detective anxiously waiting for his verdict.

"You can bet your ass this chick is fried and freeze-dried now, ace. We got a full match. Usually the bullet lead will frag or deform too much for a positive ID with the tool marks in the gun. But this one matches up like a frickin' jigsaw."

Morgan nodded and flashed a thumbs-up. Oddly, though, he felt a hard little nubbin of regret cankering inside him.

Like any good homicide cop, he was obsessed with one working maxim: *Get hard evidence.* He knew that motive and opportunity and autopsy protocols alone were as useless as last week's *TV Guide* unless there was a definite physical link between a suspect and a corpse. Without that link, a murder investigation was virtually impossible to wrap.

210

Fortunately for his rep as a supercop, the sensational D'antoni case appeared all but wrapped from Day One.

The crime was violent and brutal and perfect fare for the bucket-of-blood tabloids: The Teflon-coated, armor-piercing "cop killer" bullet, fired pointblank, had turned multimillionaire Keith D'antoni's rugged profile into an arabesque on the wallpaper behind him. Nor was there any doubt in Morgan's mind that the lab crew had already gut-hooked their fish. A comparison microscope had established exactly which Browning parabellum had fired the slug; a neutron-activation test to detect primer gunshot residue had identified the hand that had most likely fired the gun. Not only was the weapon now safely locked up in the police evidence room—Morgan was also convinced it had been surrendered to him at the crime scene by the murderer herself.

Not that Ursula D'antoni had actually admitted killing her husband. But neither had she denied it.

So far she had shown neither remorse, confusion, fear, nor even interest. She was not in shock, had passed a thorough physical, and was declared legally sane by the court psychiatrist. The death of her husband simply did not seem to concern her. She just passively refused to let herself be assimilated by all the investigative fuss around her. Physically speaking, she was not what Morgan would call your typical traffic hazard.

Hers was a more subtle, sloe-eyed beauty that left glowing retinal afterimages when he closed his eyes. Subtle . . . yet the sheer erotic force of her felt like nothing he had ever experienced.

Now Lofley's voice sliced into his pleasant reverie with the invasive weight of a coroner's bone-saw. "Any glitches turn up during the post?"

Morgan shook his head. "M.E. verifies that cause of death was massive gunshot trauma to the brain."

"She got a rap sheet?"

"Zip. I ran her through our computers and the NCIC files. Not even a traffic citation."

"Entropy requires no maintenance," suggested Lofley

cryptically. He bent over the microscope again like a monk over his alms. "Who knows? Maybe she offed her old man because he liked to go out dick trawling."

Morgan had abandoned his perch on the corner of the nearest desk and was heading toward the door. "Whatever. Just make sure you personally tag that slug and file it away in the evidence room. I don't trust that nimrod clerk of yours."

"Ja, mein herr," grunted Lofley without looking up.

For the rest of the day Morgan tried to stop thinking about Ursula D'antoni. But it was like trying to stop his tongue from exploring a broken tooth.

He considered himself an efficient jobber, not a scanner of human souls. He was known as one of the bounty hunters: that one-sixth of any big-city police department that is routinely responsible for 80 percent of the arrests. Fellow cops admired his investigative technique but resented his overtime pay.

Still, this case troubled him. One fly in the ointment was the complete absence of a clear motive. He had canvassed the entire neighborhood yet turned up not one tale of wife abuse or infidelity on the part of Keith D'antoni. Nor was there evidence that *she* had a lover waiting in the wings. And Ursula D'antoni was an heiress who was far wealthier than her husband, so money had not been the motive.

But motives were not Morgan's bailiwick. What really troubled him was the sexual force of her, which pulsed from her willowy body like radioactive motes.

He had first felt it a week ago. Morgan had responded to a call from the prowl-car team that had originally investigated a neighbor's report of a gunshot coming from the D'antoni residence. The couple lived up in the Heights, a plush glass-and-redwood dwelling with a crushed marble cul-de-sac, sunken den, and velvet-and-damask furniture.

An ashen-faced uniformed cop had pointed him back to the den, where his partner was keeping a wary eye on the woman above the muzzle of his police .38. She was sitting on the floor under a varnished oil painting of some naked little Hindu god. A scattering of silk zazen cushions and pretty origami roses surrounded her. Her husband's mangled head rested in her lap. The weapon was still in her right hand, though she wasn't aiming it at anyone.

"She won't drop it, Lieutenant," the patrolman explained. "I don't think she hears me."

She had looked up at him when Morgan entered the room. For a moment, a mere micromoment shorter than the space of a heartbeat, he stared into those eyes the color of crushed berries and felt an archetypal revulsion and fascination. That moment passed and then his back broke out in cool sweat. He felt his eyes quivering as if he had splashed shampoo into them, and a fuzzy white noise filled his head.

But that, too, passed. Now he felt his pulse fire boosters, his breathing quicken as if he had just dashed up a flight of stairs. His throat pinched shut, and warm blood crept up the back of his neck. His legs trembled as though his calves had just turned to water.

All of it seemed like a visceral prelude to something bigger—the physical component of a dangerous mental insight. For during that moment he also suddenly understood something, glimpsed a few lines of psychic graffiti.

It was nothing he could state neatly as a law. Rather, it was a realization that everything in his world had somehow, suddenly and definitely, changed forever in a radical paradigm shift of perception.

Then she talked to him, and the dangerous insight was forgotten. Her voice slid down the bumps of his spine with the tickling grit of a cat's tongue.

"I love Yama," she told him, looking up at the painting as she spoke. "He knows that death is the greatest gift Shiva has ever given his children." Then she surrendered the weapon butt-first.

She looked at Morgan again and smiled a dreamy, fey smile. Abruptly, he felt his penis engorge with hot blood. It was suddenly so hard that it twitched with each heartbeat. His response shocked him so deeply that, for the first time in years, Morgan was forced to pull the laminated Miranda card out of his pocket before he could read her rights to her.

* * *

"Twenty years now I've been practicing criminal law, yet only recently did I comprehend the truth, Reno: 'Evil' is a point of view, not an immutable fact of nature."

It was an odd opening remark. Morgan looked a question at Eric Coleman across the wide pecan veneer of the lawyer's desk. The silver-templed attorney was quaintly dapper in a Harris tweed jacket and burgundy Countess Mara tie. But a patina of nervous perspiration coated his brow like glazed plasticine.

Morgan shrugged. "Whatever. 'Evil' isn't my usual turf."

Coleman nodded, leaning closer across the desk in his growing urgency. He rubbed a knuckle across his mustache. "No, it's not, is it? Evil is a cause, and you deal with effects."

The remark left the cop groping for words. The ormolu clock on the desk ticked off at least ten uncomfortable seconds while he tried to orient himself. Coleman had called him last night at home and asked—his normally suave voice oddly strained—to see him. As a rule, Morgan considered lawyers the most accomplished liars since Simon Peter denied Christ. But he made a rare exception in the case of Coleman. The man was brilliant but absolutely straight-arrow when it came to trial advocacy. Besides—the client he wanted to discuss was Ursula D'antoni.

Yet this meeting was clearly unorthodox, if not exactly wrong, and both men knew it. The crucial discovery phase of the legal process was approaching, when the prosecution would be required to detail, for potential defense rebuttal, precisely what evidence would be introduced into trial. For the defense attorney and the case officer to meet like this would usually be considered potentially compromising for either side.

Normally Morgan would have refused, even a request from Coleman. But something almost . . . plaintive in the man's voice had struck a resonant chord of curiosity within the cop.

By now Morgan was thoroughly baffled. "Did you call me in to discuss metaphysics or Ursula D'antoni?"

Actually hearing her name had the same effect as slapping

Coleman with a wet towel. He started, then leaned back in his chair.

"Ursula? She's . . ."

His voice trailed off. For some reason Morgan was convinced the man had been about to say "innocent." Instead, Coleman now said emphatically, "She *won't* be prosecuted."

The almost childlike petulance of the lawyer's tone surprised Morgan even more than the words.

"Are you saying . . . do you mean you have proof she's innocent?"

He hadn't meant to be so blunt. After all, he would soon be squaring off against Coleman as a witness for the prosecution. But Coleman was clearly not interested in the usual niceties of legal punctilio.

"She hasn't admitted or denied anything," said the attorney. "Nor do I care if she did it."

"You don't care?" repeated Morgan woodenly. For a moment he wondered if this highly respected lawyer had finally stressed out and gone soft between the head handles. Then a more likely possibility occurred to him: The model family man had knuckled under to midlife crisis and become infatuated with his mysterious client.

Morgan slid that thought to the back burner of his mind. He said, "Well, I agree they won't pin Murder One on her. There's no clear intent and sure's hell no sign of malice aforethought. But whether you care or not, the forensics evidence *is* damning."

"All-peering science," said Coleman scornfully. "DNA fingerprinting, mass spectrometers, thin-layer chromatography . . . I'm not talking about guilt, I'm talking about justice. She *won't* be prosecuted, do you hear me?"

The attorney's voice climbed an octave or two up the scale, startling the cop. The man's obvious desperation now struck Morgan in its full force. He watched, his heart beginning to scamper in his chest, as Coleman reached into the wide top drawer of his desk. He slid an eight-by-ten matte-finish color photo across toward Morgan.

"Look at her," said the attorney. "Really *look* at her."

Morgan did look. He gazed long and hard into those huge, almond-shaped, sloe eyes. Cool sweat broke out in his armpits, and it felt like flying neutrinos were invading him. Again he had the absurd feeling—as he had on that first night he saw Ursula D'antoni—that he should look away before his retinas were seared.

But he couldn't look away. Staring into her eyes made him feel that he was watching a poisonous but lovely serpent undulating across crushed velvet, that he was watching the rhythmic beauty of death itself. For a moment he felt a last-gasp feeling of panic, like when he was young and in bed at night and his leg would fall into the crack between the wall and the bed, where the bogeyman lived: There was always that moment between the realization and the motor act of pulling his leg out, when his blood iced over in helpless fear as he wondered if he'd be in time or pulled under forever.

Suddenly, with no visceral segue, he was hard—a boner more intense than a morning piss hard-on. But this time the turn-on didn't stop there: He felt that familiar, tightening tingle between his rectum and his testicles, the signal that he was on the threshold of an orgasm. For a moment the room went blurry, as if he were seeing it through a wet windowpane.

Finally, mercifully, Coleman pulled the photo back across the desk and placed it lovingly into the drawer again.

"She wants to see you," he announced. "Tomorrow morning."

Morgan hadn't felt this unsated since high school, when heavy makeout sessions had left him with a bad case of lover's nuts. It was at least thirty seconds before he could meet the lawyer's gaze. "See me?"

Coleman nodded. "At Central Lockup. She refuses to request bail, you know. And she says we should go together." At the mention of seeing her, the attorney smiled for the first time since Morgan had arrived.

"But why?"

Coleman leaned back in his chair again and let the clock tick out another silence that grew embarrassingly intimate.

"Because, Reno," he finally replied, "she wants you to."

That night Morgan finally drifted down a long tunnel into sleep around two o'clock and woke up in his battered Morris chair several hours later with a crick in his neck. I won't go, he decided. The hell do *I* care what she wants? But at nine sharp—red-eyed but freshly shaven and showered—he met Coleman downtown at Central Lockup.

Maybe it was just his imagination logging some overtime, Morgan told himself—but the hard-boiled cop who led them back to the conference area almost seemed to . . . resent their visit. Morgan's suspicion was confirmed when the guard, a perpetual curmudgeon whom he had never seen crack a grin in the past ten years, now smiled almost shyly as he spotted Ursula D'antoni waiting for her visitors behind the plexiglass divider.

But Morgan forgot about the cop—and about everything else—when she flicked those crushed-mulberry eyes on him. Her black hair was pulled into a heavy Psyche knot over her nape. Detainees awaiting trial were permitted their own clothing, and she wore a cool green shirtwaist dress and white kid sandals.

"Ursula," he heard Coleman's adulatory voice saying beside him, "I brought him."

She nodded. It was just one curt but graciously regal forward tilt of her head. For the first time Morgan noticed, when she closed her eyes, how the lashes curved sweetly against her cheeks.

"I knew you would," she replied, and again the sound of her purring contralto moved up and down Morgan's spine on tiny geisha feet.

Morgan parted his lips to speak. But staring into her unwavering gaze, it was as if everything Freud had termed "defense mechanisms" had suddenly switched to inoperative mode. All his thoughts skittered around inside his skull like frenzied rodents, refusing to be caught. Her eyes bored even deeper into his, probing him to his core, and now a door slammed shut deep down inside him—slammed shut on everything his life had been, on everything he had ever believed.

"You do understand," she said with quiet urgency, "that we all serve Yama?"

"No, I *don't* understand. Who is Ya—"

"Shush!" she cut him off impatiently. "Yama is the Hindu god of death. His cousins, Eros and Thanatos, are locked in their final, fatal embrace. Don't you sense it? All mankind has developed a collective subconscious wish—a universal wish not to exist."

A sense of alarm seeped through Morgan, a primitive revulsion he could not yet focus. He felt dizzy, as if a few pints of blood had just been drawn out of him.

"At the very moment when a man has a climax," she went on, "his heart stops beating. You *must* understand this— you go inside of a woman seeking death, not pleasure!"

One part of him knew that what she was saying was insane. But that didn't matter anymore. He knew only that he wanted what she wanted. Now police work meant nothing. There was only her and the inexorable forces that threatened her unless he intervened.

She understood what he was thinking and offered him a little quicksilver smile. For a moment her mulberry eyes seemed to glow like LED numerals.

"Sit down," she invited him, and he had to because his legs were suddenly turned to rubber by the force of his orgasm.

"Any chance," Morgan remarked, three days after the meeting in Central Lockup, "you could run the D'antoni test again?"

Dez Lofley shot him a puzzle-headed look. "Why? It's been run twice already."

"I'm just skittish, is all. The DA can't turn up any sign this woman ever even bounced a check. The entire prosecution is going to hinge on those lab results. As for the defense, maybe Eric Coleman could try for an insanity plea—she's muttered some strange shit about Hindu gods and whatnot. But Coleman prefers acquittals. That means he's surely going to request backups while he hammers away at his favorite theme: the unreliability of forensic science."

"Whatever pops your corn, ace. I'll run it. I just wonder sometimes if these defense jerkoffs ever take the time to smell what they're shoveling. No number of instant replays can change the final score."

"Let's hope so," said Morgan. He turned to leave. Then, as if remembering something incidental, he turned back to the technician.

"By the way: Coleman wonders if you could stop by his office."

Lofley, who was monitoring an effluent spewing into a gas chromatograph chamber, glanced up at the homicide detective. "Why me? What's the caper?"

Morgan shook his head. "Nobody tells me anything."

Lofley's forehead runneled in a frown. "This sucks some major kielbasa. A lab tech for the prosecution talking to a lawyer for the defense—in private?"

"Why not? Afraid you'll take a bribe?"

Lofley studied him for a long minute before he shrugged. "The whole world's going insane—I'm just proud to be part of it. Yeah, okay. I'll stop by."

"Your Honor, we simply do not know how it could have happened," explained County Prosecutor Jared Maitland. "All we do know is that Lofley removed the bullet from the evidence locker for a final backup analysis. After this, apparently, he didn't notice it was gone at first because he assumed—" Maitland paused and corrected himself. "Because he was *sure* that another lab tech had filed it away again. We have a trace on it, but so far nothing's turned up."

Judge Hiram Neusbaum frowned as if his private chambers had suddenly been occupied by a troupe of not particularly funny clowns. His normally avuncular gaze now radiated official reproof as it shifted from Maitland to Morgan to a thoroughly miserable-looking Dez Lofley.

"A discovery proceeding is *supposed* to itemize evidence,

gentlemen. Are you telling me you don't have any? What about this"—he glanced down at the stack of briefs and depositions in front of him, sifting through them—"this neutron-activation test?"

"Yes, Your Honor," said Maitland, "the test to detect primer gunshot residue. Only . . ."

He trailed off for a moment and stared at Lofley, who visibly flushed. "There was apparently a sampling error. The polythene vial containing the specimen removed from Mrs. D'antoni's skin was somehow . . . mixed up with another vial."

"But can't *that* test, at least, be duplicated?"

Maitland winced. "That's impossible, Your Honor. It would require a second sample. I'm told that primer residue adheres to the skin in measurable quantities for only about forty-eight hours at most."

A grave silence filled the chambers. Again Judge Neusbaum glared from one man to the other, doling out the full measure of his disapproval.

"Mr. Coleman," he finally announced curtly, "I believe the next move is yours."

Coleman looked oddly strained for a lawyer who was about to carry the day. Consistent with her apathy throughout the proceedings, Ursula D'antoni had opted not to attend today. Now Coleman said quietly, "I request dismissal of all legal proceedings against my client, Your Honor, on the grounds of insufficient evidence for an actionable cause."

Maitland deferred by lowering his eyes. Judge Neusbaum aimed a final withering glance at Dez Lofley.

"They say even a blind hog can root up an acorn now and then, Sergeant Lofley. How a forensics technician in your position of responsibility could be so grossly incompetent *twice* in one case defies the imagination. I'll be sending a memo to Internal Affairs about this. Charges dismissed."

A few minutes later, as Morgan and Lofley were exiting together from the municipal building, a lone sob hitched in the lab tech's chest. His eyes met Morgan's.

"I *want* her, Reno," Lofley confessed in a whisper, his face a study in abject misery.

Morgan nodded his understanding. "I know you do," he said gently. Making Dez the fall guy had not been necessary after all, Morgan realized: He was still thinking of the eight-by-ten photo of Ursula D'antoni he had spotted under Judge Neusbaum's stack of depositions. "Don't we all?"

But he also realized that Ursula was right. It wasn't pleasure they wanted from her—it was their own death they sought, that moment at the peak of orgasm when the heart stopped beating, the brain quit thinking, and the body was merely a twitching corpse, a rag puppet dancing toward blessed oblivion. It was a universal compulsion that only a few could yet comprehend—Yama's disciples. Eric Coleman spoke the straight word: Evil was a point of view, not a fact of nature, and murder was Shiva's greatest gift to his children.

Again he looked at Dez, and pity roiled his guts like the churning of digestive gears. Clearly the lab tech was shattered by grief. Unlike Morgan and Coleman, he could not grasp what Ursula truly represented. He was sick of life but, in his ignorance, afraid of death—afraid of that which he secretly desired with an intensity like hell thirst.

Morgan felt the reassuring weight of the snub-nosed police .38 in its chamois holster under his suitcoat. He gripped Lofley gently by the elbow and nudged him toward the unmarked beige sedan at the curb.

"Let's take a little drive into the country, Dez," he said soothingly. "You need to stop thinking so much."

THE ROOM WHERE LOVE LIVES

Grant Morrison

---

*I*t is with great regret that I commence this, the final account of my adventures with Aubrey Valentine. Readers who have followed the exploits of Aubrey Valentine from my first published account, *The Bleeding Whispers,* through to our most recent, *Mystery of the Flayed Mirror,* will be familiar with Valentine's singular skills in the field of occult investigation. I had hoped that our association would continue well into the future but, sadly, events have overtaken my wishes and it falls to me, as Valentine's chronicler, to bear the bad tidings to his many admirers.

So it is with heavy heart that I have assembled this final tale from the testimony of the Bedlow family, from Valentine's last statement, and from my own eyewitness account of the Monday Street horror. I can only pray that it will stand as a fitting tribute to the unusual life of the finest man I have ever known and one I was proud to call my friend.

The house on Monday Street was built late in the reign of Queen Victoria. A solid and imposing townhouse, it looked out across a quiet and tree-lined avenue in the heart of London. Almost as a reflection of the era of its construction, the house, while exhibiting a conservative, classical facade to the outside world, contained within its walls an eccentric profusion of rooms and chambers. Dusty alcoves below stairs gave onto narrow corridors connecting one room with another. There were secret rooms tucked away like forgotten, unopened letters. Faded wallpaper in the basement, the attar of dead flowers, mirrors cataracted with thick dust.

And the house had passed through several hands before it finally became the property of a Dr. Bedlow and his family.

While it would not be true to say our story began with Mrs. Bedlow and her daughter, it seems appropriate to begin the narrative with their unfortunate discovery of what we came to know as the Rutting Room.

Mrs. Bedlow had spent an afternoon shopping, at the close of which she collected her eighteen-year-old daughter, Imogen, from the movies. Imogen's friend Giselle Barnes was to spend the evening with the Bedlows, and she accompanied them home in the car.

The girls hurried to Imogen's room, while Mrs. Bedlow went directly to the kitchen and dumped the contents of her bags onto the table.

A wedge of sunlight draped itself across table and floor like a flag, and Mrs. Bedlow paused to observe the dust motes moiling in the gauzy light. There was something unusual about the movement of the particles; they seemed to follow some subtle organizing pattern. Like iron filings on paper, the dust motes arranged themselves into spiderweb formations. These then exploded, unable to sustain coherence, and were rearranged into new configurations. She admired this restless choreography for some time before the effect faded and it seemed as though her eyes had been deceiving her from the start.

She stocked the fridge and cupboards and prepared a snack for the girls. Carrying a small tray, she began to climb the stairs. Now she could feel a movement, a pulsation in the air. She touched the wall and her fingertips registered a deep, thudding concussion. It seemed as though the pipes beneath the skin of paper and plaster were pounding with a slow, metronomic rhythm. She had a brief vision of gas mains, water pipes, and electric cables carrying arterial blood through the substructure of the house. The pulse quickened and Mrs. Bedlow felt her own heartbeat accelerate to match it. Sweat broke across her forehead and she was aware of a spreading dampness at her crotch, an involuntary, exciting, lubrication. She bit her lip and forced herself to the top of the stairs, reeling dizzily.

"Imogen," she said, and her voice was hoarse and breathless, preorgasmic. She had spoken her daughter's name as though it were the name of a lover. She approached the door of Imogen's room and stopped short.

The door handle was swelling and contracting slightly, inflating and deflating like a lung. And the sounds that came from beyond the door had no place in a girl's bedroom.

Slowly Mrs. Bedlow reached out to touch the keyhole. It was wet, leaking a musky sexual fluid. She raised her fingers to her lips and licked at them. She closed her hand around the warm, pulsing door handle and opened the door.

The whole room inhaled, drawing her into its suffocating heart. The smell of animals in heat. Smell of stained sheets and stale come and heated flesh.

"Look at me, Mummy," said Imogen, giggling.

She was bent over the bed, moaning and salivating. Giselle Barnes, kneeling, worked her hand between Imogen's legs. They both turned to look at Mrs. Bedlow, eyes heated to incandescence.

"Oh, God!" was the best Mrs. Bedlow could manage before the girls descended on her, tearing at her clothes.

There was a sustained note of shame in Mrs. Bedlow's voice as she recounted these events to us. That shame, quite clear in her words, was entirely absent in her demeanor. She sat in the kitchen, wearing a loose robe that was parted to reveal her pale body. Her legs were slung over the arms of a chair and she continued to masturbate slowly and compulsively as she talked. Sometimes she paused to wet her fingers in her mouth. She looked up at us with desperate eyes.

"You must help us," she sobbed. "We can't stop it. We can't stop it, and my daughter's still up there." Then she seemed to lose control again, eyes closing. The rhythm of her hand became more insistent as she drifted into memory.

"It was so beautiful." She sighed. "It was like she was trying to get back into my womb, headfirst . . ."

Valentine eyed her coldly. I wondered if he ever experienced any human emotion now. I could not remember the last time I had seen him smile. He touched his brow with his bandaged left hand, always a sign that he was thinking deeply. There was silence, broken only by the chopped breathing of Mrs. Bedlow.

"Where exactly is your husband now, Mrs. Bedlow?" Valentine asked.

She jerked her head toward the ceiling. "With the girls. With *it*. He can't control himself. None of us can. The room just wants us to fuck and fuck until we die."

I looked at Valentine as he removed his duffle coat.

"I must examine the room before I make my decision," he said.

Mrs. Bedlow got to her feet. I could see the dreadful exertion in her eyes. She was driven to seek sexual gratification by any means, and it clearly took a massive effort of will for her to restrain her urge to assault us.

"I'm frightened to go near it but I want to so much," she said. "It was only my husband who managed to push me out of the room on that first day. If he hadn't, I'd still be there." Her hand crushed her breast, fingers teasing the swollen nipple. "I'd still be there."

"Quite," said Valentine curtly.

We climbed the stairs.

"Can you feel it?" Valentine hissed.

I nodded. It was impossible not to be aware of the percussive thumping in the stairs below our feet. The room, whatever it was, had anchored itself deeply into the fabric of the house, extending roots into the infrastructure. Its power was unmistakable. My own pounding erection demonstrated that. I tried to imagine what it would be like to stay here night after night, as the Bedlows had done, slowly succumbing to that dreadful carnal hunger. I will never know how Mrs. Bedlow finally summoned the strength of will to contact Valentine and myself.

Mrs. Bedlow whined and whispered lewd endearments.

Again I glanced in Valentine's direction, but his eyes were fixed on some unguessable horizon. I could not help but wonder how the power of the Rutting Room was affecting him. Since the horrible death of Angela, his young wife, some years ago—as recounted in *The Affair of the Highgate Shroud*—he had been resolutely celibate, almost sexless indeed. Nothing could fill the gap Angela's death at the hands of The Mysteries had left in his soul. If anyone could tackle the hideous sexual energies of this monstrous room, it was surely Aubrey Valentine.

"Here," said Mrs. Bedlow. She pointed to the door and backed away. Bracing her weight against the far wall, she selected a golf umbrella from the hatstand and slid the handgrip into herself. Weeping madly, bending and unbending her legs, she rode the wooden shaft. Her eyes clouded over. She crooned our names, begging us to join her.

"Poor Mrs. Bedlow," I muttered, trying to push away the thoughts that bubbled into my mind.

Valentine ignored her cries and faced the door.

"Are you ready?" he said. I nodded, unsure, and he motioned for me to stand behind him. He reached out and gripped the door handle. It stiffened in his grip, becoming tumescent. Without further hesitation, he threw the door open and we confronted the room.

The first thing was the smell: a vast reeking perfume that spoke of reeling, desperate nights and polluted innocence. It was the bleak perfume of all blighted desire. This first olfactory shock was followed by the visual horror. The scene within the room recalled some image from Bosch.

Giselle Barnes, in the soiled tatters of her dress, was servicing three naked men. Imogen Bedlow giggled and drove a policeman's baton repeatedly into her own bleeding anus. As we watched, the tableau collapsed and its elements reformed. Now the men were locked in a knot of buggery and fellatio, while the girls sucked and tore at one another.

Valentine gestured to one of the men. "Bedlow?" he said. I nodded.

Imogen, on all fours, backed up and impaled herself on

her father's penis. The eminent Dr. Bedlow gripped the girl's shoulders and pulled her back roughly. At one point he managed to turn his head to face us. There were tears in his eyes. "God help me," he cried, and before he could say anymore, one of the other men mounted him from the rear.

"It's monstrous," I said. It was monstrous, but I could not deny the black excitement I felt.

"But look there," said Valentine, pointing upward. The walls of the room were shifting through strange geometric patterns. I felt I was watching some nightmarish four-dimensional origami at work on the architecture of the place. The patterns on the wallpaper flowed into suggestive shapes. Wet slits opened in the walls, gaped, and were sealed.

And at that moment the door slammed shut in Valentine's face. He produced a kitchen towel from his pocket and wiped his brow.

"Who are the other men?" he said calmly.

Mrs. Bedlow looked up from the floor. "Giselle's father," she said. "And a policeman. They were all trapped there." Then, unable to retain restraint, she withdrew the umbrella handle and rubbed her wet thighs with her hands, baying "Fuck me!" again and again and again.

Valentine strode toward her and, with one precise movement, rendered her unconscious. Then he slung her over his shoulder and we left the house.

We were in our room at the YMCA and Mrs. Bedlow sat drinking instant coffee. Soberly dressed now, there was scarcely anything about her that recalled the nymphomania of several hours previously. Nevertheless, she appeared to be in deep shock. The heat had gone from her eyes, leaving a glassy blankness.

"What are we going to do about my daughter?" she said.

"When was your last period?" Valentine said.

Mrs. Bedlow looked up from her mug, frowning. "Months," she said. "I thought it was another baby . . ."

"I doubt very much that you're pregnant, Mrs. Bedlow. I

believe that the room induced in you and your daughter and the Barnes girl a state of super-receptivity. It made you like itself, a fucking machine, unable to orgasm or to replicate. Coitus for its own sake."

She began to sob, and I reached out to take the coffee mug from her numb fingers.

"What *is* it, Mr. Valentine?" she said. "What is it? What's it doing to my daughter?"

Valentine ignored the question, perhaps not daring to tell her the truth.

"What do you know of the history of the house, Mrs. Bedlow?"

She dabbed at her eyes with a tissue. "Not much. Before we moved in, it belonged to some old woman. Her son said something about it being a kind of private hospital before that. A clinic or something. That's all I know. If there was anything else . . ."

"Stop!" Valentine said abruptly. I could see he was onto something. "Monday Street. Of course! I knew I recognized the name." He turned to face me. "There's a book in my large suitcase," he said. *"Cults of the Pandemonium.* Would you be so kind as to fetch it for me?"

I threw open the battered valise and rummaged through a debris of dog-eared paperbacks, quickly locating *Cults of the Pandemonium.* Its luridly colored cover depicted a gorgeous naked hermaphrodite dancing, while a shadowy figure beat upon a tomtom. I tossed the book to Valentine and he flipped through its pages.

"I should have known!" he said. His eyes scanned a page. "Erich Horney. My God. Horney was a disciple of Wilhelm Reich. He worked at the Organon Institute in Maine in the late '40s, before splitting with Reich in 1952."

We listened intently as Valentine summarized a brief biography of the aptly named Horney. He had adapted many of Wilhelm Reich's sexual theories and taken them in unusual and, some thought, unethical directions.

"His dream was to create something which he called the Horney Chamber," Valentine explained. "This seems to have been a more extravagant version of Reich's orgone accumulator. Basically, Horney intended to create a room which could harness sexual energy, which he believed was an expression of the fundamental forces of the universe." As he spoke, Valentine paced up and down the room.

"He claimed to have succeeded in building a prototype in 1965, but development was hampered by the fact that the room's mechanisms could only be properly activated by an act of 'indefinitely long' sexual intercourse. Nevertheless, by judiciously employing four porno actors, Horney claimed that his chamber was able to absorb and redirect sufficient sexual energy to power the flight of a small gargoylelike homunculus.

"His ultimate ambition was to create a room which could have sex with *itself,* thus producing an unlimited supply of power. A perpetual-motion sex engine."

Valentine threw down the book and looked directly at us. His face was flushed with excitement.

"Horney was certified insane in September 1974 and was taken into the private care of a Dr. Monteuil, who owned a small convalescent clinic on Monday Street."

"Good Lord!" I exclaimed, unable to think of anything else to say.

"And the room?" Mrs. Bedlow said. "My daughter's room?"

"I think we can safely assume that a fully functioning Horney Chamber was built, Mrs. Bedlow. Perhaps Horney died before he could put the room into operation and it has waited all these years for a trigger. Something to turn the starting handle, as it were."

He paused and lifted his bandaged hand to his brow.

"Does your daughter have a boyfriend, Mrs. Bedlow?" he asked.

She nodded, realizing the implications. "It's not what you'd call serious," she said. "They met on a school trip to Belgium. They exchange letters . . ."

"There we have it," Valentine said gravely. "Those nocturnal adolescent yearnings: our trigger."

"But what can we do?" Mrs. Bedlow said. "How can we stop it?"

Valentine sat down facing her and took her hands. He fixed her eyes with his own.

"I haven't told you everything, Mrs. Bedlow," he said.

I felt a tremor trip down my spine. The sky outside our room seemed to thicken. Shadows curdled in the haunted corners of our anonymous room.

"There are certain powers and dominions in our universe," Valentine said. "I can say only that they come from *outside* and that they are inimical to humanity. Sometimes we catch glimpses of their manifestations on this plane of being. They travel in many shapes, all hideous. They come howling through our blackest dreams, feeding on our fears and doubts.

"We call them The Mysteries, and I have dedicated my life to fighting them. They destroyed the only woman I have ever cared for, and now they have taken possession of the activated Horney Chamber. They will try to use its energies to create a window, through which they can enter our world *en masse.*"

"But my daughter . . ." Mrs. Bedlow began. Valentine silenced her with a gesture.

"Your daughter, your husband, and the others are nothing more than raw material to The Mysteries," he said. "They will use them to destruction in order to power the room. When they have exhausted all the possible combinations of the human frame, The Mysteries will push them beyond the limits of flesh. They will become expressions of pure desire, without stable form."

Mrs. Bedlow was sobbing uncontrollably now, and she managed to say only six words: "What are we going to do?"

Valentine stood up.

"You're going to stay here, well away from the house," he said, and then looked at me. "We are going to take the fight to The Mysteries."

I think I will always remember Valentine the way he was at that moment. It is the picture of him that I will carry with me to the grave: Valentine, framed by the window, cast like a statue in shadow and light. His hawklike, scarred face, his leonine hair, his angular shoulders bent with a burden of melancholy. This memory remains clear, like a snapshot of a long-lost perfect day. And, in my mind, he will never fade nor grow old.

"Let's go," said Valentine, picking up his bag.

The light inside the house had taken on a curious red cast. The air had congealed into a bloody miasma that caught in the back of the throat and reeked of sweat and sex.

"Will we be strong enough to fight it?" I asked. Already my penis was knocking against the door of my trousers, stiffening into a club. I found myself watching Valentine's buttocks shift under his jeans.

"This is only a residual effect," he said. "The real power is in the room itself. It's anchored itself to the house in order to function more efficiently as a gateway for The Mysteries. We must prevent that from happening."

As we climbed the stairs, the sound of the room became louder. It was moaning. A deep bass note vibrated through the walls and floor.

"I'm afraid, Valentine," I admitted. "I can feel itself insinuating its way into me. What if I can't control myself?"

"Then try to enjoy it," he said grimly.

We stood outside the door. Valentine reached into his bag and transferred a number of items to his pockets. Finally, he selected a brace of Band-Aids from a silverplated tin.

"I'll be looking beyond the real," he said. "You must be my eyes if I need a description of events on this plane." Thus saying, he fixed the strips of sticking plaster over his eyelids.

I wiped my brow and picked up Valentine's bag.

"Ready?" he said, and, before I could reply, the door was open and we were swept into the Bacchanal.

The first thing I saw was the young policeman. His body was no longer his own and had become a mere engine of unfocused lust. The Mysteries had worked their enchantments upon his flesh and transformed it to suit their own ghastly purpose. His body seethed, like a bag of skin filled with serpents. Mouth and nose were fused into a single glistening slit with staring eyes on either side. His eyebrows had grown together into a thick pubic mass at the crown of this rudimentary vagina. His tongue thrashed from his transformed face, flicking thick liquid onto the bodies of his fellow revelers. Heavy extrusions surged out of the young policeman's torso, searching for receptive orifices before subsiding back into his rippling musculature. His penis was extended, fractal-branching into a cat-o'-nine tails that flailed and penetrated men and girls and the very walls of the room with indiscriminate abandon.

Giselle was pounding her fist repeatedly into a gaping, flaming hole at the base of the policeman's spine. When I caught a closer glimpse of the girl's hand, I realized that it too had suffered a monstrous transformation, becoming a blunt, glistening phallus. The other men and Imogen were not so radically altered, but I could not help but be aware of the way in which their skin seemed to slide and flow.

This, then, was the scene that greeted me when I entered the room. I will not lie; I wanted to retch, but at the same time I was stimulated to the threshold of my self-control. Here was pure flesh, pure desire, set free from all restraint and given uninhibited expression. All the impulses that drive the human animal were here distilled and unleashed.

The room itself was no less active than its occupants. Every object strained at the limits of its construction. Chairs, tables, toys, furnishings: All these things ached with a newly revealed eroticism, each attempting to form of its substance some representation of cunt or cock. The walls, floor, and ceiling were alive. Suffused with a rosy glow, they extended stalagmite dildoes upon which the occupants of the room pleasured themselves. Vibrating gashes blinked open in the walls, eager to be filled.

My mind and body reeled, and I could no longer tell whether I was in Hell or in Heaven.

I glanced at Valentine, blindly surveying the room, and tried to describe what I was seeing. I knew that he saw something quite different. His "sealed vision" permitted him to penetrate to the normally veiled essential nature of things. He saw the naked room.

"My God!" I heard him say. "The taint runs deep . . ."

He raised his bandaged hand toward the tall, narrow windows on the far side of the room. I forced myself to look beyond the carnal chaos to those open windows. The scene there bore no relation to the cityscape one would have expected to see from that perspective. Instead of chimneys and treetops and clouds, I found a nocturnal sky, filled with strange liquid stars. Silhouetted against these dream constellations, I discerned vast structures. The windows of these threatening buildings were lit with a whole new spectrum of unearthly colors. The buildings spat vast streamers or aurorae into the sky, and I heard sounds I cannot explain. For just a moment, it seemed, I was granted a vision of a world beyond known philosophies. A world where amniotic seas raged through living cities.

"What is that place?" I said. "What are those buildings?"

"They're not buildings," Valentine said, and he began to unwrap the stained bandages that covered his left hand.

It pains me to confess that, at that moment, I lost all control. Something pushed me back and I fell. The room roared and fluxed around me, and I raised my head to see Imogen Bedlow's lips fastened around my erection. I slid in and out of her mouth and could feel strange cold spaces at the back of her throat. As she gorged herself on me, her own father took her from behind and, almost as quickly, Barnes was upon *me*. Worse was to follow as I helped him to divest me of my clothing. With writhing, lactating nipples, he fell upon me and drove himself into me. I abandoned myself to the delirious, monotonous rhythm of the bewitched room.

Giselle and the young policeman seemed to be fusing together somewhere in the center of the room, creating a new and fabulous organism. I saw a shrieking, deformed thing rearing up toward the ceiling and collapsing like a wave. It was beautiful and glorious, a living Henry Moore sculpture carved from bleeding flesh. It strained for heights of gratification I could scarcely imagine, and I watched it pass into the palpitating substance of the room itself. Then I collapsed, hovering on the brink of orgasm for what seemed like endless hours.

Suddenly Imogen was torn away from me. I looked up through a red fog to see Valentine pushing her back against the wall. She tongued the air, pleading with him to abuse her. Calmly, Valentine removed a key from his pocket and placed it in the girl's mouth. Her eyes closed in bliss and she began to suck on the rusty key. Valentine ignored the hands that scrabbled at the zip of his trousers and turned the key in Imogen's mouth. I swear that I heard the clacking sound of an ancient lock. Imogen's eyes snapped open, like switchblades. She began to scream.

For a moment, the spell was broken. Barnes and Bedlow pulled away from one another in disgust and horror.

"Get them out of here!" Valentine shouted. I tugged at my trousers and tried to restore some dignity to my appearance.

"Forget your trousers!" he cried. "Just get them out!"

Ignoring my nakedness, I managed to push the others out of the room and onto the landing.

I paused at the threshold and turned. Valentine lifted his uncovered left hand. It was withered horribly, like the hand of some mummified king. This, I knew, was another legacy of his most dreadful confrontation with The Mysteries. Angela had died and Valentine had lost the use of his hand. It had, however, become for him a potent object of power. He placed birthday-cake candles on the tips of each finger and lit them. Then he lifted his Hand of Glory in preparation for the final battle.

"Valentine, for God's sake!" I whispered. "You can't fight them alone."

"I'm not alone," he said. "Get out now, while you still can. The only way to stop them is to use the room's own power. It'll destroy you if you stay."

The air was filling with strange viscous streamers. Pearlywhite, like semen floating free of gravity, this substance filled the air around us. Thin tendrils glistened and sang.

"They're coming!" he said.

"I can't leave you to fight them alone . . ." I tried to say again.

"Out!" he yelled, and the door blew shut in my face.

"May God help you, Valentine," I whispered.

There was a moment of calm in which I heard Imogen Bedlow weeping softly, and then a surge of power shook the walls and I was thrown down the stairs.

I recovered my senses to see Barnes and Bedlow kissing passionately on the landing. Imogen crawled between their writhing bodies, licking and sucking at whatever she could find. Eventually she sandwiched herself in such a way that both men could fuck her simultaneously. I struggled with the urge to join them.

There was a great ululating sound from the Rutting Room and I ran back up the stairs. I could not leave Valentine to his fate. With shaking hands, I opened the door for the last time.

Of Giselle Barnes and the young policeman, no evidence remained, except for a shuddering cube of stressed flesh.

Valentine hung suspended and naked in the center of the room, thrashing at the heart of a twitching web, a great spidery crucifixion. Filaments and protrusions extended from every corner of the room to penetrate his mouth and rectum. His pelvis bucked and his penis slammed like a piston in and out of a soaking orifice that the room had manufactured for itself.

"Valentine!" I shouted, but he did not respond. His body spasmed automatically. The far wall no longer existed, and in its place there was a vista of staggering abnormality, through which those monstrous "buildings" came lurching. Faces were scorched into walls. Leering, childish drawings appeared and were erased by unseen hands. The word "SUBMISSION" was scrawled with some diarrheal substance that faded into bilious smoke. Saliva ran from the walls. I felt that I was simply an observer in the midst of a battle I could not comprehend.

I looked up to see Valentine extend his Hand of Glory. The tiny candles flared, and shredded paper began to rain down from the ceiling. The room's breathing grew more rapid and the walls flushed red. The same color spread across Valentine's skin like a rash. His own breathing was synchronized with that of the room. Together they ascended toward some unendurable climax. The Mysteries reached into the room, spreading a scabbed, diseased shadow across the windowsill.

There was one ineffable moment when everything paused at once, and then Valentine threw back his head and screamed.

It is to my eternal shame that I fled from the room and did not stay to help my friend. Instead, I joined Barnes, Bedlow, and Imogen for a final mesmeric orgy. Her bruised lips locked about me and I was lost.

When I awoke from my wet dream, it was to find Valentine standing over me. The fingertips of his left hand were charred to matchsticks.

"I'm sorry . . ." I began.

"It's all right," he said. "They're gone, for now, and there was nothing you could have done to help. That door has been sealed forever."

"Thank God," I muttered. The unconscious bodies of my recent lovers lay tangled on the floor. "What have I done?"

Valentine shook his head. "More lives destroyed by those monsters."

"But what about you?" I said.

He simply turned and walked back toward the door that opened onto the Horney Chamber. At the threshold, he paused and looked down.

"When Angela died, I thought *I* had died to love," he said. "I was cored, hollowed-out. Now it seems I've found the thing that was lost to me."

"The room?" I said, barely articulating the words.

He nodded. "I was enflamed," he said quietly. "I transformed the room into an instrument of purest love. The carnal and the spiritual united. The Mysteries had managed to pervert the room's true inclinations. I restored them."

I knew then what he was about to say.

"The Horney Chamber, powered by love, opens out into innumerable worlds. It can be folded through dreams, into unimaginable universes," he said. "Rainbow skies and blue, raging storms of tear-stained love notes. It's all out there, old pal."

He smiled at me. "That's where I'm going."
He reached out and laid his ruined hand on my shoulder.
"Goodbye," he said.

He opened the door. From within, I heard the sound of a great sighing. The room was filled with light; spring mornings and new rain, scented black chiffons, red lamps swinging in the sweat of the night. All the colors of desire, all love and longing expressed in one eloquent rush of charmed air.

"Goodbye, Aubrey," I said.

And Aubrey Valentine stepped into the room where Love lives and closed the door, and I never saw him again.

BLACK CARS

J. L. Comeau

You comfortable back there, Mr. Winslow? Great. How was your flight? A little turbulence, yeah? Just let me stow your bags in the trunk and I'll be right back.

Wow, cold out there tonight. Dulles is always windy. So where're we headed? Oh, yeah. That's your girlfriend's house, right? Good-looker, mmm-mmm, great skin. Oh no, I'd never say anything about her in front of your wife, Mr. Winslow. No way, no way. Did you tell anyone about your little sidetrip here to D.C.? No? Smart man.

Whoa, here comes the rain. Better turn on the wipers.

You look sorta cold, Mr. Winslow. Just between you and me, I keep a little flask of cognac in the glove box for my best customers. Want a little snort? Sure, let me fix you up. Warm the old bones.

That's better, huh? More? Here.

Hey, how did you like calling my car direct on this cellular phone? Convenient, huh? Thanks, I like this new car, too. Yeah, it's a real switch from driving that old taxicab of mine. They call this a Black Car. Luxury sedan. They're real popular up on Capitol Hill now.

Beg your pardon? Naw, I only drive nights. Sleep days. I've got cat's eyes, you know? Night eyes. Sun kills me. Burns my brain. And there's business out here after dark, let me tell you. A lot of monkey business, too, if you know what

238

I mean. Things can get pretty weird sometimes, but I don't really give a shit what people do as long as they pay me what they owe. I'm a driver, not a cop,· right? Yeah, gotta make that living first and foremost. But it can get weird. Believe me, I could tell you some stories.

You really want to hear one? Well, let's see . . . There's so many—Oh. I've got one for you. We drivers swap tales, you know, mostly bull stories about hot babes in the backseat inviting us to join them or wild lies about huge fares and tips that never happened. Stuff like that. We all do it. Anyway, one story I kept hearing again and again was about a couple living in a luxury suite at the Willard, that classy hotel around the corner from the White House. I'd been hearing about this wealthy couple for years, about how they'd hire out a Black Car for an entire night. Hey, that's a driver's dream. Thirty bucks an hour for a whole night can turn into one hefty chunk of green. Then, on top of that, this particular couple were said to tip a hundred percent, so you can understand why all of us drivers were eager to book those two, right?

Well, at first I thought the stories were a bunch of brag and crap like the rest, you know, because none of the guys who'd ever transported this couple were still driving. But I'm an ambitious kinda guy and I keep my ear to the rail, so to speak. So a few months ago, one of the other drivers told me that he'd heard the couple lived in Suite 302. That's all I needed to know. I hustled my backside over to the Willard Hotel that same night, trotted myself up to 302, and shoved my business card under the door. On the back of the card I'd written: Call me for the best ride of your life.

Two days later Mr. Murdock called me.

He booked me for that entire night, eight to five. It was a Saturday and I had a lot of business already booked, sure, but hell, I'd have cancelled my subscription to the resurrection for a chance at that kind of dough, ha. So I farmed out all my previous bookings to the other drivers and didn't say a thing to anyone about the Murdocks. I like to play my business sly, you know? Keep my best customers to myself. Black Cars are competitive as hell; we'd steal each other's clients in a heartbeat. It's expected. Business is like that, right?

So, to get back to the story, I buzzed home for a shower and got all decked out in my best suit. Gray Italian double-breasted job. Sharp. I thought I looked like a million bucks when I pulled up in front of the Willard at eight. But then I saw the Murdocks and realized I might as well have worn a leisure suit from K-Mart. Brother, they were something to see.

They kind of flowed down the front steps of the hotel like melting butter. Smooth. Clothes you wouldn't believe. Mr. Murdock and his wife looked as different from each other as an eagle and a cat, but somehow they seemed perfect together. Complemented each other, right? He was as dark and tall as she was fair and tiny. Like a storybook king and princess, you know? Perfect. Could have been in their thirties or sixties, no telling.

I was kinda nervous when the doorman ushered them into the car. I'm from a working-class background, grew up in the Virginia suburbs. I was afraid my manners might offend them. Well, the Murdocks put me right at ease, talking to me the way you would talk to someone across a dinner table. Friendly. Told me they wanted a tour of the city. I thought that was pretty strange, since they were residents, and said so. They laughed and Mr. Murdock said, We want to see *your* interpretation of the District. We want you to show us things we've never seen before.

I figured he wasn't talking about the Washington Monument or the Lincoln Memorial. So I took a chance. I headed northwest across the city toward what they call the Crater District.

You familiar with the Crater? No? Hey, let me tell you, it's unique. Half blast zone, half upper-middle-class residential district. It's where the two parts of Washington, D.C. come together. Sandwiched in between burned-out buildings and deserted lots are big renovated homes that the owners bought for a song. Yuppies, right. Thought they were smart because those great big houses are located two blocks from the business district and two blocks from the subway. They

were sure the whole area would get cleaned up and renovated when urban renewal rolled in, but they were wrong.
Now they're stuck out there in their fancy houses butted up
to the worst kinda urban blight. Rats big as ponies, know
what I mean? The residents did manage to get rid of most of
the prostitutes who hung out there when they moved in, but
nature abhors a vacuum, right? A whole new variety of
prostitutes moved in. Transvestite hookers. Guys all decked
out like chicks.

What's that? Oh, yeah! They're gorgeous-looking! You
wouldn't believe them, all made up and dressed in glitter
and spandex and legs like you never saw. They stand around
on the corners competing with the crack dealers for attention as the cars drive by. They come out at night, yeah, just
like the rats. Just like me, ha.

Well, I drove the Murdocks over there for a look, thinking
that either they'd get pissed and that would be the end of it,
or they'd get a kick out of the Crater circus. I've picked up
my share of rich types, and one thing I've found out: Kicks
are hard to find when you've got tons of dough. They get
bored when they can have anything whenever they want it,
right? So what the hell, I took a shot.

As it turned out, the Murdocks loved the Crater. They
made me circle through the area for hours, and let me tell
you, when you drive slow through the Crater in a brand-new
Black Car, you arouse some interest from the locals. Christ,
the hookers and the dealers were all but chasing us around
the block. They can smell money, you know.

The Murdocks stared and gawked and gave each other
long looks, asked a lot of questions. I told them about the
transvestites' business, how they took their clients into the
alleys and abandoned buildings, and sometimes the johns
came back out in body bags. Screams and gunshots are night
music around there. The residents don't even bother calling
the cops anymore. The cops won't come. What's the point,
right? I made the Murdocks keep the doors locked, of
course; it's dangerous as hell in the Crater after dark. Yeah,
stabbings and shootings and all that kind of stuff. Bad place.
The yuppies stay shut up in their houses behind barred

windows once the sun goes down. But for several hundred bucks, man, I'm willing to hang tough for a few hours, know what I mean?

Nothing much happened that first night with the Murdocks. At five the next morning, I took them back to the Willard and they paid me. Five hundred and forty bucks. Doubled the fare, can you believe it? Just like I'd heard. And then they booked me for the following Saturday night. The Crater's kink business hit the target dead-on. The Murdocks were mine.

How're you doing back there, Mr. Winslow? Warm enough? Good. Sleepy, huh? Yeah, the rain and the wipers are kind of hypnotic, aren't they? God, I love driving in the rain. Slicks away all the ugly, know what I mean?

It was raining that second Saturday night when I picked up the Murdocks, too. Raining like hell. They carried a couple of big leather satchels with them and I stowed them in the trunk. I was afraid the weather might drive the Crater sex and drug circus indoors, but those hookers and dealers, they're hard cases, I'm telling you. They had their corners covered like always. It was just like being in an old forties film that night, the dealers all slouched down in trenchcoats and snap-brims, the hookers hawking their skinny bods through transparent plastic umbrellas. Streetlamps puddled lights on wet asphalt, traffic lights blinked through the downpour. Weird. Surreal, like Mr. Murdock said.

We eased through the district for about an hour, up one street, down the next, through the alleyways. Caught a hooker and his john in the headlights. They were busy doing commerce up against the wall of an old abandoned building. Didn't even look up at us. That's the attitude in the Crater. Nobody gives a shit. The Murdocks didn't say anything either, but I glanced at them in the rearview mirror. They were smiling.

While we rolled around the Crater in the rain, Mr. Murdock told me that he and his wife were from somewhere in Europe, don't ask me where. Said they were in the custom furnishings business, that his family had been making chairs and sofas and stuff for centuries. Very exclusive clientele, royalty and ultra-rich, you know. I asked him how much his cheapest piece would cost me. A hundred grand, he says. Can you imagine? Hope it's made of gold, I said. Christ.

So anyway, we drove around and around, past the same hookers and dealers who were getting a little pissed with all our looking and no buying. Want some crack? a dealer on a prime corner shouted at us. What the fuck's up, man? he said. Disgusted, right. Gotta make that living. Mr. Murdock told me to keep going, so I did. On and on. He and his wife nearly had their noses mashed against the back window, gawking. They whispered back and forth and I watched them in the rearview. I got the message quick that it was the hookers that interested them, not the dealers.

So all of a sudden this leggy black guy in a white curly wig and glitter makeup runs right out in front of the car and whips open his shiny plastic raincoat. Nothing but a red sequin G-string on underneath. I had to slam on the brakes. Nearly slid right into the bastard; couldn't have missed him by more than a foot. He came running up to the Murdocks' window, all girly and breathless, and tapped a three-inch plastic fingernail against the glass. Open the window, Mr. Murdock told me, so I buzzed it down halfway. Hookers have blades in those big pocketbooks they carry, you better believe it.

I'm Tina, the hooker said in this weird, cotton-candy high-pitched voice. Wanna date? he/she asked, flipping these big fake eyelashes all crusty with silver glitter. A real hot little number, I guess, if you're into that kind of thing.

Well, Tina trotted in place, bending over at the window, red spike heels clattering on the wet pavement. C'mon, she kept saying, be a sport. I'll do ya both, she told the Murdocks. I'll do ya both real good, sucking and smacking those big frosty lips, you know, putting on a real show to clinch the deal.

And it worked. Mr. Murdock opened the back door and let Tina into the car. I didn't like that much. Never know what kind of crud those hookers might be infected with, right? But hell, I'm making plenty of cash, so who am I to complain? I just put the car in gear and started rolling.

Jesus, Tina was all over them, rubbing and smooching and slobbering, so Mr. Murdock pushed her back in a gentle way and started asking questions like where and how much and so forth. Tina batted those wild eyelashes and told me to kill the headlights and pull back through an alleyway off of 10th Street and drop them at the entrance to a big hulking cavern of a burned-out church back there. Huge stone building that looked a thousand years old. Mr. Murdock asked me to pop the trunk as he and his wife and Tina got out of the car, and they picked up their satchels and disappeared into the rain.

I didn't like sitting alone in that dark, wet alleyway, I can tell you. A big dirty rat loped across the road right next to the car dragging some kind of dead animal through the dirt. Nasty. Christ, you can't imagine what might be lurking out there in the dark in that kind of place, you know? And the rain kept coming down, plunking on the roof, visibility zero. I hit the auto-lock key. The Murdocks could damn well bang on the door when they wanted back in, I decided. I wasn't going to get my damn throat cut.

I kept wondering as I sat there in the dark, waiting, what the hell do people like the Murdocks want with a fifteen-buck transvestite street hooker when they can afford the classiest call girls and gigolos in D.C.? Kicks, I figure. Thrills, right?

Mr. Winslow? You awake? Oh. I thought you'd fallen asleep back there.

Well, about an hour or so after I let Tina and the Murdocks out, I heard a man screaming somewhere out in the night. I had the windows shut tight, so I can't tell where the screams came from, but man, I started to get nervous. Real nervous. I glanced at the dash clock. After midnight. I decided that if they didn't come back in another fifteen minutes I'd blow the horn and wait another five. Then screw it, I was out of there, dough or no dough. Can't make a living if I get stabbed or shot to death, right?

But ten minutes later, here they come, running through the rain carrying their satchels. Just the two of them, Mr. and Mrs. Murdock. No sign of Tina, naturally. That's the way it usually goes. After everybody gets their jollies, the hooker splits for the curbside again pronto. Gotta make that living, right? Get right back at it.

I popped the lock and the Murdocks piled into the backseat, dragging their satchels in behind them. They seemed happy; Mrs. Murdock's usually pale skin was all flushed and pink. She looked beautiful, young, eyes all glittery like Tina's makeup. Excited. Mr. Murdock told me to drive them back to the Willard, and I slid out of that black alley like Cisco Crisco, slow and easy.

Well, I wheeled it out of the Crater and delivered the Murdocks back at the hotel at a quarter to one. Shit, I thought, not much dough tonight. But Mr. Murdock lays a thou' on me. My eyeballs almost fall outta my head, right? I can depend on your discretion, can't I, Mr. McClung? Mr. Murdock said. You betcha, I told him. I can be plenty discreet for a grand, I'm telling you. Less than five hours' work, too. Christ.

As they left, Mr. Murdock told me they had some business that would take them out of town the following week, but he wanted to book me for the week after. Great, I said, sure. So two weeks later we went back to the Crater and picked up another vestie hooker, same type, tall and leggy, young and slender. Light cocoa color. The Murdocks seem to be turned on by skin color, right? Look, Agatha, Mr. Murdock told his wife while he pawed over the hooker, what lovely texture. So soft. Then Mrs. Murdock started rubbing the guy's chest and legs, too. Kinda made me sick. Not to my taste, you know. I got different ideas about kicks. But hell, I drove them over to the burned-out church again and they went off to do their weird thing, then I took them back to the Willard. I make my thousand and everybody's happy.

Well, this goes on every other Saturday night for about ten weeks, and then things change. Things always change, right? Mr. Murdock told me he had a business proposition to discuss. My ears perked right up because I'm an ambitious kinda guy, and I'm always game for more dough.

You okay back there, Mr. Winslow? You look a little sick. Yeah, I thought you looked kinda pale. We're almost there. You want me to go on with the story? Okay.

So anyway, Mr. Murdock tells me he's interested in younger men, you know, adolescents. Yeah, he's a chicken hawk, wants a little chicken. That's what they call the under-age male hookers: chickens. Well, I knew right where to take the Murdocks, just a couple of blocks over from where we picked up the vesties, right? We cruised a while and Mr. Murdock located a tall, good-looking blond kid in a pair of low-slung jeans and no shirt. Lifted weights, you could tell right off. Muscular, you know. Kinda like yourself, Mr. Winslow, wide shoulders, good body, good tone. Except that the kid's arms were all tracked up from popping junk. But you're going to find that on pretty much all the chickens or else they wouldn't be out there hustling. That's what I told Mr. Murdock. He didn't like the needle tracks, but he invited the boy into the backseat anyway.

The kid was clever, you could see it in his eyes. Before he hopped into the car, he checked out the Murdocks and me real good. Wary as a tomcat, this kid. Been around, you could tell. Once he was in the car, he smiled at the Murdocks, big green-eyed cat grin, sneering. What's your pleasure? he asked Mr. Murdock, and Mr. Murdock leaned forward and told me to take them to the regular place, meaning the abandoned church.

Hey, the kid said, I thought we were going to do this right here in the car, man. Mr. Murdock didn't say anything, just stared straight ahead while we rolled toward that dark tunnel of an alleyway. No! the kid yelled, starting to panic, I don't work this way, man! Calm down, Mr. Murdock told the kid, there's no reason to get excited.

Well, the kid started to open the door and Mr. Murdock grabbed him by the back of his neck and whacked his head up against the door post hard. Blood covered the side of the kid's face and he looked around, stunned, like a shot dog, you know? Not his face, Alton! Mrs. Murdock hollered. Don't ruin his face! Mr. McClung, Mr. Murdock called to me as he was struggling with the boy. I need your help, Mr. McClung.

I didn't like it one bit, let me tell you, but the Murdocks are my best customers, so I turned around and conked the kid on the top of his head with my portable credit-card imprinter and he dropped like a sack of potatoes. Bam, out cold. Open the trunk and help me carry him up to the building, Mr. Murdock said, so I popped the trunk, then got out and slung the kid over my shoulder. While the Murdocks got their satchels, I locked the car up. Hated the idea of leaving it in that dark alley untended. Who knew if it would even be there when I got back?

So I followed the Murdocks through the dark up to the church, right? I was so damned worried about my car that I didn't even think about what kind of weird shit the Murdocks had in mind, I just walked behind them carrying the kid through the weeds and the trash. Christ, that building was dark. All echoey and creepy inside, you know? Mr. Murdock flicked on a little penlight to light the way. Rats and roaches and big hairy spiders skittered away from the light as we moved down what I supposed was the aisle between the pews, although all the pews and fixtures got ripped off a long time ago. Just a big room with high ceilings and a filthy plank floor littered with used condoms and liquor bottles. Nice joint, huh? The Church of Twisted Scenes, ha.

So Mr. Murdock told me to drop the kid in the corner of a little room behind what used to be the altar. The kid was moaning, starting to come around. I asked Mr. Murdock what else he wanted me to do, and he said just to go on back to the car and wait for them. I was glad to be getting out of there, let me tell you, and I turned to leave as fast as I could. As I headed for the doorway, I saw Mrs. Murdock kneeling over one of the big leather satchels. She'd spread a white cloth on the floor next to a couple pairs of rubber aprons and gloves and was busy laying out what looked like doctor's tools: scalpels and drills and dental picks and stuff.

Well, let me tell you, I hustled out of that place and back to my car, which was waiting in the alley in one piece, thank God. A miracle. I locked myself in and sat waiting for the Murdocks, trying to ignore the screams that came from the church. Hey, nobody notices screams in the Crater. Just a little night music.

So anyway, about an hour later I see the Murdocks coming back to the car, and I noticed that their satchels looked a lot fuller than they had earlier. Sides all bulged out, you know? And they felt heavier than when I stowed them in the trunk the first time. Smelled funny, too. Like biology lab in high school. Ugh.

When we got back to the Willard, Mr. Murdock laid two grand on me and patted my shoulder. Good man, he said. I know I can trust you, Mr. McClung. I suppose you understand about our little business now, don't you? he asked me. Yeah, I said, I guess I do. We like to mix business and pleasure when we can, he said with a weird smile. Fine, I told him. It's okay by me.

What was that, Mr. Winslow? I can hardly hear you. You're slurring your words real bad. Huh? Oh, yeah, you're right. This isn't your girlfriend's house. We're going to make a little stop. Uh-huh. Right. This is the Crater. No, now don't get upset, I know you're having trouble moving and talking. It's the stuff the Murdocks gave me to put in the cognac. It's to relax you.

What? Yeah, I know it's dark. This is the alley I was telling you about. See the old abandoned church over there? Wait a second and I'll come around and get you.

Here you go. Just let me get you up on my shoulder and lock the door. It's okay if you holler. Nobody's going to come. Nobody cares. I'm really sorry about this, Mr. Winslow, but I gotta make a living, right? You're not much of a tipper, to be perfectly honest, and you've got just the kind of skin the Murdocks are looking for. They're in the custom furnishings business, like I told you, and they produce their own leather—the most supple and exotic leather in the world, right? Get their kicks and their rare skins at the same time.

Me, I got a two-thousand-dollar-a-week coke habit. That's why I'm so talkative, I guess. Cocaine does seem to go right to my yapper. Keeps me hopping for dough, let me tell you, and the Murdocks keep me rolling in the high numerals.

So, here we are. Business is business.

What's that? No, your girlfriend's not going to tell anybody anything. I'm going over there right now to tell her that you want me to transport her to a little rendezvous with you, which is true. She knows me from all those times I drove you both to dinner and back, remember? I'm going to bring her here to the Murdocks, too. She's got a great complexion, Christ. Maybe the Murdocks will save you for later and do her first so you can watch them peel her alive. They'd really get off on that. That's probably how it'll go.

Okay, I'm going to let you down now. Can't sit up against the wall here? All right, just slump forward, it doesn't matter.

Here come the Murdocks now.

Hey, Mr. Murdock, Mrs. Murdock. He's the one I've been telling you about. Yeah, he's prime, isn't he? Wait'll you see the girlfriend. She's a beaut. Huh? Right. Twenty grand for the both of them. They'll make you a nice sofa and chair, ha.

Well, Mr. Winslow, it's been nice doing business with you, but I've gotta get back on the road now, pick up your sweetie. And I'll send your wife my card if they ever find your body. You being a veteran and all, she'll probably plant you right here in Arlington Cemetery. I do funeral processions, too, you know.

Yeah, gotta make that living first and foremost.

Right?

AUTHOR BIOGRAPHIES

John Edward Ames

Ames has published twenty novels, including *Buffalo Hiders*, *Spirit Path*, *The Unwritten Order*, and *The Asylum*. The Louisiana resident also writes westerns under the name Judd Cole.

J. L. Comeau

Comeau is a writer and writing instructor whose work has appeared in *Hottest Blood*, *Women of the West*, *Borderlands 2* and *3*, *Year's Best Horror XIX*, *Best New Horror 2, 3* and *5*, and others. The District of Columbia resident is currently working on a novel.

Matthew Costello

Multigenre author Costello has written science fiction including *Midsummer* and *Time of the Fox*, horror including *Wurm*, fantasy including *The Wizard of Tizare*, mainstream thrillers like *Home*, and nonfantasy including *The Greatest Games of All Time*. He lives in New York.

Don D'Ammassa

D'Ammassa, from Rhode Island, is the author of *Blood Beast* and a forthcoming book about horror fiction. The full-time writer has had short stories in the anthologies *Hotter Blood, Shock Rock, Chilled to the Bone,* and *Souls in Pawn,* as well as various horror magazines. He regularly reviews books for *Science Fiction Chronicles.*

Ron Dee

Dee's several novels include *Succumb* and *Blood.* He has also been published under the pseudonym David Darke in such novels as *Shade* and *Horrorshow.* The Missouri resident has sold stories to many anthologies, including *Phobias 2* and *The Ultimate Dracula.*

Michael Garrett

Garrett's first novel, *Keeper,* has been optioned for filming. His short stories have seen print in *Fear Itself, Shock Rock I* and *II,* and others. He is an Editorial Associate with *Writer's Digest* magazine and co-editor of the *Hot Blood* series. He lives in Alabama.

Jeff Gelb

Gelb is a California-based editor of the *Shock Rock* and *Fear Itself* anthologies, and co-editor of the *Hot Blood* series. He is the author of *Specters,* and is a frequent contributor to comics magazines like *Comics Buyers Guide, Comics Interview* and *Overstreet's Gold & Silver.* The former columnist for *Radio & Records* has had short fiction in *Scare Care* and other anthologies.

Nancy Holder

Nancy Holder, of California, has sold two dozen horror and fantasy short stories to *Borderlands, Greystone Bay, Women of Darkness, Pulphouse, Obsessions, Cold Shocks, Still Dead, Narrow Houses,* and others, and has been awarded the Horror Writers of America Stoker Award for best short story. She has also sold thirteen romance and two mainstream novels. Her books have been translated into more than fifteen languages.

Chris Lacher

Lacher is no stranger to short horror stories, as the editor of *New Blood* magazine and a contributing editor to *Iniquities.* He is the co-editor of the *Nasties* horror anthology and a frequent contributor to such anthologies as *Scare Care* and *H2ORRORS.* He lives in California.

Bentley Little

Californian Little is a respected D. H. Lawrence scholar who claims to have worked in various carnivals and strip clubs throughout the Southwest. He is the author of *The Mailman, Death Instinct, The Summoning,* and the Stoker Award–winning *The Revelation.* His latest novel is *University.*

Elizabeth Massie

Massie has had horror fiction printed in *Women of Darkness, Obsessions, Borderlands, Year's Best Fantasy and Horror, A Whisper of Blood, Dead End: City Limits,* and more. Her first novel, *Sineater,* will be appearing from a British publisher. The Stoker Award–winning writer lives in Virginia.

Graham Masterton

England's Masterton is hard at work on several new horror novels, including *Burial, The Sleepless,* and *Flesh & Blood.* He has had over fifty short stories published, including the award-winning "Absence of Beast." He is the editor of the acclaimed *Scare Care* anthology.

Rex Miller

Butcher, next in the series of *Chaingang* novels, is slated for publication in late 1995. Missouri's Miller is the author of eleven novels, two nonfiction books, two teleplays, and some fifty short stories, including ones in *Fear Itself,* the *Hot Blood* books, *Shock Rock II, Forbidden Acts,* and a forthcoming anthology featuring Will Eisner's *The Spirit.*

Grant Morrison

Scotland's Morrison is the acclaimed comic book writer of the groundbreaking Batman graphic novel *Arkham Asylum,* plus such series as the Invisibles, the Doom Patrol, and Animal Man. His story in *Hotter Blood* was nominated for a Bram Stoker Award by the Horror Writers Association.

David J. Schow

California's Schow is an award-winning writer of short fiction. His latest published collection was *Look Out He's Got a Knife,* and waiting in the wings is *Black Leather Required.* His latest novel is *The Shaft,* and most recently Schow has penned several screenplays, including *Dial M* and *The Crow.* He writes a semi-regular column for *Fangoria.*

John Shirley

California's Shirley is the author of more than seventeen books under his own name and a dozen more under pseudonyms. His best-known books include *City Come A-Walkin'*, *Heatseeker*, *Cellars*, *Wetbones*, and *The Brigade*. He is also a successful songwriter who fronts his own band, the Panther Moderns.

Melanie Tem

Tem, who resides in Colorado, is the author of *Prodigal*, *Blood Moon*, and *Wilding*. Her short fiction has appeared in *Final Shadows*, *Cold Shocks*, *Snow White Blood Red*, *Women of Darkness*, *Best New Horror II*, *Dark Voices*, and others.

Steve Rasnic Tem

Tem has sold over 180 short stories, with recent or forthcoming tales in *Metahorror*, *In Dreams*, *Stalkers 3*, *Psycho Paths 2*, *New Crimes 3*, *The Daedulus Book of Femme Fatales*, *Gauntlet 3*, *Snow White Blood Red*, and more. He lives in Colorado.

Thomas Tessier

Connecticut's Tessier is the best-selling author of *Rapture*, *Finishing Touches*, *Nightwalker*, and more. His latest novel, *The White Gods*, is due soon, along with a collection of his "tales of panic."

Graham Watkins

Watkins, who resides in North Carolina, is the author of *Dark Winds, The Fire Within, Kaleidoscope Eyes,* and the upcoming *Parasite*. His script to "Hillbettys" has been optioned for Roger Corman's New Horizons/Concorde Films. His short fiction sales include *Shock Rock, Fear Itself,* and *Deathrealm*.

Julie Wilson

From Maine, Wilson is a former professional model who is exploring new career directions as a writer. Her *Hottest Blood* story represents her first published work.

BOOK YOUR PLACE ON OUR WEBSITE AND MAKE THE READING CONNECTION!

We've created a customized website just for our very special readers, where you can get the inside scoop on everything that's going on with Zebra, Pinnacle and Kensington books.

When you come online, you'll have the exciting opportunity to:

- View covers of upcoming books
- Read sample chapters
- Learn about our future publishing schedule (listed by publication month *and author*)
- Find out when your favorite authors will be visiting a city near you
- Search for and order backlist books from our online catalog
- Check out author bios and background information
- Send e-mail to your favorite authors
- Meet the Kensington staff online
- Join us in weekly chats with authors, readers and other guests
- Get writing guidelines
- AND MUCH MORE!

Visit our website at
http://www.kensingtonbooks.com